You'll Probably Need Stitches

Stories and Selected Fiction

Robert Gerard Hunt

TABLECHAIR

"Dynadormophis Up" did not originally appear in *Analog*.

"Hostel is a Homophone," "Trumpet Lessons,"
and "You'll Probably Need Stitches"
did not originally appear in *The New Yorker*.

"The Plexus Tuxedo Project" did not originally appear in *The Atlantic*.

Designed by Arthur T. Rodenberg

Published by TableChair Books
TableChair Books is an imprint of TableChair Media.

ISBN 979-8-9881048-0-3

Printed in The United States of America

2 3 4 5 6 26 25 24 23

Contents

GROWING UP

Confidentially...   8

Every Boy Does Magic   12

Grandpa, Sasquatch and Me   17

Cafeteriphobia   23

Broadway Boogie-Woogie   27

The Vinyl Frontier   33

Bombs Away   37

Green Machine   40

You'll Probably Need Stitches   43

Cans 'n' Stuff   48

Anxiety in Bee Minor   51

A Summer Place   54

Death By Piano   57

The Annotated Edward Cramer   61

Altar Boys Gone Wild   68

You've Got to Hide Your Love Away   72

Trumpet Lessons   76

The Rise and Fall of the Edward Hannon Band   80

The Plexus Tuxedo Project   85

Tablechair!   90

The Reluctant Athlete   94

A Nearly Perfect Circle   100

Turkey Bowl   105

COLLEGE DAYS

I Say Potato, You Say What? 112

Hip Hop 117

I Once was a Man who Lived in a Shoe 121

Stranger Danger 127

Loving in Fall 132

Focus Study 136

ADULTHOOD (apparently)

The Dark Sides of the Room 142

Deebies! 145

Alice in Limaland 149

Smile 155

The Mighty Pegasus 158

The Old Man and the Sea 163

Hostel is a Homophone 167

Kill the Wabbit 174

Sweet Home, Perstai 177

Ice Folly 182

If It's Tuesday, This Must Be Africa 186

Con Market – Manet Cork – Knot Cream 190

Wait, Wait 193

Everybody Clap Your Hands 197

FICTION

Dynadormophis Up 204

Good Friday 210

Weird but True! 214

Trick or Treat 222

Black Friday 2050 226

Two Minutes for Holding 230

Three Days of Darkness 235

ACKNOWLEDGEMENTS 241

GROWING UP

Confidentially...

This is a cautionary tale, a story of how ignorance and the nuances of language can combine with coincidence to convey an unintended message of a mortifying caliber. It is the true account of a boy who was unaware that the unpleasantness confronting him was a consequence of his own actions, for he knew not what he was doing. Thankfully he remained in this state of immaturity for several years, allowing his fragile psyche to recover from the staggering truth when, at last, the individual links merged into an undeniable chain of events.

To appreciate the predicament fully, we must begin in the middle. Our protagonist – let's call him, say, Bobby – is a quiet second grader at a Catholic elementary school. He is in the class of one Miss M., a teacher beloved by most students and yet prone to a certain foulness of mood when crossed. It is the very same Miss M. who once made a spectacle of her displeasure with Bobby's older brother (whom we shall call B.J.) and the sloppiness of his desk by dumping B.J.'s accumulated possessions onto the floor before his peers. B.J. stood there stunned and uncomprehending, wondering why Miss M. did not simply order him to clean out his desk rather than unleashing her pent-up fury. But Bobby does not know about this darker side of his instructor, nor can he conceive that he is about to similarly provoke her ire.

It starts with a glare. Miss M. is sitting at her desk grading papers when she abruptly looks up and directs a stern look of disapproval at Bobby. She summons him to the front of the room with a voice that is uncharacteristically harsh, the sort of tone that educators reserve for unrepentant troublemakers. But troublemaker is not an accurate description of Bobby, whose childhood neuroses have already fed a budding Catholic guilt (and vice-versa) to foster a timidity that renders him nearly incapable of willful defiance. No, our hero is not the sort who tries to get away with anything. The domineering nun who taught him in first grade has already nipped his ego in the bud. So it is with great bewilderment that Bobby warily approaches Miss M.'s desk.

He is confused by her words, which he will be unable to recall upon later reflection. She does not come right out and say what it is that has upset her, but she is obviously irritated and maybe even angry. As she prattles on, Bobby tries to think of what he might have done that could have warranted such a reaction, but like a child trying desperately to invent meaningful sins while in line for confession, he comes up with nothing. He looks down at his shoes and endures his teacher's wrath until he is dismissed to his seat. Naturally, though he cannot think of any transgression by which he would deserve such a strong reprimand, he nevertheless takes it for granted that he does indeed deserve it. Bobby is worried and puzzled. The worry will fade as second grade resumes without further incident, but the puzzlement will last for years.

The Mystery of Miss M.'s Anger remains unsolved as Bobby grows older. The curious incident engages his mind now and then, especially whenever he reminisces about second grade, and over time it becomes the defining experience of that academic year. Still, its meaning stays elusive. What could he possibly have done to offend his teacher so deeply? Then, one day years later, the adolescent Bobby finds a clue. Preserved among the various ephemera of his youth is an essay that he wrote in second grade, and while the evidence it provides is by no means conclusive, it is certainly suggestive. The unconventional topic of the paper is, of all things, the experience of taking a bath.

Here is where we must travel backward in time to the genesis of our story, for the causal chain truly begins with our protagonist sitting before the living room television watching cartoons. Though he is no more than five or six years of age, he has developed an ear for language and an appreciation of how certain words sound in juxtaposition with other words. In one cartoon, he sees the Sphinx comment on its existence with the admission, "Monotonous, isn't it?" For weeks afterward, Bobby will carelessly insert the word *monotonous* into his everyday conversation with great amusement, only dimly aware of its meaning. Then there is a Bugs Bunny cartoon, and another lexicographic gem gleams before our young hero's eyes. "Eh, confidentially," intones Bugs as he conspiratorially begins to offer advice to his hapless victim. Something about the unfamiliar word appeals to Bobby, who files it away in his mental dictionary with the understanding that it sounds very good at the beginning of sentences.

Some time later, Bobby is sitting at the family room table with pencil in hand, staring up at the ceiling in search of the right words for the essay that Miss M. has assigned. He is to write a personal narrative about a common experience, and so he has decided to address the universal practice of bath-taking. For Bobby, it is not a frivolous topic, as taking a bath involves much more than getting clean. In fact, personal hygiene is a mere by-product, because the real purpose of taking a bath is cramming the tub with all the boats, army men, and other assorted toys that can be hauled into the bathroom. There are wars to be bravely fought, races to be gloriously won, and potential drownings to be melodramatically thwarted. All of these remarkable scenarios unfold in the solitude of a bath. But how can one express all of this in a few words?

Aware that not everyone is in the habit of taking toys into the bathtub, Bobby decides to emphasize his bathtime preference for play. *Let's see,* he thinks to himself. *When you're out with your friends, you say that you are playing with friends. But when you're alone, then you are by yourself. So when you are playing alone, you are playing with...who else? Yourself!* He scribbles a few words onto the paper, silently rereads his effort, and decides that something more is needed. Not much, just a dash of something to give the sentence flavor. Bobby frowns in concentration. *What are some good words I know?*

And now we fast-forward to the adolescent Bobby, still holding the essay that he wrote back in second grade. The days of simply learning how to read are long behind him, and he has gained the ability to discern shades of meaning and realizes that many texts can have multiple interpretations. Furthermore, he has a surer command of his vocabulary than he did when he was seven. It is with a shudder of horror, then, that within this enthusiastic composition about the pleasures of the bath, he finds the following sentence:

Confidentially, I like to play with myself.

Suddenly the contemptuous grimace of Miss M. surfaces to the fore of his older-but-wiser brain. Maybe, just maybe, the mystery has finally been solved.

And so, dear reader, I leave you with this gift. Always remember the lesson that I – er, I mean, that Bobby – learned that day. When you use words that you do not understand, you will at the very least sound like an idiot, and at the worst you might make somebody very angry. Oh, and it can be rather embarrassing, too.

Confidentially, it's a lesson I'm still learning.

Every Boy Does Magic

llusionist Penn Jillette once revealed to *Tucson Weekly* that his estimation of magic was changed by James "The Amazing" Randi, who taught him that it is an honorable profession provided that audiences are fully aware they are being deceived. I suppose the vast majority of those who bothered to tune in to *The Rock 'n' Fun Magic Show*, a gaudy spectacle featuring Bill Cosby, Doug Henning and the Hudson Brothers that aired in the fall of 1975, were cognizant that they were being exposed to illusions rather than manifestations of the supernatural, Henning's wide-eyed proclamations that "anything is possible" notwithstanding. I, however, was only seven years old, an age at which I accepted almost everything at face value. Even though I understood that all magic was some sort of a trick, I totally bought into the false drama that Henning employed to heighten the effect of his most dramatic stunt.

"Not only is this the first time this escape has been attempted since Houdini did it, it's the first time it's ever been tried on television," intoned a sober host as he stood before a glass tank filled to the brim with water. "And remember, it's being done live at this very moment. If this looks dangerous to you, believe me, it is." Henning then emerged from the wings, striding purposefully in a rust-colored robe with the confident air of Christ on his way to give what-for to the temple desecrators. Stripped down to a pair of orange trunks, he was hoisted by his padlocked ankles and dangled over the tank. "And now, Doug is going to take four deep breaths – and hold the last one."

As Henning was lowered into the tank, a digital timer was superimposed upon the proceedings. A pair of assistants secured the lid of the compartment and descended from the platform, allowing a curtain to rise and envelop the tank. This was when the host really earned his paycheck.

> **1:00** *"Now remember, it's twice as hard to get a deep breath when hanging upside down, and don't forget – don't forget that this is live."*

> **1:19** *"As far as I'm concerned, this is scary."*

> **1:25** *"I can hear churning water, but I don't know whether he's out of the manacles or not. I really don't know."*

> **1:43** *"How can anyone hold his breath this long?"*

Just after the two-minute mark, a robed attendant darted offstage and returned seconds later holding an axe.

> **2:14** *"Two minutes, fifteen seconds. Doug can only hold his breath for two minutes and thirty seconds. This man standing here is our emergency squad. If anything goes wrong, he's ready with his axe. Let's hope we don't really need to use him, but time is running out!"*

> **2:35** *"Something's wrong – get the axe, go up there. Smash the glass! Drop the curtain!"*

At two minutes and thirty-nine seconds, with the robed attendant having already taken his backswing, the curtain dropped to reveal an empty tank. Silence. Expressions of awe and laughter, then vociferous applause and a standing ovation when the axeman dropped his implement as well as his robe, revealing the mustache-framed, goofy smile of Doug Henning. I could almost hear my racing heart as I exhaled sharply and fell back into the couch cushions.

I didn't like being cruelly misled into thinking that someone I admired was on the verge of death due to an escape stunt gone awry. I also felt a little stupid for having believed it. On the other hand, I was impressed by the illusion and the degree to which I could be distracted by artful staging and patter. Obviously, Henning was free from the contraption long before I even suspected it might be possible. That element of magic, the misdirection and subsequent surprise, enchanted me. I thereafter embarked on every introverted young boy's required rite of passage: a little dabbling in prestidigitation.

I started slowly, consulting children's books that detailed basic tricks requiring only household objects and a little practice. Soon I became proficient in the mystifying art of pushing thumbtacks into balloons without popping them, but I lacked the dexterity and patience to do the necessary preparation for peeling a pre-sliced banana. After trying out these tricks and whatever else I was able to accomplish with the likes of matchsticks and handkerchiefs, I was ready for stronger stuff.

I found what I was looking for in an amusement park gag shop, nestled in a bin next to the rubber pencils. The finger guillotine was a sleek little prop that was cheap and easy to use, plus it allowed any kid to create a seemingly impossible illusion. Its instructions advised stoking an audience by using the unsharpened blade to thwack a carrot in half, which was easy enough to do if you took care to avoid the thicker carrots. Once you convinced folks that the device could render anyone a digital amputee, you stunned them by placing your index finger in the hole and passing the blade clean through it. At least that's how it worked provided that you set the trick blade to "finger" instead of "carrot". I forgot to do that once, and it's a wonder I didn't break my finger. I'm not surprised that you don't see too many of these gizmos being peddled to kids these days.

Observing my passion for sleight-of-hand, my parents indulged me with a generous order from the Marshall Brodien TV Magic Catalog. Though one of the gags proved to be a dud (Smoke From Your Fingertips was nothing more than a tube of clear goo that was supposed to effervesce from your artfully waved hands), I was thrilled with the rest. There was a hollow, metal cylinder that looked just like a stack of nickels when you put a real one on top of it, allowing me to thrill spectators by changing nickels into dimes. There was a pair of plastic bowls with a clear disk of the same diameter that enabled me to apparently change water into rice. A cleverly designed coin chamber gave me the ability to seemingly push nails through a half dollar. The inarguable highlight, however, was the magic box.

The magic box was a red and black, cardboard cube with doors that opened on the front and top. Thanks to a mirror that crossed the interior diagonal and concealed half of the cube's volume, it was a snap to make any small object vanish or unexpectedly appear. It was an absolutely great illusion, one that looked so good it could stupefy the skeptical. It also required very little practice to employ effectively. Ultimately, it was my unwillingness to commit myself to more than a half-hour of practice that ended my brief experience as an illusionist. That and the fact that I began to perceive most magicians as more annoying than entertaining. My magic box went on the shelf.

But it didn't go away. I just moved it to a different shelf – one within a cabinet at my elementary school. In the world of education, I found that the occasional illusion can keep kids thinking. It can also help smooth over awkward moments. One year, I had to confiscate a small item from a student who would not put it away during a lesson. The day ended with both of us forgetting to resolve the incident. When the next morning arrived and I remembered I had something that belonged to that student, I had a hunch he would mention it the moment he walked in the room, and so I concealed the contraband in the magic box. Sure enough, my unwitting student entered the classroom, approached my desk, and politely asked if I would return what belonged to him. I maintained the soberest demeanor, while inwardly I was as delighted as a little boy whose shipment of Marshall Brodien magic had just arrived. Without saying a word, I produced the magic box, opening its doors to reveal its apparently empty interior as my student looked on quizzically. Then I closed the front door, reached in the top, and withdrew the item he had requested. His expression was priceless.

Word got around the class about the trick, and I subsequently pulled a few more things out of the box and made a few things disappear. Perhaps it would have been most educational had

I revealed the perceptual science behind the illusion, but I maintain that I was still on honorable ground. The kids knew they were being deceived; they just weren't sure how. And me? I got to amaze a captive audience with little to no practice required.

Take that, Henning.

Grandpa, Sasquatch and Me

My paternal grandfather died at the age of 86 when I was twelve years old. Given the fact that he lived just around the next block during the entire time I knew him, it seems only natural that I would have many memories of our brief time together. Yet, sadly, I cannot recall any specific moments that we shared. I only remember what it was like to sit quietly in his tiny living room when Dad and I would stop by for a visit. The two of them would drone on about topics that did not interest me at all, and I would pass the time by rocking in a swivel chair and scanning the latest *National Enquirer* that had been left on the end table. Sometimes there would be something interesting on the TV, but most often not.

I can only remember Grandpa as a mysterious and taciturn widower, Grandma having died when I was six. He did not live alone, though, as he had a faithful dachshund named Gidget for companionship. A highlight of visiting Grandpa, one might think. But as much as I found my grandfather to be remote, his little dog was completely unapproachable. Apparently, she had once suffered abuse at the hands of youngsters, rendering her hostile toward anyone who happened to be in the same peer group as her former tormentors. Between Grandpa's perpetual frown and his vicious wiener dog, I didn't care to linger when we visited.

Not that there weren't subtle signs that there was far more to this man than his introverted nature suggested. The white tank top undershirts he favored in summertime revealed a faded rose tattoo, a real curiosity in an age when getting inked was a badge of nonconformity. I tried not to stare at it, just as I averted my eyes from his hand that was missing half of its pinkie finger. For many years I mistakenly believed that it had been mangled in a train coupling. Lord knows where I got the idea, as the dull truth was that Grandpa had simply got his finger caught in a factory machine press. Perhaps my brain just embellished the romantic character that started to form in my mind as I grew older and heard tales of my late grandfather.

Raising half a dozen kids during the 1920s and 30s could not have been easy, and Grandpa did whatever he could to make ends meet. Most famously, desperate for a job to support his family, he managed to secure employment as a typing instructor despite the fact that he did not know how to type. How he got the job remains a mystery, but he apparently managed to bluff his way through the obligation by a regimen of self-instruction that kept him one lesson ahead of his students. During another lean period, he was literally down to his last dollar, which he gambled on a tip book from a bar. Amazingly, the investment paid off handsomely enough to get him by.

I learned that he eventually was a successful seller of cemetery plots, a somewhat ghoulish profession for which he was once rewarded with a tie tack in the shape of a shovel. He had a spotlight mounted to his car in order to find house numbers while canvassing neighborhoods in the evening. Somehow the very idea evokes the melodrama of an old EC horror comic book. I can only guess that anyone who could manage to make a living persuading people to open their doors at night and buy a cemetery plot must have been born to sell.

I found out that against all stereotypes, it was Grandpa who cooked breakfast for my father when he was young, setting a hot plate and a steaming mug of coffee before his youngest child every morning. I laughed at the story of Grandpa's ire upon finding his car blocked by a double-parked vehicle, which he subsequently removed by starting his own automobile and pushing the obstacle out of the way. But I'm glad I wasn't around to see the legendary poker night when he is said to have expressed his disgust at a bad game by hauling all of the gambling paraphernalia down to the basement and tossing it into the coal furnace. I am told that one of my cousins possesses evidence of the incident by way of a collection of singed poker chips.

So much I could have asked him, if only I had grown a bit older before he died. But we never had a whole lot to say to each other, or at least that's how I remember it. For the longest time, well into my adulthood, I had the impression that I was barely noticed by Grandpa. I was, after all, the last of his twenty-two grandchildren, and surely the novel thrill of grandfatherhood must have worn off by then. But then I found a trio of letters, written to me during his annual wintering with my aunts and uncles in California, that tell a different story. Perhaps he never did say much to me in person – maybe he never felt comfortable doing so – but he took the time to put into written words the very things that any grandchild would want to hear:

> San Diego, Calif.
>
> Jan. 8, 1977
>
> Dear Bobby:
>
> I liked your letter with the drawing of a ten dollar bill. Did you deposit your Christmas money in the bank?
>
> I'll bet you received a number of nice gifts on Christmas Day. Did you get a sled? I hear that Lima has been getting a lot of snow, so a sled will be a lot of fun.
>
> I wish you could be with me when I take my walks along the ocean. There are many big ships coming and going, and also many jet passenger planes and Navy planes. Many people take their lunches with them and either lay in the sun or go bathing, and the children play in the sand.
>
> There has been a lot of snow in the mountains, and a lot of parents take their children up there to play in it.
>
> I will look for another letter from you soon.

A big hug and kiss for you, and love and best wishes to all.

Grandpa

P.S. I ma learning to use Norma's new electric typewriter, so please excuse mistakes.

Have you made any more plans to capture Bigfoot?

How funny it is for me to read that letter today. I don't even remember writing letters to Grandpa, which I'm guessing I might have done only at my parents' urging. Why I would have drawn a ten-dollar bill is beyond me. I do, however, recall my boyhood fascination with Bigfoot. I took it for granted that he was real, and I once detailed how I might take him captive with the aid of Dad, Grandpa, and the hostile hound Gidget. I am certain that Grandpa's dry humor went right over my head when I first read his letters.

San Diego, Ca

Dec. 14, 1977

Dear Bobby,

I enjoyed your nice letter and the interesting drawings. Thanks a lot for the Christmas seals.

We went to Richard's house in Oceanside last Sunday, and Gidget was very happy to see me. She is a lot of company for Richard, and he will hate to give her up when I return to Lima.

Richard and Dave and Lee Ann and their kids are coming for a week in San Diego, and we will be at Lee Ann's parents home for Christmas dinner.

I hope you will get everything you want for Christmas.

I read in the newspaper that Bigfoot has been seen in Oregon. I will watch for any more news about him, and let you know. It does not seem likely that he will be in Ohio until about next summer.

Glad that you like the snow. People with children drive up in the high mountains here and bring snow home in the trunks of their cars. Rather silly, I think.

Thanks a lot for the Christmas seals.

Write again real soon.

Love and best wishes,

Grandpa

P.S. You are a very good letter writer.

Why, that isn't the Grandpa I remember visiting! How could I have read words like those and so quickly forgotten them? But then I was quite young, too young to see the humor and too unsophisticated to appreciate how carefully my grandfather had written in a style that was easy for me to understand. The thought that he took the time to write when he could have spent a few more moments relaxing in sunny California would never have occurred to me.

The last letter, written within two years of his death, reflects a change in tone. Grandpa recognized that I was a little more grown up, being ten and all, and perhaps it was time to address me differently. He still, however, took delight in providing me with Bigfoot updates.

San Diego, Calif

March 12, 1979

Dear Bob:

I enjoyed your recent letter and am glad you are doing well in school, even tho you do not like it too well. It is best to have a good education.

It looks like bad weather is about over in Lima, and you can have a lot of fun with your bike. Are you going to play ball this summer?

The last I heard about Bigfoot, he was seen somewhere in Idaho. If he ever comes to Ohio, we will put Gidget on his trail.

We took a long ride in the mountains yesterday. Many wonderful things to see.

I have reservations for my trip home on the 7th of April. Will be happy to get back.

Love and best wishes to all,

Grandpa

I regret that I never knew Grandpa better, but I am very grateful to have the letters that he wrote to me so long ago. Not only do they prove to me that my grandfather did, indeed, have great affection for me, but they also provide me with a valuable lesson. It's always a good investment of time to put your love of others into writing. You never know when those words will communicate what you no longer can.

Cafeteriphobia

A big cafeteria. That's what you need if you're planning on running an institution that teaches children from first through eighth grade. St. Gerard, my elementary and middle school alma mater, met that requirement with room to spare. As a little kid, our cafeteria seemed like a cavernous space, an immense and spare rectangular room so large that its flat and featureless ceiling was supported by more than half a dozen pillars. If the prospect of attending a school that included students twice your height and age didn't already make you feel small, being herded into the cafeteria for the first time erased any vestiges of pride.

For a hall that admitted plenty of sun through great windows along its length, the St. Gerard cafeteria was run with chilling efficiency. To this day, if I were to walk through its far entrance, I could show you the exact path that we were expected to follow as we wound along the perimeter in single file toward the serving area. There we would pick up the molded plastic trays upon which a small group of cafeteria ladies – some nice, others indifferent, and a few downright intimidating – would deposit the various components of the day's meal. We picked up our milk last, dutifully inserting the half-pint carton into its designated tray compartment, and proceeded toward the seating area.

That was where they assigned their sternest and stoutest personnel, I believe, no-nonsense disciplinarians whose directives would be followed without question. It was they who marshaled us down the farthest seating row until it was filled to capacity, then subsequent rows would be seated in like fashion. Due to this system, you always knew who would be sitting immediately to your left and right, but there was no telling who would be sitting across from you. Consequently, students tried to manipulate their place in the lunch line to ensure proximity to at least one friend, or else it could be a conversationally awkward lunch. If things turned out badly, you might even find yourself sitting opposite strange kids from the grade above you.

There was one day during one of my earliest years at St. Gerard when, through no fault of my own, I was detained at the beginning of the lunch period, thus preventing me from lining up with my peers. To my horror, I arrived at the cafeteria as the eighth graders were approaching the serving windows, leaving me no choice but to meekly take a spot at the end of their queue. The seating area matron ensured that I followed the conventional arrangement, and I spent that lunch staring down at my tray and wondering if the eighth graders were laughing at me, or maybe they always laughed at everything.

I recall being a fairly happy kid when I was very young, but somewhere along the line I endured a brief period of socially crippling neuroses that may have had their genesis in the St. Gerard cafeteria. To the adults in my life, it seemed absurd that I should worry about "getting in the wrong lunch line" at school, but the specter of total ostracism was a real and reasonable fear to me. Soon my paranoia was manifesting itself in truly irrational ways, leading me to such bizarre suspicions as the idea that my own breathing might not be involuntary, and if my respiration really did depend on a certain degree of consciousness, I might expire in my sleep on any given night. It was a challenging time for my poor parents.

Crazy or not, I was responding to an atmosphere that certainly had its oppressive qualities. For example, there was a total segregation of students who packed their lunches from those who purchased a school lunch. Why, I have no idea, except that to do otherwise might have thrown a wrench into the precision mechanism of the rigidly enforced seating system. Packers sat at a totally separate set of tables, and because they were only a small minority of the student body, there was a measure of pathos in their lonely uncrumpling of lunch bags. I felt sorry for

24

them. I eventually befriended one of the packers in fifth grade, and though we became good friends outside of the cafeteria, we were destined to never share a lunch conversation.

Students were generously allowed seconds of certain items now and then, I imagine because of unintended surpluses. Generally, they were dessert items like peanut butter bars or cookies. Midway through my St. Gerard career, in a rare moment of assertiveness coupled with an embarrassing misunderstanding of leftover distribution, I gratefully accepted some sort of confection and brazenly announced, "I'll have another one."

Teachers and other adults who work with children, remember to err on the side of caution when you suspect impertinence from your charges. A quick and kind explanation of why my request had to be denied would have sufficed, but the grizzled hag whom I addressed eyed me with the outrage of Dickens' Mr. Bumble regarding Oliver Twist begging for more gruel. "Oh no you won't!" she snapped, and my cheeks flushed with shame. Taking a cold seat at my assigned row, I silently vowed to never again phrase a request in such a presumptive manner.

Even if every adult who staffed the cafeteria had been as gentle and caring as Mr. Rogers, any kid can tell you that the greatest threat to one's well-being exists in the unpredictable actions of other kids. Stan Smithers put me off white milk for at least a year when he inexplicably picked his nose and deposited a morsel of snot into my open half-pint. I remember that he did this gleefully and without the slightest duplicity. He seemed to deeply enjoy the look of sheer revulsion and anger that I must have assumed upon witnessing his transgression. It took me a long time to get over it. Every time I raised a glass of milk to my lips, I couldn't help imagining a gooey, green glob floating invisibly within it.

Remarkably, I ate eight years worth of lunches in the St. Gerard cafeteria without ever knowing the profound personal significance of my surroundings. The space looked sterile and utilitarian at best to me, with one particularly garish wall upon which was mounted an electronic BINGO board. I was totally ignorant of the fact that our lunch tables rested where rows of pews were once bolted to the floor, that our trays were filled where an altar once stood, and that decades before we wolfed down tater tots, my parents had walked down an aisle between the pillars as a newly wedded couple. How was I to know that my home rooms through fifth grade were situated above and below the modest sanctuary where Mom and Dad were married? It never occurred to me that the building I knew as the church was not yet built when they attended St. Gerard.

I never found out about this fundamental piece of my own history until many years later. I wonder if it would have made a difference had I known the former sanctity of the space we called our cafeteria. Maybe it would have made that day with the eighth graders a little less scary. Perhaps I would have shrugged off the tart reprimand of Mrs. Bumble. And if only I had known that Stan Smithers was putting his snot in my milk in the very room where my parents had exchanged vows, I might have given the kid what he deserved.

That's right, Stan. I know you're out there, and I haven't forgotten. You might want to keep an eye on your milk.

Broadway Boogie-Woogie

I remember my Great Aunt Peg as a kindly old woman who seemed to be in a perpetual state of amusement. She ambled about with her stout frame and white hair, her sparkling eyes framed by glacial grooves of laugh-worn wrinkles, her cherubic mouth always somewhere on the continuum from Mona Lisa grin to tooth-baring smile.

Her infectious laugh was gentle and silly. It began with a short, guttural warning, followed by a cascading repetition of rollicking chortles. *A-hill, hill, hill! A-hill, hill, hill, hill!* If you didn't happen to think that the object of her outburst was funny, it was no matter to her – she just went on *a-hill*-ing, and you couldn't help but be amused yourself by that silly laugh.

She was a childless widow by the time I came along. Though she lived only a block away, I never visited her, as it was the custom for her to visit us. Then one day, by circumstances I do not recall, I found myself the sole guest in her modest home.

I was perhaps nine years old, and I must have known I was due for a visit of some length, for I remember bringing along a small collection of treasures to show and tell. We sat before a coffee table in her ordinary living room, sunlight filtering through the window from the quiet intersection that bordered her corner house. I embarked on a detailed lecture concerning the assorted items I had arranged on the table. Aunt Peg sat patiently and attentively through my thoughtful discourses on the merits of one trading card over another and the means by which my portable slide viewer worked.

"Oh, how 'bout that, it has a little battery inside," she enthused, "a little battery, a-hill, hill!"

When at last I had exhausted my knowledge and fell silent, Aunt Peg was ready to take her turn. She fixed her whimsical countenance upon me and asked, "Have you seen my tent room?" Her casual tone made it sound as though she was referring to something everyone had in their homes. Nonplussed and inquisitive, I followed her into the hall.

Something caught my eye along the way, an optical interference that felt totally out of context. I heard Aunt Peg's footsteps stop as she turned to find me staring into her bathroom.

"Oh, you like the wallpaper? A-hill, hill! My nephew Bob put that up for me, too."

Her nephew Bob. I felt a twinge of jealousy at the mention of his name, for I, too, was her nephew Bob, only I was still being called Bobby by everyone. Aunt Peg's Bob was a mystery to me, someone to whom I was not related in any obvious way and whom I had never met. He did not live here in town, that much I knew, and it was clear from the way that Aunt Peg spoke of him that she was very fond of him.

What kind of man was this Bob? If the bathroom wallpaper was any indication, he was certainly unlike anyone I knew. The pattern was an aggressive, black-and-white tessellation of trance-inducing op art, all dissolving chessboards and the suggestion of checkered spheres that seemed to expand from the wall in bulbous apparitions about the towel rack. Sitting on the toilet must have been a trip into psychedelia, leaving the occupant with a sense of being lost among a sea of holes. I decided then and there that, whomever he was, I liked Bob.

With my senses somewhat scrambled, I followed Aunt Peg down the hall to a doorway from which dangled a curtain of stringed beads and plastic gemstones. She parted the colorful obstacle, and I stepped into another world. A rosy warmth suffused the space, bathing a simple card table and chairs with a crimson glow. The unremarkable furnishings were dominated by great swaths of burgundy fabric that drooped from the four corners of the ceiling and gathered in the center above a hanging tiffany lamp. The effect was surreal. I felt as though I was inside a carnival fortune teller's tent.

"Isn't this something?" chortled Aunt Peg. "Bob dreamed it all up and did it all himself. Now I can sit under a tent any time I want, a-hill, hill!"

"That's really neat!"

"I'll say! And that's not all!" She gestured toward a tall box with dark, wooden sides and a rectangular section of beige material stretched over its near face. "Can you guess what this is?"

I had no idea. Before I could think of a response, Aunt Peg pushed a button on a nearby stereo console, and the box came alive with sound and light. Multicolored pinpoints glowed and pulsated to the steady rhythm of a pop song.

"Wow! He made that?"

"Yep. Now I can sit in my tent room any time I want and watch the lights and listen to music. How about that?"

We sat down and played a few games of Go Fish. I kept glancing at the swirling colors of the stereo speaker, wishing secretly that Aunt Peg would notice my admiration and give the fascinating creation to me. It didn't seem likely, though. She seemed as delighted by the coveted object as I was.

In the course of the afternoon, I learned that the mysterious Nephew Bob had left his mark throughout the house, adding elements of dramatic flair and progressive décor here and there. There was a once unremarkable wardrobe, formerly of a pedestrian brown finish, now antiqued and concealing a television behind its distressed panel doors. And the coffee table at which we had sat earlier turned out to be anything but ordinary. Underneath the newspapers and magazines that cluttered its glass surface was an oval pedestal made from an old washtub, its interior filled with artificial plants that could be observed through the tabletop.

"This is Bob's, too," beamed Aunt Peg as she pointed toward a framed print near the stair landing. "See if you can guess what it is!"

I gazed up at an abstract painting composed of large white rectangles bordered by smaller quadrilaterals of yellow, red and blue. It was an appealing pattern, but I could not discern what it was supposed to represent, if indeed it symbolized anything at all. "Did a kid paint it?" I ventured. It seemed plausible.

"Oh, no," chuckled Aunt Peg. "This is a famous painting by a famous artist, and it shows what it's like in New York City. Pretend you're a bird flying over the Empire State Building and all the skyscrapers, and you can look down and see all the streets. See all the yellow taxi cabs? If you squint your eyes like this, it's almost like a real picture. Isn't that somethin'?"

"Wow!" Now that she explained it, I saw everything she could see. In fact, I couldn't stop seeing the concrete idea behind the geometric abstraction. Never again would I be able to look upon the image as a mere jumble of rectangles; from now on I would be soaring high above the crowded streets of NYC. "I can see it now! How did you figure that out?"

"Bob told me all about it, a-hill-hill! He says you wouldn't believe how exciting a big city like New York is!"

I turned to study Aunt Peg beaming at the painting with childlike fascination. She, herself, was a totally accessible portrait of happiness. Her unassuming house was full of wonders in which she delighted. Whether it was the vibrancy and whimsy of the decor that endeared these treasures to her or the mere fact that they were created and installed by her beloved nephew Bob I could not tell. But sharing them with me and seeing my awed reaction seemed to please her as much as anything could.

Before I began my short walk home, I felt a surge of curiosity about the mad interior decorating genius who had transformed her home into an eccentric art museum. "Aunt Peg, is Bob going to do any more neat things in your house, like the tent room?"

30

Her ever-present smile waned for just an instant. "Bob lives in San Francisco now." Then her effervescent enthusiasm bubbled over again. "But he told me in his last letter that he's finally going to be able to come back and stay for a visit sometime soon!"

As it happened, I never did meet Bob, nor did I return to Aunt Peg's house. She continued to attend our various family gatherings, and as I grew older, she began to regress. By the time I was a teenager, she had moved into a nursing home.

Hindsight affords me the knowledge of just how unsophisticated Aunt Peg was. She was one of the jolliest, friendliest people I've ever known, yet she was blissfully ignorant of much of the world. That there might be any significance to the flamboyant dress of her nephew Bob, his flair for progressive interior design, and his abandonment of the intolerant Midwest for the friendlier surroundings of San Francisco was absolutely beyond her comprehension. Did she know that the painting he hung in her living room was a mass-market print of Piet Mondrian's *Broadway Boogie Woogie*? Probably not. Tragically, that childlike perspective included a literal faith in the words of others. She truly believed that Bob would return one day.

I was in my late teens when I last saw Aunt Peg, my one and only visit to the nursing home. It was a dark and unpleasant place filled with offensive odors and unsettling noises. The only thing worse than the atmosphere was the shock I felt upon encountering Aunt Peg, who had been transformed from a stout picture of jollity into a bony and defeated wretch. Her thin wrists were secured to the armrests of her highback chair, in which she slumped forward and glared. She was experiencing a reaction to her medication, we were told, causing her to inhale sharply and suck her puffy lower lip into her mouth every few seconds. My mother tried to offer pleasantries and maintain a positive outlook, but Aunt Peg was unyieldingly bitter.

"No...no...I never..." she wheezed, "hear from Bob...he...never comes."

It was a horrible visit, compounded by the fact that the situation was unlikely to improve. When at last it was time for us to leave, I leaned over and kissed her forehead. "Goodbye, Aunt Peg."

She continued to wheeze and draw her lip into her mouth, her head bobbing backward with every inhalation. Her eyes remained fixed at some distant point, and the spotted backs of her clenched hands rose up from their restraints.

"Goodbye, Bob."

The Vinyl Frontier

tar Trek or *Planet of the Apes?*

That was the paralyzing decision that I had to make one afternoon in 1975. I stood transfixed before brightly colored boxes, my brow furrowed with the anxious knowledge that whichever option I chose, it would come at the expense of forfeiting the other.

Star Trek or *Planet of the Apes?*

Both playsets looked fantastically inviting, especially when accessorized with a quartet of eight-inch action figures. I studied the pictures and tried to envision what exciting scenarios I might be able to create with these tantalizing toys. Did one of the choices offer more hours of fun? Might I grow tired of one of them sooner than I imagined? Did one road lead to sustained happiness, while the other ended in unforeseen regret? My nostrils flared.

Star Trek or *Planet of the Apes?*

My mother and father stood nearby, patiently observing their youngest child's angst. We were standing in a long aisle within the vast establishment known as Children's Palace. The mere sight of its turreted facade had thrilled me to my very capacity for excitement, for I had seen television ads for the store and yearned to visit it like a prospector dreams of El Dorado. In my hometown of Lima, toys were confined to a small department within stores that sold an array of goods. The concept of a big box retailer dealing exclusively in toys was like hearing tell of a swimming pool filled with chocolate milk. Yet here in Columbus, I was standing within a genuine Children's Palace.

Children of today have no point of reference to comprehend this wonderland. A recent simulacrum would be Toys 'R' Us, yet its wares lacked the charm of a Children's Palace at the dawn of the disco era. In 1975, toy store stock did not include endless titles for rival video game systems, nor did glossy boxes concealing computer software line the shelves. All of the items for sale offered a tactile experience, and to see row after row of board games and bikes and models and Hot Wheels and Rock 'Em Sock 'Em Robots and many gizmos hitherto unseen was overwhelming in the most euphoric way. Not to mention dolls, Barbies, and all things pink, if you liked that kind of thing. It was like a preview of heaven.

Both of the items I coveted were manufactured by Mego, the same firm that would later unleash Captain and Tennille and KISS action figures upon a jaded public awash in the peculiar trends of the Seventies. The outfit would have made Eli Whitney proud, minimizing production costs by sticking different heads onto interchangeable articulated bodies. Apparently in some cases, overstocked heads for unpopular lines were reused for later products. According to collector Michael Rogers, that is how the Paul Stanley figure came to be topped with the painted noggin of Daryl "Captain" Dragon. One can only wonder what happened to the heads of Toni Tennille.

In hindsight, the most amusing thing about my childhood dilemma is the fact that I am not, nor have I ever been, a Trekkie, a Trekker, or whatever it is that devotees of the U.S.S. Enterprise like to call themselves. Neither can I lay claim to any enthusiasm beyond casual amusement for the *Planet of the Apes* franchise. Yet the merchandise beckoned to me with all the persuasive power of brand name recognition. At a list price of about $15 for either option (no small sum in '75), I had to choose carefully.

I considered the *Planet of the Apes* Treehouse. A little spare in design, but it included a barred cage in which to detain prisoners, which looked like fun. The open architecture offered plenty of opportunities for violent confrontations that would end with a character plunging to his death, which also sounded fun. A hatch in the roof provided further possibilities for high-altitude hijinks. But the coolest thing about the playset was that it was meant to be inhabited by *Planet of the Apes* action figures. There is something fundamentally irresistible about talking simians wearing bandoliers and brandishing rifles. Really, who wouldn't enjoy owning a set of eight-inch, articulated apes?

The *Star Trek* action figures, on the other hand, were far less interesting, though the resemblance to their TV counterparts was impressive. The U.S.S. Enterprise Action Playset was a vinyl-sheathed hexagonal box that opened to reveal a rather crudely interpreted bridge set. Minimally detailed furnishings included a bulky captain's chair, a pair of stools that looked more like snack tables for the captain, and a boxy object with symbol-laden decals that was meant to represent a complex control console. A slot behind the viewscreen was intended to receive any of a dozen cardboard inserts featuring illustrated scenes of mediocre quality. Overall, it was a less enticing package.

But...it had one redeeming quality that I found absolutely fascinating. A rectangular box housing a rotating cylinder represented the famous transporter room. Like a closet with its door removed, the space was enclosed on three sides. The cylinder had a panel of its exterior cut away, allowing one to place an action figure inside a quarter of the interior. Opposite this was an identical, hidden compartment. The outer surface of this container was plastered with dazzling, black and yellow, op-art stickers. Atop the whole affair were three buttons. By setting the cylinder spinning with the center button, you would perceive what appeared to be an electrical pattern superimposed over the action figure. The other buttons stopped the cylinder cold at either the occupied or empty compartment, enabling a convincing illusion of disappearance. It was a great little magic trick, and I could not resist it.

Only eBay knows what price I might have commanded one day had I kept my U.S.S. Enterprise Action Playset and my Kirk, Bones, Spock and Klingon figures in decent condition. As it was, I handled them roughly, popping off the characters' heads and extracting the rotating cylinder from its transformer room housing for closer inspection. I lost the guns and the utility belts among the assorted detritus of my toy drawers. Even if I could have located all of the various components, it would have taken some effort to restore everything to collectible condition. I guess I just didn't have a sufficient amount of respect for the *Star Trek* crew.

All these years later, I am older and wiser. In my maturity, I realize the decision I should have made. Keep the U.S.S. Enterprise, but man the spacecraft with Dr. Zaius and the rest of the denizens of *Planet of the Apes*. Now *that* would have been cool.

Bombs Away

Born during the Depression and raised in the years of scarcity that lasted through WWII, my father was accustomed to amusing himself by inventing games using whatever materials were at hand. He played war by tossing coins onto his bed, pennies as privates and higher denominations representing officers. Those that landed face-down were killed in action. He once pretended a jar of cherries was a passenger plane, dropping the glass container onto cement and narrating the gory aftermath. When there was nothing else to do, Dad could be found shooting his arrow straight up into the sky with a naive confidence that it would never return to its point of origin.

Years later as the father of six children, Dad still retained a measure of satisfaction in the invention of a simple diversion. I was indulged with shelves and drawers full of toys, yet I do not think that I enjoyed the best of those items any more than I did a crude entertainment that Dad fashioned from a discarded cardboard box. It was a long, flat box, the sort that might have once contained a small folding table. With the aid of a ruler and a ballpoint pen, Dad adorned one of its broad sides with a map of a generic town. The fictitious city featured crisscrossing streets, numerous buildings, an airport, and a busy seaport, all rendered with the endearing precision of an amateur draftsman.

It was a short trip from Dad's basement worktable to the bottom of the steps, where we placed the box before ascending the stairs. Once we reached the top, we turned around and sat. Dad and I divvied up the ammunition: a small cache of colorful, plastic darts. We took turns throwing them down to the silent city, which looked like a distant metropolis from our vantage point.

The overall layout was discernible, but it was difficult to make out the small details. Dad and I were pilots on a bombing run, and our objective was to inflict maximum damage to military targets while leaving civilians unharmed. Half of the fun was throwing the darts, and the other half was running down the stairs to see what we had hit.

The bay was populated with a number of vessels ranging from aircraft carriers and battleships to much smaller speedboats. Hitting any of them was considered a great victory, as was managing to land a dart tip in any of the planes scattered about the airfield. Also meritorious was blowing up one of the circular oil silos, a detail inspired by the enormous containers on the outskirts of our real-life town. Most of the time, though, our bombs struck elsewhere. There was a hospital, clearly visible from the top of the stairs due to the bold cross Dad had drawn on its roof, and I'm afraid that it was the recipient of collateral damage from time to time. I mean, they weren't exactly smart bombs that we were dropping. Some of mine missed the cityscape completely, embedding themselves in the bottom step or ricocheting off the basement floor. Yes, it was dangerous business, but we were up to the task.

Our faux town included a school, which I believe Dad intended to be another taboo bomb destination. However, as I was not enamored of my educational experience, I rather relished the idea of my school being obliterated. I think Dad took as much delight as I did in the occasions when we reached the end of the stairs and discovered a dart lodged smack in the middle of our little town's sole institution of learning. "No school! No school!," I would shout with the enthusiasm of a boy waking up to a raging blizzard, "Can't go to school because there is no school!"

Undeveloped acreage was still available along the perimeter of the box, and Dad allowed me to add my own streets and edifices in an unrefined style that clashed with the neat aesthetic that he had established. It looked as if the zoning board had been kidnapped and lawless citizens had built amok. Free to add new targets to our bustling town, I enhanced the airport with a few more planes, drew some more ships in the bay, and plotted out a modern suburban neighborhood with winding streets that rebelled against the orderly grid of the city.

My crowning touch, though, was simply to modify one of Dad's rectangular buildings by adding the label J.C. Penney Outlet Store. Having accompanied my parents on many trips from Lima to Columbus, I had spent what seemed to be an accumulation of many hours waiting for Mom to finish shopping there. I found it quite trying, as the store was vast yet held little merchandise that appealed to me, and so I would exhaust whatever interest I had in the place within ten minutes. Mom saw much that was worth exploring, however, and inevitably Dad and I would pass some time sitting in the dismal lobby before retiring to the car. To me, the J.C. Penney Outlet Store was a military objective of greater strategic importance than planes, ships, and oil tanks.

Sometimes, for added excitement, we turned off the lights for a night bombing run. With only our mental perception of the darkened basement and muscle memory to guide us, we cast our weapons into the blackness and listened intently. A distant *thup* signaled that one of our darts had at least hit the box, though precisely where was impossible to say. Often, we heard the clatter of a bomb striking and sliding across cement, and once in a while we were startled by the hollow clang of an errant missile bouncing off the furnace. Lights back on, we scrambled down the steps to assess the damage, both to our little town and to whatever else we hit in the basement.

Eventually Dad's dart-throwing diversion was riddled with holes, and the box began to lose its structural integrity, but by then we had successfully completed many missions together. I was fortunate to have a childhood that included plenty of opportunities, wonderful vacations, and a wealth of material goods. As nice as all of those things were, none of them were better than sitting at the top of the stairs with Dad, tossing plastic darts into a cardboard box.

Green Machine

don't remember exactly when I learned to ride a bicycle, but I'm pretty sure I was the last of my peers to acquire the skill. I have a vague notion that it wasn't even necessarily my idea. Somehow, we ended up borrowing an old and rusted girls' bike with training wheels, a literal vehicle for shame and embarrassment. I knew that the whole world was watching me as I wobbled up and down the sidewalk. *Ha, ha! Look at that kid who hasn't learned how to ride a bike yet!* I kept my head down, tried to keep my balance, and wondered how I had unwittingly fallen behind the rest of the pack. Like every childhood drama, it seemed terribly important at the time.

My first experience with human-propelled vehicles was the classic tricycle, which by all accounts I heartily enjoyed. It was the standard, all-metal model with a runner between the back wheels. I am told that it was stolen from our front yard one night, a heartless thievery that I do not recall, yet I am willing to cast blame upon the anonymous robber for activating latent neuroses. If ever I am called to plead my case before a jury, I'm blaming whatever I did on the tricycle thief.

I never had another metal tricycle, but sometime shortly afterward I became the proud owner of a Big Wheel, the definitive tricyclic transportation of my generation. With its ultra-low seat and right-wheel handbrake for spinning out, I had great confidence in the coolness of my ride. It made a wonderful noise as its hollow, plastic wheels sped across concrete, a sound so distinctive that my grandfather once claimed he always knew that Dad and I were coming around the block for a visit when he heard the distant rumbling of my Big Wheel. I was perfectly happy with it, but there did come a day when I was physically too big for it. Marx Toys, maker of the Big Wheel, was ready to meet my needs, ready with a product that was to the Big Wheel what the Big Wheel was to old-school tricycles.

The Green Machine was a beautifully engineered contraption of elegant design. A recumbent tricycle with a bucket seat, it featured a broad axle in the back and a simulated mag wheel up front. It looked really sleek. But the coolest thing about a Green Machine was its absence of a steering wheel. In its place was a pair of side-mounted, stick-shift controls, which rotated the rear axle. Pull the left control back while pushing the right control forward, and you would turn left. Shift in the other direction to turn right. Although the pedals were fixed to the front wheel just like a Big Wheel, the rear-steering mechanism of the Green Machine meant that its front wheel was always straight as the plastic chassis. Consequently, one never had to deal with the annoying variation in pedal distance that accompanied every Big Wheel turn.

Oh, how I loved my Green Machine. Taking it out for a spin was the purest of joys. Sitting so close to the ground while getting the most out of its efficient drive design gave a thrilling illusion of speed. Its left-right shifters allowed an economy of motion that could not be afforded by a steering wheel. Truly, the Green Machine returned maximum locomotion for a minimal investment of effort. For someone like myself, a natural adherent to paths of least resistance, it was a blissful marriage. I was comfortable. I was cool. I was one with my Green Machine.

Since the distant days of the ancient book of Ecclesiastes, mankind has noted the transitory nature of all things, whether painful or pleasurable. "To everything there is a season," wrote its author and much later sang The Byrds, and all the turn-turn-turning of that front wheel, albeit never to the left nor right, eventually took its toll. There is only so much stress that plastic can endure. My last ride on a Green Machine came to a rolling halt immediately after I felt a strange lack of resistance in the pedals. Suddenly my legs were pumping like crazy, yet I was decelerating. The shaft of the pedal assembly had broken loose from the wheel's worn core. It was a devastating impotence.

Dad knew how much I loved the Green Machine and did everything he could to restore its operability, but the strongest compounds he applied could not withstand the force of pedaling. At that point, I don't even know that you could buy a Green Machine anymore, just as Big Wheels were disappearing from toy department shelves. Nor were replacement parts available. Alas, not with a bang but a whimper, my Green Machine was totaled. As with my stolen tricycle and outgrown Big Wheel, it was time to move on, whether I wanted to or not.

Surely I knew how to ride a bike by the time my Green Machine died? I would like to think so, yet the chronology is hopelessly jumbled in my mind. It is quite possible that I failed to learn this basic skill simply because I didn't have to. Really, with the comfort of a cool, recumbent tricycle at one's disposal, who needs to bother learning how to balance on two wheels? Having no other choice, I had to conquer my ineptitude. And believe me, riding a rusty girls' bike with training wheels is a strong motivator, so strong that I barely recall the learning process. One day I couldn't ride a bike, and then one day I could. Or at least that's all I remember. Perhaps I've repressed the struggle.

But I do remember my Green Machine. I know the exhilaration of neighbor's lawns whizzing by and the roar of the wind in my ears. I can still feel the rear axle responding to my grip on the stick-shift controls. I can summon vestiges of the pure joy I experienced speeding along as the sun set on many a summer evening. And the child inside me, for better or worse never far away, still hopes that one day he'll ride again.

You'll Probably Need Stitches

The house in which I grew up had aluminum downspouts that descended from our gutters and curved away from the foundation atop beveled cinder block. They channeled rainwater adequately, but they were prone to rust and had sharp edges at their openings. Not much of a hazard for most people, but if you were an eight-year-old boy running around the perimeter of your house at top speed, they could be dangerous. I was surprised to discover this fact one summer afternoon, and I was further stunned when my bloody leg failed to elicit any sympathy from my mother but instead earned me a reprimand.

"Well, if you hadn't been running around the house instead of watching where you're going, this wouldn't have happened," I recall my mother scolding me as she tended to my injury. She probably tempered her criticism with compassion, but only her cool rebuke remained in my memory. Somewhere among my developing dendrites and synapses I stowed away the lone nugget of wisdom I managed to cull from the experience: If you're hurt, don't tell Mom. It was a maxim that was destined to lead me astray.

Some time later, I was idling away the long hours of another summer afternoon a few doors down in the back yard of a friend. My memory has not preserved precisely what we were up to that day, but it probably involved yet another imaginative adventure on the unanchored swing set that would tilt ominously whenever we dared to swing simultaneously at top speed. We could see a few unweathered inches of post rising from the ground as we held our legs tucked underneath our seats at the start of each arc. Rushing forward, we would feel the opposite posts tug at the ground behind us when we reached maximum altitude, and in my mind I could see the whole rickety shebang careening forward to hurtle us toward our premature deaths. Gosh, it was fun.

Novelty intruded upon this particular episode of our perilous routine in the form of a summons from an adjoining yard. It was the call of a stranger, a girl standing on the other side of a chain-link fence that separated my friend's back yard from that of the house on the opposite side of the block. In all of our many hours of playtime upon the swing set, I had never seen anyone emerge from that house. My friend didn't seem to be any more acquainted with her than I was.

"Look at this," she beckoned, holding aloft a strange leather object with dangling beads that looked as though it might have been the end product of a summer camp craft project. She was oddly devoid of enthusiasm and seemed to take no pride in the item. "You can have it. Here."

I glanced at my friend and looked back at the girl, who, I realized, was gesturing toward me. I felt an undefinable discomfort that pressured me to respond, a social obligation of sorts. In retrospect, I wish that I had possessed the maturity to simply thank her for her kindness and politely decline, as I truly had no desire to possess the rather unattractive ornament she was offering. This simply did not occur to me, however. It seemed like the friendly thing to do was simply to accept her gift, which I could discard later. I gallantly approached the fence to appease her.

There was a border of tall shrubs that ran along the opposite side of the fence, thick enough that it prevented us from standing any closer than several feet away. Our small arms could not reach across it easily. Thus, in order to effect the transaction, it became clear to me that I would have to give myself a boost by wedging the toe of my tennis shoe into one of the chain links and pulling myself up. A moment later, I was stretching across the hedge, and the girl placed her bizarre relic in my grasp.

The incident was over in seconds and would have merited no space in my long-term memory were it not for the confluence of my clumsiness and the fence installer's carelessness. As I retreated from my outstretched position, my shoe slipped from its hold, and I made a short but sudden descent upon the top of the fence. In most cases, this would have resulted in no greater harm than a tender bruise, but I had fallen on a fence that had been installed upside-down. The sharp metal twin prongs that would customarily fix the netting to the ground instead pointed upward along the top rail. One of them punctured my left side, just below the armpit.

I knew instantly that I was hurt and reflexively clamped my arm against the wound. A searing pain began to shoot through my side, but neither my friend nor the stranger seemed to notice the severity of my injury. I must have skewered myself gracefully somehow. But one thing was immediately obvious to me: I had certainly hurt myself stupidly. This was far worse than absentmindedly catching my leg on a downspout while running around the house. Mom would be furious.

"What were you thinking?" I imagined her interrogating me. "Didn't I tell you that you are not allowed to climb fences? What are you doing accepting gifts from strangers? Just look at the hole in your shirt! That's it! No more foolishness! You are grounded for the rest of the week!" The worst possible disciplinary consequences began to sprout in the fertile soil of my paranoia. If you're hurt, I remembered, don't tell Mom. But this was serious! And then I saw my way out – I would tell Dad instead. Dad would understand.

I muttered a badly improvised lie about suddenly realizing I had been out playing longer than I was allowed, ran from the back yard and frantically pedaled my Big Wheel home. Bounding up the porch and entering the living room, I startled my grandmother by loudly demanding to know the whereabouts of my father. The news I received was devastating: he was out fishing at the reservoir and was not expected to return for at least another hour. I sank down in a chair, my left arm pressed stiffly against my side, and mulled over my options. There was only one, really. I would just have to wait until Dad got home.

We made a peculiar tableau, Grandma and me. She sat quietly in her usual spot watching yet another game show and casting an occasional suspicious glance at me. It was, after all, an oddity for me to accompany her in this fashion, yet there I was, a solemn model of rigidity staring with grim fascination at Paul Lynde camping it up on *Hollywood Squares*. My attentiveness did not diminish during the commercial breaks, determined as I was to remain in a catatonic state until my father returned. I deftly swatted away her feeble inquiries concerning my well-being.

"Is there something wrong?" Grandma ventured with narrowed eyes.

"Nope!" I countered as nonchalantly as I could manage. I would not crack under pressure.

Several minutes passed before Grandma spoke again. "Are you sure you're alright?"

"*Yes!*" I hissed distractedly, furrowing my brow as if all this chit-chat might make us miss a priceless *bon mot* from the center square.

A further silence ensued, and before Grandma could formulate another question, Mom entered the room. She stopped at the sight of her mother and son transfixed before the television. I flattened my arms against my torso and tried to ignore her skeptical gaze. Just keep looking at the TV, I told myself, Dad is bound to come home any minute.

"What's wrong?"

"Nothing," I croaked, unnerved by Mom's extraordinary perception. I could feel my resolve quivering.

"C'mon," she prodded. She sat down on the couch and eyed me with an intensity as strong as the steely gaze that I kept concentrated on the television. "When you're sitting in the living room watching game shows with Grandma, there's something wrong. Out with it."

"I think game shows are interesting." It was a valiant last effort, but Mom was not to be deterred. She demanded an honest explanation. I bit my lip and tried to resist, but it was no use. I had to come clean. "Well," I sniffed, "I got this cut."

With that, I stood up and lifted my numb arm above my head. Mom blanched at the sight of my blood-soaked shirt. "What did you do?!" her voice rose, and I dizzily tried to find the right words.

"I...I fell on these spikes on the top of the fence-"

"Fell on these spikes?!" She whisked me into the bathroom and opened my shirt, dabbing at my side rapidly with a warm washcloth until she located the wound. Her muffled gasp conveyed to me a mixture of shock, concern, and great annoyance.

"I'm sorry, Mom!" I pleaded. "Is it bad?"

My mother was no doubt trying to keep her own composure as she replied, "Well, you'll probably need stitches!" Surely, she foresaw a trip to the emergency room, possibly the necessity of a tetanus shot, and most likely she feared that there could be even more to my injury than her cursory examination had revealed. But all I heard was the unfamiliar word *stitches*. It sounded awful.

"Sss...ssstiches?" I trembled, my eyes wide with rapidly increasing anxiety. With no further clues as to the meaning of the word and its implication for my prognosis, I assumed the worst and began to panic. I envisioned a team of surgeons laboring over my battered body as they attempted to save my life by employing some extremely painful procedure. My last reserves of rationality drained like the blood from my paling face, and I cried as I had never cried before.

Perhaps a hypnotist could extract from my mind the repressed memories of what followed, but my brain has seen fit to shut the door of recollection at this moment of catharsis. I did indeed have to get sewn up at the emergency room, but I do not remember the experience except for the fact that it was nowhere near as awful as I had feared. And therein was the one and only good thing to come out of our traumatic ordeal: practical knowledge about the wisdom of staying calm and the dangerous futility of panic. It was a lesson that I would not soon forget.

Not for a few years, anyway, until the time I was leaning out the back of our station wagon as the tailgate door swung shut, causing the window to shatter against my head. But that's another story...

Cans 'n' Stuff

The street on which I was raised runs nearly three quarters of a mile, a straight line along its entire length. We lived almost dead center, whence I could pedal my bike a satisfying distance in either direction. On the west end of the avenue lived Big Ed and Little Ed, a father and son whose nicknames reflected their seniority but not their relative size. Big Ed, as I recall, was a quiet, gray-haired man of small stature. Little Ed, however, was bigger in every way, from his large frame to his frizzy, black hair, which framed a happy-go-lucky countenance. They would have been an odd couple under any circumstances, but for a brief period of time they were business partners. They ran their unique venture from a tiny and disheveled storefront at the eastern terminus of our street.

Cans 'n' Stuff was surely one of the stranger establishments to have emerged in my hometown. Its eclectic stock was an outgrowth of its proprietors' respective hobbies. Big Ed collected beer cans, a fad of rising popularity in the seventies. Little Ed collected record albums, singles and related memorabilia. Naturally, they opened a shop that sold used records and beer cans. It was, perhaps, one of the greatest moments in the history of entrepreneurial zeal executed without so much as a shred of market research. What, after all, was the target demographic of Cans 'n' Stuff? Whom did Big Ed and Little Ed envision as their customers?

Herein was a lovely irony, for it so happened that, despite the presumably limited appeal of Cans 'n' Stuff, the quirky endeavor held great appeal to another pair who lived smack in between the Eds and their silly shop: my father and me. I don't know that Dad and I had a whole lot in common with Big Ed and Little Ed, but we did share their peculiar elder/younger – beer can/record album preoccupation dynamic. Imagine, a little bit of father-son heaven opening up right at the end of your street. I was too young to recognize its improbability. I just knew I liked it, and so did Dad.

Long before the term man cave was admitted to the popular lexicon, Dad had created a peaceful refuge of sorts in a corner of our unfinished basement. A work bench sat under the darkened window that used to look out over the back yard before its view was obstructed by the crawlspace of our addition. Plenty of illumination was provided by a hanging bank of fluorescent lights. Though the furnace, water heater and fuse box surrounded the space, Dad added little touches of manly decor that made his "workshop" comfortable. He nailed old license plates to the exposed floor beams and taped calendar images of faraway places to the sides of storage boxes. Stacks of *National Geographic* and *Popular Mechanics* filled a utility shelf. And somewhere along the way, Dad decided to paint the wooden shelves affixed to the upper half of the foundation walls a vibrant orange. Within these eye-popping display units, he assembled his beer can collection.

"Someday," Dad was fond of intoning as he gestured toward his collection with a sweep of his hand, "this will all be yours, son." It took me a few years to discern his wonderfully dry and gentle sense of humor. He never took his hobby seriously, although it is true that some of the rarities he possessed had the potential to escalate in value. As was the custom among collectors, Dad's cans appeared to be full, their pull-tab tops unmolested, but their concealed undersides had puncture holes that allowed for the draining and enjoyment of their contents. For my father, half of the pleasure of a beer can collection was the opportunity to try new beers, and the other half was derived from the colorful and often amusing packaging art. Any monetary value was just icing on the cake. Or perhaps foam on the beer.

Among the more memorable brands I recall was Olde Frothingslosh, a tongue-in-cheek product of Pittsburgh Brewing Company featuring Iron City Beer in a series of novelty cans emblazoned with retro cheesecake portraits of the hefty Miss Olde Frothingslosh. From the same brewery came Hop'n Gator, a lemon-lime flavored beer said to be inspired by a mixture of suds and Gatorade. Dad also had the requisite can of Billy Beer, the shameless self-exploitation of President Jimmy Carter's notoriously backwoods and beer-swilling caricature of a brother. Alongside a beer calendar and a festive Miller High Life poster, the collection added a cheery touch of whimsy to the otherwise drab basement. On many evenings, Dad could be found contentedly puttering away down there to the tinny sound of a baseball game or classical music on his portable radio.

Meanwhile, I was starting to look beyond the records I had found in the house and began exploring my own musical interests. Little Ed, long admired by me since the days he had been a jaunty high school chum of my big sister Diane, graciously heralded the opening of Cans 'n' Stuff by presenting me with a promotional gift: an 8×10 black-and-white glossy of the *Ed Sullivan Show*-era Beatles and a 45 of the KISS standard "Rock and Roll All Nite." Unsophisticated as I was, I quietly disregarded the photo while prizing the single, which I errantly spun on my turntable at 33 and 1/3. Having only seen yet never heard KISS, the resulting monstrous sludge that thudded from my speakers seemed credible enough, bizarre as it was.

Soon Cans 'n' Stuff became a regular destination for Dad and me. Big Ed and Little Ed must have loved it when we walked through the door. Fathers and sons enjoyed a few moments of enthusiastic talk about fields of interest that seemed to captivate no one else. In fact, I do not remember ever seeing another customer in the shop, though surely it must have attracted its share of curious passers-by. Perhaps I was always too occupied by the business at hand. Dad and Big Ed chatted about cans while Little Ed promised to keep an eye out for the records I coveted. We always left a few cans and albums richer.

In the end, however, our occasional patronage could not sustain the short life of Cans 'n' Stuff. I can't imagine it ever turned a profit. But for an all-too-brief season, Dad and I knew a place down the street that seemed like it had been created just for us. Big Ed and Little Ed, your business may not have succeeded in the traditional sense, but you certainly were a hit with us. Even now, I smile to think of the time we spent idly perusing your bygone establishment. And believe it or not, we still have those records and cans.

Anxiety in Bee Minor

E-M-B-A-R-R-A-S-S-E-D, *embarrassed*. That's what I felt when I was eliminated from my school's inaugural spelling bee in the first round. I was also I-N-F-U-R-I-A-T-E-D, *infuriated*, because I never wanted to be a part of the competition in the first place. As I saw it, spelling bees were not potential pathways to academic glory but rather protracted exercises in dodging humiliation. You hang in there as long as you can, take your best guess when necessary, and wipe the sweat from your brow when someone else gets knocked out on a word you didn't know, either. That's under the best circumstances. At the other end of the spelling bee spectrum is the real possibility of making a shameful mistake and inducing self-inflicted P-S-Y-C-H-O-L-O-G-I-C-A-L T-R-A-U-M-A, *psychological trauma*.

Despite my reluctance, I had trudged up to the stage with the rest of the seventh and eighth graders and haplessly plopped down onto my assigned folding chair. The gymnasium seemed uncomfortably full, mostly due to the presence of the rest of the student body and what seemed like the entire faculty and staff. That included my mother, who worked in the office. She gamely chalked up my lack of enthusiasm to the general pattern of surly behavior that was emerging in my early teens. I imagine that she was glad to be there. I just wanted to be anywhere else.

There were quite a few of us crammed onto the stage, and so it took a while before I was forced to approach the microphone. Most of my peers had sailed through to the second round with no apparent difficulty. I hoped that I could at least do that. But when the proctor gave me my word, I was flummoxed by a pair of vowels that seemed like they were out of order no matter which one I put first. Always a visual learner, I closed my eyes and conjured up my two options. First they both looked wrong. Then they both looked right. Then I pounced on one of the variations with absolute certainty. A second later, I preferred its alternative. A bead of sweat trickled down my back. I had a fifty percent chance of survival.

What was that word, you are wondering? It was *flouride*. Or *fluoride*. Yes, F-L-U-O-R-I-D-E, *fluoride*, which I now say with absolute certainty only because my word processor's automated proofreading feature will not allow me to remain ignorant on this point. But by God, I'm looking right at *fluoride*, and it still doesn't look right to me, but then neither does *flouride*. Which is to say that I was truly traumatized by the event. It doesn't seem to matter how many times I try to commit the proper spelling to memory. Ask me again tomorrow, and I'll be indecisive about it. It's a true mental block.

You may further wonder just how it is that merely enduring the minor embarrassment of exiting a spelling bee early could translate into irreparable cognitive dissonance. Perhaps the mere experience, in itself, does not. But my mortification was exacerbated by Mom's reaction to my failure. She was convinced that I had misspelled *fluoride* on purpose in order to leave the stage as soon as possible.

This created a dilemma just as vexing as the unsatisfying vacillation between *ou* and *uo*. On the one hand, I was accused of being deceitful when I had actually been honest. I did not like the idea that my mother might think I was lying when, in fact, I was not. But if I asserted my innocence, I would also highlight my ignorance. *Yes, Mom*, I saw myself admitting glumly, *I really am that stupid*. And so I had to decide between two unappetizing choices. Did I want my mother to believe that I was dishonest yet smart, or truthful yet dumb? Deceitfully intelligent or nobly ignorant? *Ou* or *uo*? What's the difference?

Ultimately, I settled on feebly dismissing her allegation, a purely Machiavellian move by which I intended to cull the best of both options. In telling her that I did not intentionally misspell *fluoride*,

I was assuaging my conscience by declaring the simple truth. I realized, however, that countering her claim with a further falsehood might be exactly what she might expect from her darkly clever son. If I really wanted her to believe me, I would have to repeatedly and indignantly emphasize my honesty. But I didn't really want her to believe me quite so much. So I only spoke the truth once. After that, I ignored the whole affair, and if Mom continued to believe that I really could spell *fluoride* and was sufficiently shrewd to find a way to get myself tossed out of an event I loathed, that was not my fault. I had told her the truth, for goodness' sake.

Who would have thought that a silly misspelling could morph into an ethical morass? What would Freud have made of its implications? Here's a neurotic kid who seeks the approval of his mother (a goal conventionally achieved through consistently exhibiting honesty) by remaining duplicitous so that she might overestimate his intelligence. Either way he wins, and either way he loses, which means that he neither wins nor loses but instead remains imprisoned in a psychological purgatory. This, then, mirrors the duality of his humiliation upon the spelling bee stage. If he spells *fluoride* correctly, he gains the admiration of his peers and maintains his ego, yet he must endure a further round upon the stage. By misspelling *fluoride*, he is encouraged to leave this crass exhibition of which he desired no part, but he also looks like an idiot. It is simultaneously a hollow victory and a beneficial defeat. Which is to say that it is neither, an eternally unresolved conundrum that will render him forever incapable of remembering how to spell *fluoride*, despite the fact that it's printed right there on every blessed tube of toothpaste he's squeezed every morning ever since.

Is there a cure for my curious mental malady? Perhaps writing about my psychosis will purge it from my system. Perhaps. P-E-R-H-A-P-S, *perhaps*.

A Summer Place

When I was ten years old, there was simply no better place in the world than the humble campground store I knew as Barney's. It was the hub of a Michigan lakeside resort that my family frequented during the seventies. Every summer, we drove up north with the Monfort family, rented a pontoon boat, and shared a cottage that was adjacent to a tiny, private beach. I imagine that the proprietors, a couple named Barney and Eunice, considered the surrounding geography to be the main draw of their business. But while playing on the beach, swimming in the lake, riding on a boat and fishing were all pleasurable to some degree, I was happiest when I was allowed to burn a little time and money at Barney's.

It was nothing more than one long, rectangular room with a concrete floor, a place where patrons could find any convenience they might have forgotten to pick up in town as well as a ready stock of living nightcrawlers and waxworms. There were vending machines for soft drinks and newspapers, and I certainly purchased my fair share of candy there. But the real attraction for me was the front half of the establishment, which was dominated by pool tables and pinball machines.

I still remember the cool sensation of metal corner trim under my thumbs and the concave flipper buttons at my middle fingertips as billiard balls clacked from the sharply aimed cue sticks of local pool toughs. A fresh scent of pine from the sawdust swept floor permeated the air, and every few minutes you could hear the rising warble of an old, elongated spring followed by the firecracker report of the slamming screen door. There was a genuine jukebox across the room, filled with an assortment of popular 45's that became the soundtrack of my time within that sacred place. The Steve Miller Band's "The Joker," David Bowie's "Fame," Bad Company's "Rock 'n' Roll Fantasy," Foreigner's "Hot Blooded." When I hear those songs today, I find myself still ten years old and standing before a pinball machine.

It was pinball that drew me to Barney's like carpet tacks to a horseshoe magnet. Video games were primitive, home gaming systems were nonexistent, there were no personal entertainment devices to keep one dazzled with music and movies, so what else was a boy to do? I mean, besides running, playing, swimming, or fishing? Heaven, to me, was a quarter in the age of the five-ball pinball machine. Ecstasy was the hammer knock of a free game. Knowing nothing of the world and paying little attention to the recorded high scores, I fancied myself a premier pinball player. While the overgrown goons behind me wasted their lives on cigarettes and endless games of eight-ball, I engaged in the more refined pursuit of becoming a pinball wizard.

It really didn't matter what machine was available. In fact, out of the many I played at Barney's, I can only remember two specific tables. One was a Bally-manufactured KISS pinball, a hot item released at the height of the band's fame. I never really cared for their music so much as I was entertained by their image, and so a KISS pinball machine was more appealing to me than an actual KISS album. I also recall – and what ten-year old boy wouldn't – another Bally product based on *Playboy* magazine. Colorful comic art of a pipe-clenching Hugh Hefner embracing a pair of models adorned the back glass, and the start of every ball was heralded with a cheeky and flirtatious musical motif. But those themes, visual candy though they were, were almost irrelevant. Had there been machines based on quilt making or city council meetings, I would have played those, too.

Mom and Dad apparently saw little harm in my preoccupation. I suppose they figured if that was what I wanted to do with my allotted funds, and if it happened to provide me with even greater pleasure than the more conventional amenities of our pleasant surroundings, then so be it. Never was I more thrilled with their indulgence than on the day of my eleventh birthday, which happened to coincide with one of our Michigan vacations. I woke up, as was my wont, at some late morning hour, pulled on my black t-shirt with its ironed-on Alice Cooper decal, and strode confidently out the cottage door and toward Barney's. I could feel the weight of a couple dozen quarters swinging like a pendulum in my pocket, striking my thigh with the promise of more pinball than I had ever played in one day. Swinging open the creaking screen door, I flared my nostrils and drew in the sweet pine aroma. The day was mine.

It was my birthday wish to sate my considerable appetite for pinball, and boy, did I ever. My pocketful of quarters gave me hours at the flippers, and by the time I exhausted my funds, I was physically exhausted as well. I was never an aggressive player, one of those guys who manhandles the machine to the occasional tilt. Such behavior was crass and vulgar to me. If you were good enough, I reasoned, you didn't need to do that. All of my exertion was in the fingers and wrists, not a taxing effort at all unless you carry on for hours. When I finally walked away from Barney's, my arms were aching. At last, I had had enough.

There were other wonderful things on that day as well. Mom and Dad gave me one of the big gifts for a boy of my age that year, a Kenner Millennium Falcon, the gold standard of *Star Wars* toys. I received plenty of well wishes along with the traditional chocolate cake. And that evening, I sat in a lawn chair and looked out over the lake, holding a blazing sparkler as distant heat lightning illuminated the horizon. I exhaled a satisfied sigh and stretched my aching arms. What more, I pondered rhetorically, could anyone possibly want?

Death By Piano

Among the indignities that Brian suffered during his teenage years, accompanying his kid brother to our piano lessons must have been one of the most painful. The eight years that separate us were a vast chasm in those days, and we had little in common beyond our genetics and home address. My brother seemed aloof and foreign to me then. As neurotic and quirky as I was in my formative years, Brian must have seen me as an inscrutably strange and pesky little alien for whom he was occasionally responsible. Every week, we would amble down the street with piano books in hand, ready (or not) for another lesson with Mrs. O'Neill.

A wall of bookshelves and a large picture window defined Mrs. O'Neill's front room, where Brian and I would take turns sitting on the sofa during each other's lesson. Sometimes I would peruse the small stack of children's books and comics while Brian played, but more often I tilted my head back upon the sofa cushion and gazed at the ceiling, which sparkled with a dusting of golden glitter. I would let my eyes relax their focus until the sparkling ceiling dissolved into an infinite cosmos, and the music whirled around me like orbiting planets as I stared into the outer reaches of the universe. Then it would be my turn.

Mrs. O'Neill was a nice teacher, perhaps far too nice for anyone who lacked the self-discipline to take practicing seriously. It made my lessons all the longer for Brian, who had to endure my many false starts and ignorance of key signatures. Again and again he would witness Mrs. O'Neill correcting my finger posture, waiting patiently for me to identify an interval, and demonstrating the rhythm of a triplet ("Trip-el-LET, trip-el-LET").

She wrote my assignments in a little notebook, only to have me return each week showing minimal mastery of the pieces I was supposed to practice.

I actually loved playing the piano, but devoting the time and effort to correctly interpret sheet music was monotonous to me (which is probably why I remain an atrocious sight reader). What I really wanted to do was noodle around and experiment, learning how to invent arrangements of tunes I knew and how to compose songs of my own. Whenever I did sit down to practice, I would rush through my assignments so that I could play what interested me.

Over time, I developed a small repertoire of original phrases and segments that I would play repeatedly on our upright Baldwin, which was never in tune. In fact, I have no memory of a tuner visiting our house, though I did hear stories of the cantankerous man who used to service our piano. He would inevitably break a string and loudly complain that our piano was "a piece of junk." This behavior rapidly wore thin for my parents, who ceased calling him and never got around to hiring someone else. As a result, our piano never sounded quite right. In particular, the high A produced a shrill dissonance all on its own, as though it had been transplanted from a honky-tonk upright.

This combination of an eager yet inexperienced pianist and a detuned instrument could be lethal to the ears. I eventually stopped taking lessons, because...well...what is the point if you're not going to practice? But I never stopped playing, and once free from the constraints of a formal musical education, I indulged my creativity with abandon. Outside of using the soft pedal and avoiding late hours, I made no concessions to the mental health of my family. If I enjoyed playing one of my compositions, I would repeat it as many times as I liked. Whereas I had little tolerance for repetition when it came to practicing anything assigned to me, it did not bother me to keep going over any troublesome parts of numbers I had written myself. It is a tremendous credit to the patience of my parents that they never requested me to stop. But oh, how they must have suffered.

Brian has made no secret of the fact that a specific composition of mine became anathema to him. The piece was cobbled together out of various segments with which I had been experimenting, and it ran over four minutes in length. I played it a lot.

The composition begins with a pleasant and melodic motif, unless one happens to play it on a piano with a dissonant high A. That key practically screams its individuality, ringing out three times in the opening five seconds. The introductory statement is followed by some alternating chords with low octaves learned from listening to Robert Lamm's piano solo on *Chicago at Carnegie Hall*, which is further emulated by the ensuing staccato ascension of the same chords. This was particularly annoying to Brian, as I always delivered this segment with all the passion my fingers, wrists, and forearms could muster.

There follows an odd sequence with booming C octaves that is either an extremely fast march or bizarrely metered boogie-woogie, or perhaps something else entirely. It includes rapidly descending right-hand arpeggios that eventually slow into the mellow middle of the piece, a few seconds of contemplative jazz. This soon transforms into a foot-stomping cadence that evokes Elton John's *Too Low for Zero* era. Then, it's back to the breakneck march. Or boogie-woogie. Or whatever it is.

Three and a quarter minutes into the number comes the showstopping highlight, six measures of sheer bombast featuring a loud series of descending octaves. I would hold down the damper pedal and punch the keys ferociously, creating a reverberating wave of sound that echoed off the kitchen cabinets and rivaled the most clamorous church bell ringing of Old Europe. By this time Brian would be driven close to the brink of madness, unable to concentrate on anything due to the mind-numbing intrusion of a pianistic monstrosity that he knew all too well. And remember, I was doing this years before John Tesh started making money using basically the same concept.

The last blast of this segment barely decays before the finale, a variation on the opening theme that provides unifying closure to the whole composition. Then there is the unsettling ambiguity of the hanging final chord, which is at last resolved with a cheeky, four-note scherzo. For what is cooler than lampooning one's own pomposity? Or more pompous, for that matter?

The old Baldwin is gone now, but the pieces that were hammered out on its strings live on in our minds and our muscle memory. Like the unconscious routine of tying one's shoes, Brian and I can summon old favorites from our fingers so long as we don't pay too much attention to what we're doing, otherwise we may find ourselves inexplicably lost in the middle of a routine we thought we thoroughly understood.

To this day, Brian can perfectly replicate a beautiful little number that takes me right back to staring at the infinite cosmos from the comfort of Mrs. O'Neill's couch. And sometimes, when Brian is visiting and I'm feeling mischievous, I'll sit down at the piano and play the opening notes of the haunting composition that still lingers in my brother's mind like an immortal and malevolent phantasm.

He smiles indulgently and good-naturedly when I do this, noting, "It's really not that bad, it's just that you played it again and again and again..."

But of course I did, Brian. Practice makes perfect, you know.

The Annotated Edward Cramer

When children express their boundless imagination in writing, the results can be bizarre. I was regularly reminded of this as a teacher of elementary-age students. It was my privilege to observe their literary development at a formative stage, when their novice attempts to emulate various styles sometimes merged with their limited background knowledge to surreal and unintentionally humorous effect.

What I tried to remember when evaluating student narratives is how incredibly strange my own attempts at storytelling were at that age. As unusual as some of the student work I encountered was, none of it surpassed some of my juvenile efforts in their breadth and depth of sheer weirdness. Take, for example, "The Glass Eye," a macabre stab at humor that I wrote circa second or third grade. Its off-kilter flavor is apparent even in its byline, as I attributed the work to Edward Cramer.

Whatever compelled me to adopt a pseudonym is now beyond my ken. All I can say is that I'm certain the moniker had almost no significance to me other than having the vague authorial ring I thought my own name lacked. Did I think a pen name would increase the likelihood of readers taking my work seriously? Who can say? As evident in the following paragraphs, it's hard to get inside the head of Edward Cramer.

The Glass Eye

By Edward Cramer

One day a man was fixing some pipes. He was a plumber. Suddenly, he heard something rolling down a pipe. He picked it up and saw that it was a glass eye. "Now how did that get there?" he said, puzzled. He finished his work and asked everyone if they had lost a glass eye. They all said no.

I love that second sentence. There's nothing more endearing in a child's writing than totally unnecessary exposition. Incidentally, this mysterious setup is about as realistic as the story gets. It's all high-concept from here on out.

"I feel like a stupid Cyclops!" he said to himself. The plumber didn't know what to do. He put the glass eye in his pocket.

I'm sure I must have felt quite clever inserting this mythological reference. A youthful fascination with monocular creatures and prosthetic eyes was probably the kernel from which the entire story grew.

The next day he was fixing some pipes when he heard something rolling down a pipe. He picked it up. It was a glass eye. Now he had two glass eyes. He asked everyone if they had lost a glass eye. They all said no. He put the glass eye in his pocket and forgot about it.

Just what might the plumber place in his pocket that he would not forget? It would have to be something pretty weird...

Now the same thing happened over and over again, day after day, week after week. The plumber had forty-eight glass eyes. The plumber finally took up collecting glass eyes.

Well, why not?

> *The next day he was fixing a sink and he heard something rolling down a pipe. The plumber picked it up and saw that it was a head with no eyes, ears, teeth, hair, or nose. He took the head home and put two eyes inside.*

Good heavens. I don't think a human head could make it down one of our heating ducts, let alone clear the water pipes. Must have been an industrial-grade utility sink.

> *Now each day he worked, he got more heads rolling down pipes. Finally, the plumber had twenty-four heads. He put the forty-eight eyes in the twenty-four heads.*

It's a bit like *Sesame Street*, no?

> *Two days later, he was working on a sink, heard something rolling down a pipe, and picked it up. He had one hundred teeth. This happened for four more days, and the plumber had five-hundred teeth. He put the five-hundred teeth in the twenty-four heads with the forty-eight glass eyes.*

Apparently, I had no idea how many teeth are in a typical human head. The average number is 32, and if we multiply that by 24, we produce a product of 768. A collection of 500 teeth, assuming sufficient variety, would provide only 15 complete dental sets. Now you know.

Now the plumber decided to start collecting body parts. So, as he collected body parts, he got more excited. Two months later, he had twenty-four heads with twenty-four noses, forty-eight ears, five-hundred teeth, one million hairs, and forty-eight glass eyes.

That second sentence is particularly disturbing, isn't it? It's the sort of thing you can get away with writing when you're under ten years old, but after that, beware the men in the white coats. By the way, the hair estimate is also grossly insufficient. With an average of 100,000 individual hairs on your garden-variety human head, a million strands would cover a mere ten heads. Rather ruins the story.

Now he wanted to get rid of the heads, so he flushed them down the toilet. Two months later, the plumber was fixing his own sewage pipes when they suddenly broke in half. All the heads he had flushed down the toilet came tumbling down. The plumber was stuck with twenty-four heads. He was really mad.

I don't know, if I were trying to get rid of two dozen heads, I certainly wouldn't want to take the risk of creating impenetrable blockages in my sewer line. Still, you have to admire my childish faith in the power of toilets to rid us of all problems.

The plumber took the twenty-four heads, put them in a large box, and buried them under the ground. The plumber was happy now. He finally got rid of the heads.

Two months later, the plumber had flowers in his back yard. He went back to look at them and he could hardly believe what he saw. The flowers had blossoming heads!

Now the plumber was as mad as he could get. He took his grass trimmers out and chopped the heads off the flowers. He took the heads and put them in another box.

I don't think I was sophisticated enough to pun with the word *head*. More likely I had seen a picture or cartoon of flowers with anthropomorphic heads.

The plumber went to the airport and ordered the plane to be flown from the airport in New York to the tropics in Brazil. Though for some reason, Georgia was in the way of the flight pattern. The plumber lived in Georgia and this is what happened.

Oh yes, did I forget to mention that the plumber lived in Georgia?

The plane lifted off and was in the air. It went over Georgia when half of the plane crumbled. The half that crumbled had the heads in it. The heads dropped in the plumber's back yard.

Oh, the irony! The irony!

There was nothing the plumber could do. He was stuck with twenty-four heads with twenty-four noses, forty-eight ears, five hundred teeth, one million hairs (not rabbits but hairs) and forty-eight glass eyes.

Now the plumber was piping (HA, HA!) mad. He put the twenty-four heads that had twenty...Oh, I'm not going through that again!

Now we seem to have taken a break from narrative in favor of experimenting with homophonic and occupational puns, as well as a dose of comically exasperated meta-commentary.

> *Anyway, he put the heads in a new box and put the box in the trunk of his car. He was driving his car when all the sudden (he timed it just right) a dead cow fell on his car and crushed it.*

And while we're at it, why not throw in a wacky non-sequitur? Probably inspired by Monty Python.

> *The next thing the plumber knew, he was in heaven. He looked around. In one corner was a box. The plumber went over to the box and opened it. Inside were the heads.*
>
> *"Damn those heads!" said the plumber. Right then the plumber saw God.*

A shocking use of profanity from a tender mind, decades before *South Park*.

> *"You shall pay for that," said God.*
>
> *"How?" questioned the plumber.*
>
> *"Sell your soul to the devil," replied God. So the plumber did that and paid God forty thousand dollars. "You forgot," said God, "you're already dead!"*

One can only hope that the author's take on the monetary value of one's soul is at least as woeful an underestimation as his guesses regarding human teeth and hair. And what's up with God in the role of trickster? An odd theological stance from a young Catholic.

"Oh, no!" cried the plumber.

Cue the muted *wah-wah-wah* horns here.

THE END

At last our storytelling train chugs into the station, and what a long, strange trip it's been. As I consider the twisted tale penned in my own small hand, I am reminded of the adage, "The child is the father of the man." Now all these years later, it's clear to me that I must have been adopted.

Altar Boys Gone Wild

There was that moment of silence just before Mass began, when the altar boys stood with lit candles behind the priest in a narrow hallway to one side of the altar, concealed from the congregation by a brick partition. I always felt a twinge of nervousness akin to waiting backstage before making a theatrical appearance, for in seconds we were to walk in procession along a side aisle to the back of the church, take a right past the baptismal font, and solemnly traverse the center aisle. After ascending some steps and placing our candles on either side of the altar, we would simultaneously bow beneath the crucifix and then take our seats on either side of the throne-like chair that accommodated the priest.

As self-conscious adolescents, we were well aware of the potential for public embarrassment that was offered by participating in the ritual. All eyes were upon us, and were we to trip over our cassocks or drop a wine cruet, it would not go unnoticed. So there was always a bit of tension as we waited in the wings, just the sort of mildly anxious anticipation that inspires one to create a healthy distraction. That is the only explanation I have for why I smiled at Alberto, yanked out a hair from the top of my head, and placed it in the flame of my candle.

In retrospect, my impulsive action was an example of perfect comedic timing executed at the most unfortunate moment. Just as the oily filament was immersed in fire, we heard the musical cue to begin the processional, whereupon my plucked hair burst into flame with far greater brilliance than I had expected. I saw Alberto's eyes widen in surprise as I recoiled from the combustion. And then, before either of us had a second to properly process what had just happened, we were walking out among the congregation, our flared nostrils detecting a hint of singed hair.

Had I indulged my pyromania, say, sixty seconds earlier, Alberto and I would have shared a mischievous giggle and forgotten the incident by the time we reached the altar. However, because our laughter had been suppressed due to our immediate assumption of public piety, we endured an uncomfortable containment of manic energy like a pair of corked volcanoes. Throughout the service, we sat tight-lipped upon the altar, avoiding each other's eyes. We knew that bursting out with laughter during Mass would be worse than any other gaffe we could commit, and that knowledge only increased our internal hilarity. Somehow, we made it through the service without embarrassing ourselves, though any observant congregant might have been puzzled by the stern countenances of the altar boys that morning.

One might think that I would have learned some valuable lesson concerning the incompatibility of altar boys and playing with fire, yet I confess that I was drawn toward the flame once more. It was during the eighth-grade altar boy trip to Kings Island, a reward for our faithful and dependable service. With only a little money in my pocket to procure a souvenir, I was scanning a gift shop for inexpensive items, when I happened upon a small bin of disposable lighters. They were plastic and translucent, with a reservoir of butane fuel visible beneath the Kings Island logo. I selected one with a red barrel, flicked my thumb against the ignition wheel, and observed the flame that arose at my command. It was cool, it had the tantalizing cachet of forbidden fruit, and amazingly, it was sold without question to minors.

My purchase was an end in itself, for I had no use for a lighter other than a primal fascination with producing fire. My friend and fellow altar boy, John, however, saw my new acquisition as a means to fulfill his own deviant desires. Since I now possessed a portable flame, John was inspired to conduct a sociological experiment to see if it was possible for a 13-year-old boy to successfully bum a cigarette from a stranger. If he were to succeed, we would have at hand all of the necessary tools to engage in the very adult art of smoking.

At this juncture, I am compelled to relate an amusing tidbit concerning the attitudes of our respective families toward juvenile delinquency and our susceptibility to it. There is no doubt that John was an eccentric personality, and this quality along with his occasionally inexplicable actions prompted my mother and father to perceive him as a potentially bad influence on me. I would later learn that this is precisely the same assessment that John's parents had made of me. The truth is that we were both somewhat odd by the standards of our peers, and we simply enjoyed being in the company of someone else whose mind worked a little differently.

We were not alike, however, but compatible. I was comparatively reserved and far more concerned about how I was perceived by others. John was more confident and seemed like he didn't care what anybody thought. We shared a quirky sense of humor, and John was the one who was most likely to act upon our sillier ideas. Thus, it somehow made perfect sense that he should pester unsuspecting adults for a cigarette that he hoped to ignite with my lighter.

"Do you have an extra cigarette?" John politely inquired of smokers we encountered while waiting in line for rides. "It's for my mother." This stratagem was about as effective as you might think it would be, until at last, John asked someone of sufficiently low intelligence, who kindly obliged him without so much as a raised eyebrow. We fled with our contraband, high on the adrenaline that is produced by illicit madness.

Really, that was the thrill in its totality for me. I had no intention whatsoever of smoking the thing. John, however, could not pass up the opportunity, and all that remained was the question of where to smoke in an amusement park with no chance of being observed by altar boy trip chaperones. We wound up driving the winding roads of the antique cars attraction, me at the wheel and John puffing away while huddled under the dashboard.

We had reached the end of our altar serving careers, and as I steered our chugging vehicle along the center path rail and winced at the cigarette smoke, I stared at the pink-tinged clouds of the evening horizon and pondered the future. I considered my crouching companion and thought about Alberto and our other fellow altar boys. One thing was clear. We definitely were not on the path to becoming altar men.

You've Got to Hide Your Love Away

W hat...is...*this*?!" my mother sputtered, and even though my back was turned toward her, I knew what she had found. The blood drained from my face as a nauseating wave of guilt, shame, and fear came crashing down upon my senses. It was the horrible feeling of knowing that one has just arrived at the very beginning of a long and unpleasant ordeal, brought upon by oneself. I was, as I recall, an obedient and honest child with few exceptions (perhaps my memory is selective), and this rare transgression was downright felonious in comparison to anything else I had done. I chastised myself for my stupidity. Emboldened by a successfully executed illicit scheme, I had flown too close to the sun with my wax wings, and now there was nothing to do but plummet helplessly to Earth.

As is the case with many a tale of innocence lost, the path that led to my downfall was a long and circuitous route. It began nearly a year earlier, and it was indirectly set in motion by my freshly developed preoccupation with the Beatles. I turned 12 in the summer of 1980, when Paul McCartney's "Coming Up" was getting frequent airplay. Having recently realized that a number of tunes that I liked were penned by the lad from Liverpool, I took the plunge and bought a copy of *McCartney II*. A month later while on vacation, I found discounted picture discs of *Sgt. Pepper* and *Abbey Road*. The music was a revelation to me, and as I gained an appreciation for the Fab Four, I began to particularly hold McCartney in high esteem.

I entered seventh grade that fall, and when the holiday season arrived, I took note of the publicity surrounding a new release from John Lennon and Yoko Ono called *Double Fantasy*. The coverage was soon to explode in a media frenzy following Lennon's death on December 8, which must have been right around the time the January, 1981 *Playboy* was hitting the stands. I remember this because I heard on the radio that the latest issue featured a lengthy interview with Lennon, who reportedly had said some rather caustic and uncomplimentary things about his former writing partner.

I know that I may be risking losing all credibility with judge and jury when I say that although I was certainly not averse to the more prurient elements of Hugh Hefner's infamous periodical, my subsequent actions were motivated by my high interest in reading that Lennon interview. To that end, I began a relentless campaign of badgering my father to purchase the issue, promising him that I wanted it only for the article. Lennon's death only bolstered my argument, as I noted the collectibility of the issue and its likelihood of selling out soon. Somehow, amazingly, or perhaps because *he* would be allowed to read the entire magazine (I cannot say), my father capitulated, and I still remember the notorious literature laid out on our dining table at one end of the family room.

There is a scene in *Citizen Kane* wherein a reporter investigating the death of the late millionaire is granted permission to read excerpts from the diaries of Kane's guardian, a banker named Mr. Thatcher. Seated at one end of a long table in the Thatcher Library with a lone shaft of light illuminating his reading, the reporter is under strict orders to peruse only those pages pertaining to his inquiry. The same degree of security was effected for my reading of the Lennon interview. The magazine was opened to the start of the article. Paperclips had been inserted in several places so that there would be no chance of me accidentally stumbling upon pictorial content as I made my way through pages and pages of interview. I was to remain in full view of family members until my reading was finished, whereupon I was to notify the curator to remove the periodical.

I read the article, found it illuminating, and that was that. After this triumph of reason in parenting, I thought little more about the strange endeavor. At least I didn't think about it for a little while. But my curiosity had been piqued. It was an awfully thick magazine. What, I wondered, could possibly fill the rest of its pages? Perhaps there were other articles that I would find similarly illuminating. Or other interesting stuff, who knew? I sensed that I held the golden key that would open the door to adult sophistication and cosmopolitan mores, if only I had the nerve to use it.

Of course, I did use it, embarking on a clandestine mission that revealed the hidden location of the magazine and afforded me a cursory glance at its contents. As I anticipated, I did, indeed, find the rest of the issue to be illuminating. The thing about entering the door to adult sophistication and cosmopolitan mores is that, once you cross the threshold, you can never un-enter that door. You may exit through the same door, but your brain still carries the memory of what you saw on the other side. What I had seen intrigued me enough that I thought I might learn a great deal more through further exploration of the topic. But therein was a thorny problem, as I was clearly stepping beyond the bounds of what was permissible and putting myself at risk of severe disciplinary action. Best to avoid it altogether. But then I didn't really want to.

It was a great mental diversion that carried into the summer of 1981, when the idle hours and freedom from schoolwork allowed me to hatch an outrageous plan. How could I ever acquire the time to read an issue of *Playboy* from cover to cover? The answer was simple: I would buy one myself.

It took no small measure of bravado for a boy just shy of thirteen to even consider such a scheme, much less execute it. It was absolute craziness, like the most harebrained idea for busting out of Alcatraz. But I hoped that it was so crazy that, according to the old cliché, it just might work.

And so, on a hot and cloudless day in July, as my heart rate accelerated with every push of my bike pedals, I cycled a few blocks to a party shop, located just across the street from our church, no less. Before dismounting, I took off my glasses and deposited them in the ample bag that hung from my handlebars, a large compartment that I hoped would soon contain the most forbidden of treasures. Dispensing with my spectacles was akin to adopting a disguise, for I reasoned that it would make me sufficiently unrecognizable. With my heart pounding away, I grimly stared fear in the face and strode confidently into the establishment.

Behind the counter stood a burly man whose eyebrows raised as I approached. I had already done my reconnaissance work and knew precisely what to say. I cleared my throat, dropped my voice an octave, and inquired with deadly sincerity, "Do you have the August, 1981 issue of *Playboy* magazine?" There was a pause. "It's for my father."

This was, I felt, the proper strategy to obtain what I wanted. By mentioning a specific issue, I wished to convey that my father had some unusual reason for wanting to buy it, a reason that, if pressed, I would profess not to know. I tried to appear as disinterested as possible, as though I had been sent here many times before to get smokes for the old man, and this was just one more errand I was reluctantly running. Confidence was the key. Though my internal systems were processing an unprecedented influx of adrenaline, I was cool as a corpse on the outside.

"Two-fifty," said the man, who never betrayed his own thoughts as I mechanically handed over the money. He placed the magazine in a paper bag, which I accepted as nonchalantly as I might have taken a sack of oven mitts. I turned my expressionless gaze toward the door and walked out into the brilliant sunlight, stashing my contraband in my handlebar bag and retrieving my glasses. Soon I was home and in my room, having successfully cleared the final hurdle of carrying a brown paper bag through the house. I already knew where my illicit booty was going to reside: under my dresser, which had a high enough clearance yet was so close to the side of my bed that no one could see underneath it. If anybody was going to find that magazine, they would have to purposefully stick their hand under there to do it.

And that, incredibly, is precisely what my mother did a few months later. My room was undergoing a thorough shakedown due to my inability to locate the stupid clip-on tie that I was obligated to wear to a school assembly the following day. Everything was getting torn apart. Why I didn't make a show of sticking my arm under the dresser and declaring it tie-less is beyond me. Maybe I did, and Mom was double-checking my search. In any case, the jig was up. I had no defense. And like the Beatles sang, I was gonna carry that weight, carry that weight a long time.

Trumpet Lessons

Black Monday.

My parents were disappointed with the label I had affixed to the evenings on which my trumpet lessons were scheduled. Having spent a good deal of money to purchase the instrument itself, they no doubt would have been pleased had their son expressed any measure of gratitude over the further expense they incurred by arranging private lessons. Each week they took the time to drive me to the outskirts of town so that I could spend a half hour in the presence of my instructor, a stern man renowned in my family for his success in developing the musical talents of a couple of my siblings. Despite my parents' sacrifices, I was far from grateful.

It was a dismal clash of disparate personalities. Mr. Steffman was a gifted teacher who expected his students to arrive motivated and well-practiced. Anything less was unworthy of his time. Had I the maturity and discipline to adhere to his regimen to any degree, I might have blossomed into a brass master. Unfortunately, I was a self-absorbed, sullen teen with little patience beyond instant gratification. Regular practice interfered with more important pursuits, like afternoon, early evening, and prime time television viewing.

Mr. Steffman was one of those people of whom admirers would say, "he doesn't suffer fools gladly," a curious phrase that makes an attribute of being unkind to people with whom one disagrees. Perhaps he was attempting to unearth a fragment of pride from my accumulated layers of teen apathy, a dogged disciplinarian seeking to awaken his pupil's sense of shame and in turn spark his young charge's redemption. If that was the case, it flew right over my pimply head. I sensed only contempt, which prompted me to respond with resentment. He was appalled by my laziness. I was indignant at his disgust. And so on it went, a classic vicious circle of mutual loathing.

A morbid gloom would descend upon me each week even before my mother had finished preparing our Monday dinner. It darkened my every pre-lesson activity, following me like a personal storm cloud. When at last the time for our departure arrived, I would settle into the back seat of our green Volare with Death Row resignation. There was nothing left to do then, no chance to improve my forthcoming performance, only a twenty minute ride to an unavoidable destination. As we followed the swerving road along the polluting oil refinery, I would stare out my window at its network of towers and catwalks, imagining not the reality of my backwater hometown's unsightly infrastructure but rather the cosmopolitan skyline of some distant metropolis. Someday, far away from here, the cursed trumpet lessons would linger only as repressed memory traces while I fulfilled a greater destiny. All too soon my fantasy would evaporate into nausea with the turning of our car onto my instructor's street.

I was always shown to a dining room that had just been cleared of its dishes. Mr. Steffman sat slightly behind me to my left, perusing the classified ads while sucking air through his teeth and chewing on an ever-present toothpick. A section of his newspaper lay on the floor ready to accept the contents of my spit valve. No pleasantries were exchanged as I assembled my trumpet and placed my music upon the stand. Finally, a sigh was exhaled from behind the classifieds, and I was prompted to begin playing. Often, I exceeded his tolerance for poor playing within several measures.

"Stop. Do it again."

It was a directive I heard with relentless frequency. Sometimes I wouldn't even make it through what I had just played before I was halted a second time, then a third. To emphasize the elementary nature of the music and my disappointing grasp of it, it was not unusual for him to pepper successive directions with sing-song condescension.

"Alright, Bobby, let's do it again!"

How I hated him for calling me that. It was the name he'd certainly heard my siblings and parents use over the years, but it was not what I preferred. Now and then I would hear it from a relative or a family friend, and it didn't bother me a great deal. Somehow, though, coming from Mr. Steffman, it was painful as a schoolyard taunt. I flattened my lips against my mouthpiece and forced out bitter notes. Surely the experience was as exasperating for him as it was for me.

We were both caught in an unpleasant situation. I had no desire to take lessons from him and was not inclined to practice. He did not wish to teach lazy students who were offended by his criticism. The only common interest we shared was a sense of obligation to my parents. One night he could no longer keep this fact to himself.

"Bobby," he addressed me with a clipped tone through his taut, thin lips, "I'm not doing this because I care about you. The only reason I keep giving you lessons is because I happen to like your parents."

No doubt I had provoked his comment by my continual technical incompetence coupled with a perpetually dismal attitude. It wasn't as though he hadn't tried to accommodate my interests and meet my individual needs. He had even allowed me to bring my acoustic guitar for a few lessons when he discovered I was more likely to play it than I was to practice with my trumpet. But even though the instrument changed, the hostile dynamic between us remained, and little progress was made.

None of this made sense to me at the time, however. I was stung by the implication of his frustrated comment. *I don't care about you...I happen to like your parents.*

We limped onward for a while, pointlessly enduring week after week of fruitless lessons. Near Easter time we either finished early or my parents were late picking me up, for I waited uncomfortably for several minutes inside his foyer. Mr. Steffman offered me some jelly beans, but I refused.

"Aw, c'mon," he tried again, a gesture that at once acknowledged our discord and feebly sought to establish harmony between us. Now it was my turn to toss a dagger into my opponent's soft spot.

"No, thank you. I don't like jelly beans," I lied. "I'll wait outside."

I walked out of the house into the chill of an April evening, setting my trumpet case on end for a makeshift chair. My parents would be surprised to see me waiting out in the cold.

The Rise and Fall of the Edward Hannon Band

The applause was explosive, a prolonged cacophony of shrieks and howls that reverberated throughout our small gymnasium. As teachers attempted to restore order amid bellowing calls for an encore, John and I sat on the stage and regarded the chaos we had created. We had expected to go over well, but never did we anticipate the wave of adoration that washed over us. It was all coming from the end of the bleachers along the north wall, where our eighth grade classmates were sitting. The rest of the student body craned their necks and looked back and forth in silent confusion.

We called ourselves The Edward Hannon Band as a tongue-in-cheek homage to our social studies teacher, a transplanted Pennsylvanian whose ample moustache and east coast colloquialisms were amusing to us. Plus, naming a band after someone who isn't actually in the band is ironically hip when you're thirteen. Mr. Hannon tolerated our tribute with good humor, though the quirky adoption of his name was not the key to our success. Rather, we won the approval of our peers by penning a folksy lament that pushed all the right buttons.

"Patrol Today" was two minutes and four chords' worth of self-pity that tapped right into our adolescent angst over being stuck out on safety patrol duty after a long school day. As we were all entering the classic self-absorption of our teenage years, it seemed like an important and relevant topic. Given that my very own brother not only taught science and math at our school but also organized the safety patrol, there was an enticing subtext of irreverence as well.

The children who walked to and from our Catholic school, which served grades one through eight, arrived and departed via three main arteries along a block-length stretch of Robb Avenue. The most coveted positions were at the intersection of Robb and Elizabeth Street. There, at the bottom of a flight of concrete steps between the church and the elementary building, three patrol members were stationed to handle the heavy pedestrian traffic. The luckiest among them got to operate a long, wooden gate that pivoted on a base to swing out and secure the crosswalk. Working the Elizabeth post was fun, social, and it even made you look important to the younger kids.

Much less desirable was the terminus of the block at Main Street, near the far end of the elementary building by the convent. Because only two patrol members were located here and far fewer kids used the intersection, the post was comparatively dull. The minimal activity made patrol duty seem much more like a responsibility, and consequently it was less fun.

Worst of all, however, was the lot of the unfortunate soul who got assigned to the opposite end of the block, a lonely outpost past the rectory at the West Street intersection. Although plenty of cars sped by, the post was occupied by a single patrol member, and hardly anyone used the route to leave school. On a balmy spring afternoon, the isolation and the monotony transformed minutes into hours. Everyone hated getting stuck out on West, hence the chorus of our little tune:

> *Patrol today, patrol today.*
> *I got it on West in the middle of May.*
> *It's so hot out, my shoes are turning to clay,*
> *And I wish I didn't have patrol today.*

If the lyrics sound simple, the music was even simpler. Every line of the verses and chorus was the same four-chord progression, as if echoing the punishing tedium of its subject matter. I wish I could lay claim to having done that intentionally, but the truth is that we only knew a few chords.

John and I had been taught some rudimentary acoustic guitar skills by Father Paul, a young priest whose full beard and self-darkening eyeglass lenses made him stand out in our parish like a hippie in Mayberry. He had recorded a couple albums of inspirational songs before coming to our church, where he implemented a folk mass. Once, in the course of our religious instruction, he showed us a 16mm film of one of his concert appearances, including a bit in which he wore a top hat and cape to sing "Duke of Earl." Soon the church youth were doing calypso strums on the altar, exhorting the congregation to join in on folk renditions of "They'll Know We Are Christians," "You And I," and once in a while, a Father Paul original called "Renew."

With the exception of "Do Lord," a fast-paced slice of gospel bluegrass that we found hysterically funny, John and I eschewed the religious numbers in favor of applying our limited skills toward learning a little classic rock and composing our own quirky songs. The annual spring talent show was a natural outlet for our musical interest, and so it was that we performed "Patrol Today" to a raucous ovation. Despite clearly trouncing the competition on the Applause-o-Meter, we were awarded third place (and if I remember correctly, I think John's little sister placed above us with a well-executed piano solo). Probably we didn't even deserve that, but the faculty judges likely felt some pressure to appease the howling mob. It hardly mattered, though – we were instant celebrities.

As the end of the school year loomed, our newfound popularity was reiterated in the inscriptions on our new yearbooks. *To a great kid that's gonna have a great band, too...Get your records out soon...Good luck in the future with your Ed Hannon Band...Good luck on your next album...*and so on, and so on. It seemed to John and me that we should strike while the iron was hot. With a sure-fire hit in our repertoire, it was time to work up a setlist and capitalize on our smash debut. We set our sights on the church festival, which was scheduled in early June. By some miracle of generosity or perhaps a complete lack of foresight, the festival organizers gave us an early afternoon slot on the stage in the food tent without even requiring us to audition. We were elated.

A month of furious rehearsal ensued. We went to a local pawnshop and rented an electric guitar, a bass, and an amplifier. The festival organizers granted our request for an upright piano in the tent, so we worked up some arrangements with that in mind. The pressure to put together a show fired our creativity, inspiring us to write some new tunes. John wrote a song called "Don't Applaud (Just Throw Money)" with the opening line, "We are the Edward Hannon Band..." I cobbled together a lengthy piano instrumental. We decided that we would play a couple covers, but we were confident enough in the strength of our own compositions that the set would be built mostly around original material. We would impress them with our "new stuff," then we would finish strong with a triumphant "Patrol Today."

The food tent was mostly empty as we set up for our performance; a small group of volunteers manned the grill along the opposite side. As we tuned up just before showtime, a dozen or so students settled in among the first two rows. They were there to hear "Patrol Today." Which we would give to them. After we played the entirety of our set.

I don't recall being too disappointed at the small turnout, but I do remember the terrible weight of dread and embarrassment that descended on me before we had finished playing our first number. Judging by the skeptical looks on the otherwise unemotional young faces of our tiny audience, we were not going down well at all. We good-naturedly ignored a few calls for "Patrol Today," sticking to our game plan to make 'em wait 'til the end. The longer we played, the more restless they got, and the more difficult it became to carry on. My face was burning red with humiliation, yet we persisted. Our hour-long set seemed to expand and transcend time itself, transforming into an alternate reality of anxious desperation.

Midway through our performance, we barreled through our cover of Chicago's "Dialogue," which ends with the repeated refrain, "We can make it happen." A caustic voice from the first two rows heckled, "No you can't!" By the time we reached the end of our set and finally played the hit that made us famous, no one cared anymore. Only the kind ladies working the grill offered words of support. And just like that – *pfft!* – the brief flame that was the Edward

Hannon Band was extinguished. John and I would remain good friends and continue to play a lot of music for our own enjoyment, but the church festival would be our one and only public performance.

Tucked among all the effusive praise from fellow students in my eighth grade yearbook is a short message written in a more mature hand. It reads:

> *Lots of luck in school and in whatever you do. If you make a lot of money with the band, send me a few dollars.*
>
> *Mr. Hannon*

The check is in the mail, Ed.

The Plexus Tuxedo Project

'Ve never known anyone with a greater capacity for taking himself too seriously than my old friend Matt. Admittedly, we knew each other best when we were teenagers, a time in which melodrama is often the norm. But even allowing for the emotion-scrambling potential of coursing hormones, Matt was in a class by himself. He seemed to thrive on inventing a life that was far more compelling than our mundane, Midwestern reality. It was a tendency that often alienated him from our peers.

But then it was always something of an uphill struggle for Matt. He was an alien from the start, a rare transplant from the Carolinas with a strict, Southern father whom he addressed as Sir. Some time around third grade, he appeared at our little Catholic school. He was very sociable and seemed to make friends quickly, and it wasn't long before his mother was hosting our Cub Scout den meetings from the basement of their modest home just down the street. From the beginning, however, Matt spoke in a way that seemed aimed at eliciting our sympathy and admiration. He was candid about the heart surgery he had endured as a toddler, an apparently true event for which he would gladly provide evidence by displaying his scar. As time went on, he would embellish his medical history with statements to the effect that he "technically shouldn't even be alive," that he stoically faced greatly reduced longevity, and that he had been "clinically dead" for some matter of minutes.

If that were all there had been to it, I easily could have accepted his words as those of an ordinary kid who had survived a genuinely traumatic brush with death. Maybe he could have been a little less dramatic about it, but hey, he earned the right to explain his experience in whatever manner was beneficial to him. That was merely the beginning, however. As he became assimilated into our peer group, and perhaps because the level of attention that he initially drew began to wane, he told some stories that went beyond stretching credibility and into the realm of bizarre.

For example, Matt maintained that he had written an article that was published in *Atlantic Monthly*. This was an odd claim to make within our circle of friends, especially given that it was a title that was utterly unfamiliar to us. When pressed for details, Matt said only that he had written the piece under a pseudonym, and consequently he was unable to cash the payment check, which he subsequently destroyed for fear of his parents discovering his duplicity. He told that whopper with total conviction, as though he truly believed it himself, not a trace of irony to darken his cherubic countenance.

He also confided that back in his wilder days down south (you know, about the time he would have been in second grade), he managed to covertly design and construct a small yet operable atomic bomb. This is just the sort of extraordinary claim that invites all sorts of questions once one stops staring at its claimant like he is a total loony. Matt remained adamant, though, maintaining that he knew the device worked because he detonated it, destroying a small, abandoned house in the process.

Now, the great thing about spinning a tale like that is that nearly any other implausibility you utter comes across as comparatively credible. Matt certainly knew how to push the reality envelope. If he could make himself believe that he was a clandestine author and nuclear science prodigy, then in what fantastical personal attributes was he incapable of believing? As we aged through adolescence, this quality gave him an atypical dose of self-confidence and gravitas. He expected you to believe whatever he told you, because apparently, he believed it himself.

Oddly, I knew all of this about Matt before we became close friends for a time. Sometime during our sophomore year, we discovered that we appreciated each other's sense of humor and shared a common interest in songwriting. I had recently drained my bank account to buy a Casio keyboard, a miniature-key model that was part of the first great wave of mass-produced, low-quality digital instruments. Matt started hanging out at my house, and together we wrote a dozen or so original tunes. We called ourselves Plexus Tuxedo, a name I had conceived upon seeing an anatomical drawing of the solar plexus. We were very cool.

Matt had more academic knowledge about songwriting than I did, and he taught me some useful things about structure that helped me evolve from meandering compositions to tightly written tunes. He introduced me to the hook and the bridge (which he mistakenly referred to as "the offbeat"). He had a good voice, and he was unflaggingly enthusiastic. Unfortunately, he was also an undisciplined lyricist. His penchant for melodrama often got the better of him.

A few couplets for illustrative purposes:

> *Italian girls with dark black hair.*
> *A blonde's blue eyes convincingly stare.*

And:

> *A seagull screams in joyous glee.*
> *Visions of waves will always be.*

And:

> *Like the weasel I evade them,*
> *stealing their bread and beer.*
> *Someone save me.*
> *I fear they're coming near.*

And, finally, this earnest appeal:

Won't you please listen
just 'cause he speaks Russian?
Maybe his nation
doesn't know salvation,
doesn't mean he ain't there.

Lyrics like that should have been sufficient to dissolve our songwriting partnership. But to our credit, we had fostered a mutually supportive relationship in which we could be free to create without fear of criticism. We might have eventually written something good, had not Matt's tentative grip on reality begun to erode my patience. In between songwriting sessions, he boasted of the power of his mind over his body, claiming that he could place his downturned palm over an open flame while suffering neither pain nor burns. He offered unsolicited details of alleged intimacies with his girlfriend, whom he later caught "in bed with another man," sparking a tale of confrontation that rivaled anything from the annals of daytime soap operas.

All of which was boorish, but what really rankled me was my increasing suspicion that not all of Matt's ideas were original. He called one of his tunes "The Grand Illusion," not a proprietary title by any means, but as it was already the title song of a well-known Styx album, I thought it was an odd choice. He had another number called "Fooling Yourself," which happens to be the name of another song on *The Grand Illusion*. Matt dubbed one of our co-written pieces "Your Starter For...," a title that was absolutely nonsensical to me. At the time, I did not know that it was also the name of the lead track from Elton John's *Blue Moves* album. Whenever I asked him to explain his title, he couldn't. As I later learned, the second track on Elton's album is "Tonight," thus creating a witty titular connection between the first two songs. Must have gone over Matt's head.

Eventually I was terminally embarrassed. Embarrassed by the songs we wrote. Embarrassed by our lack of talent. Embarrassed for myself when Matt looked me in the eyes and lied to me. Embarrassed for him that he was doing it. So I did my own bit of lying. I started avoiding his calls and making excuses when he did get through to me. It didn't take long for him to get the message. We never had much to do with each other after that.

Matt certainly had many positive qualities, attributes that helped him become a successful adult. He was smart and funny, and he made me laugh a lot. He listened, too, probing my fears and frustrations and trying to help me improve my life just as much as he worked to improve his own. His unquestioning loyalty was his asset, his chronic dishonesty his Achilles' heel. But the best I had to offer was my sincerity, and my own weakness was an intolerance for anything less from my friends. Every time I realized he had told me a lie, even though it was likely that he couldn't help himself, I felt betrayed and took it personally.

Like I said, I've never known anyone with a greater capacity for taking himself too seriously than my old friend Matt. Well, maybe one guy...

Tablechair!

For years, Brian and I had little to say to each other due to the icy chasm of our eight year difference in age. We had few common interests, after all. Not until I reached adolescence did our cold war start to thaw, a more or less civil diplomacy emerging in the unlikeliest of venues: on the virtual football fields, baseball diamonds and tennis courts of pioneering Intellivision video games. It was my older brother, who followed sports and occasionally actually played them, versus his nonathletic and sports-illiterate sibling in highly competitive contests of manual dexterity and hand-eye coordination. Countless battles unfolded on the color screen of our wood-paneled console television as we stretched out on the living room floor and blindly manipulated the controllers, keeping our wide eyes locked on the action.

Sometimes we were woefully mismatched, as when we faced off in football. Clearly Brian had the far better grasp of strategy. I had only one effective weapon in my pitiful strategic arsenal, a potentially devastating play that I called *The 9929 Twenty-Yard Fadeback*. Named for the four-digit code one entered into the controller to call a play that included a receiver going long, the scheme exploited a curious anomaly of Intellivision Football: its quarterbacks never threw too short nor tossed the ball out of bounds, instead firing off passes that would spiral all the way off the scrolling screen if they were not caught. By some strange compromise of gameplay design, those golden arms could accurately throw the length of the football field.

The 9929 worked like a charm, provided that I could entice a prolonged rush. I simply ran my quarterback twenty yards backward, made sure Brian wasn't in between me and my offscreen receiver, and let 'er rip. One 80-yard pass later, my isolated receiver would dash alone into the end zone. Unstoppable if you didn't see it coming. Of course, it soon became impossible for me to entice Brian into a prolonged rush. As soon as my quarterback retreated more than five yards, my brother was on the alert to abandon the rush and intercept the ol' 9929. I don't think I ever won a single game of football.

I fared much better in baseball, which required no strategic decision-making beyond deciding what kind of pitch to throw and when to swing the bat. The rest was all reflexive. If you had the chops to instantly activate any of your fielders by touch, then you were as good as anybody. Consequently, neither of us dominated in baseball. Brian would win one, then I would win one, all to the primitive, 8-bit approximation of an umpire growling *Yer out!*, which actually sounded more like some sort of digital belch.

It was tennis, though, that brought out our most intense competition. We were bitter rivals on the court, and if a sportscaster had sought a narrative suitable for dramatizing our struggle, it would have been the underdog story of the little brother who won games against big brother but never managed to take a set. Serve after serve, back and forth the advantage went, yet Brian inevitably emerged triumphant.

As the older brother, Brian usually took the high road even in the heat of battle. However, he was not above ragging his opponent when necessary, nor was I above being rattled by it. Most unfortunately, I could never match his intimidation, and he knew it. If his circumstances ever turned desperate, he could recover lost ground by shrewdly hammering away at my psyche. This was the situation he found himself in one afternoon when I made the unprecedented personal accomplishment of winning the first four games of a set. It was time for Brian to bring the mental heat.

"Thankyousomuch!" was his first volley, a smugly delivered rush of syllables that he let loose with an icy smile after winning a point. I didn't even know that I was being messed with at that point, focused as I was on continuing my streak in order to win a set for the first time ever. A few plays later, I heard it again. *Thankyousomuch!* And here I made a colossal mistake. I gave my opponent a sidelong glance that conveyed my annoyance. I might as well have slathered my leg with beef broth and kicked a junkyard dog. It was all the provocation he needed.

Now that he knew I was irritated by his new verbal tic, it was time to take the intimidation to a new and lower level. He waited until I made an error, somehow failing to return a ball that was hit right to me. *Thankyousomuch!* He was taking credit for my mistake! I was incensed, yet little did I know that my fury was the beginning of the end. While I fought harder and harder to keep my advantage, Brian was pulverizing the foundation blocks of my mental game. He knew what he was doing, but I couldn't see it. I turned to him and unleashed a torrent of protest that was mere fuel for the fire.

"Oh, come on! I made a stupid mistake! You didn't win that point, I lost it!"

Brian just flashed a Cheshire Cat grin and chuckled, and his complete lack of remorse only deepened my indignation. I was already off my game, but I lacked the maturity to compose myself and see my lead through to victory. He won the game, then another, and though he should have been the one sweating bullets, I was the one who felt like I had everything to lose. My play became sloppier. I missed more points that should have been mine. Brian took another game. I flailed about under the fear of what had the potential to be my most embarrassing loss ever. I made another stupid mistake, and then Brian let loose another one of his infernal proclamations of *Thankyousomuch!*

"Thankyousomuch! Thankyousomuch!" I blurted out in exasperation. Brian said nothing but began to laugh gleefully. "It doesn't even mean anything anymore!" He clutched his side and vibrated with mirth at my outburst. "You might as well be saying..." I grasped furtively for random words, "...tablechair!" My brother roared with laughter, but I was serious. He was about to get a taste of his own medicine.

The first chance I got, I unleashed my lethal non sequitur. Gloating over an ace, I attempted an ironic smile and vindictively whispered, "Tablechair!" This tactic failed to achieve its desired effect. Far from being intimidated, my brother was merely amused. He knew the set was his. I was clearly self-destructing. He could have remained silent for the rest of the set and won without further provocation.

But it's hard for an aggressor to resist another twist of the knife, especially when he finds it funny. And so Brian stopped saying *Thankyousomuch!* every time I made a mistake. Instead, he said *Tablechair!*

Brian won the set, 6-4.

Shameful? Perhaps. But as John Lyly observed over four hundred years ago, "The rules of fair play do not apply in love and war." Never was it more true than on the virtual battlefield of brotherly rivalry we called Intellivision Tennis.

The Reluctant Athlete

You want me to play softball in a prison?" I asked incredulously.

"I know," said Brian in a calm tone that resonated with sympathy and reassurance. We both knew that my objection had little to do with the unusual venue, and it was painfully obvious that he was desperate for players. So desperate, in fact, that he was approaching one of the last people you would want to ask if you wanted to forge a decent softball team. My brother tried to bolster his sincerity with a smile, but he could barely suppress a laugh as he tried to entice me by adding, "It'll be fun!"

"Yeah, fun," I grumbled. Brian belonged to a service organization that not only did the occasional good thing for the community but also participated in a recreational softball league. Scheduling a game against the inmates of our local minimum-security prison was a way to join the two vocations. Unfortunately, only a handful of members had signed up for the opportunity. Joining Brian in this endeavor would be the noble thing to do, but it would require a complete consumption of my pride. It was akin to taking a willing dive into a pool of embarrassment. "Let me think about it."

If athletic ability is predestined by our DNA, the sports gene is surely absent from my genetic code. If it is a matter of nurture rather than nature, then I must have been abandoned as a fledgling and raised by charity. Whatever the cause, it has always been painfully evident to everyone that I am far more suited to the role of spectator than that of participant.

Not that I didn't try. When I was about nine years old, I signed up for Catholic Youth Organization summer softball. Lord knows whose idea it was. Maybe my parents thought it would provide me with exercise and boost my overall confidence. Perhaps I actually suggested it myself on a whim fueled by youthful denial. Somehow, I wound up playing softball that summer, clad in my purple team shirt with the CYO logo on its front and an ad for a sponsoring local insurance company on the back. I had an oversize softball glove and an undersized, red-painted, wooden bat. I understood the rules and showed up for every practice. I really did try, but I was inept.

Considering my offensive play alone, I am uniquely qualified to claim ineptitude. Although I was always included in the batting order, if for no other reason than it was mandated by league rules, I struck out every time I stepped up to the plate throughout the regular season. Our coach first advised me to "choke up on the bat," then to not choke up so much, but however I tried it, all I could do was choke, period. Opposing teams were merciless with their chatter, every one of their mean-spirited utterances ridiculously unnecessary. Instead of taunting me with *hey, batter-batter-batter-SWING!*, they could have chanted *please hit the ball, please hit the ball* and it would not have made any difference.

When it came to fielding, I spent more time on the bench than my teammates. Still, I got out there for a while every game, pragmatically stuck out in right field. I always struck the little leaguer's pose, lurching forward with my hands planted on my knees and my eyes fixed on the batter. Although my physical attitude might have fooled a passerby into admiring my apparent enthusiasm, inwardly I suffered the angst of a young Les Nessman: *Please, God, don't let them hit it to me.* When the odd fly ball did come my way, I would manage to run toward the general vicinity of its descent with my arm outstretched, whereupon the ball would inevitably plunge with a thud into the grass. My frantic throws to the infield could turn a single into a home run.

Thanks to gym class, my lack of athleticism was evident not just during the summer but all year round. Once I attempted to emulate the stance of a sprinter at the starting blocks when it was my turn for speed trials. I was crouched down with all the tension of a coiled spring, and at the starting signal I suddenly catapulted forward and fell on my face. When we were made to run laps around the field, I clutched my cramping sides and cast envious glances toward our asthmatic classmate Billy, who was permitted to walk his circuits. What I would have given to trade places. Maudlin images of juvenile asthma sufferers staring longingly from their bedroom windows as their peers engaged in strenuous physical activities did not arouse my sympathy but instead provoked my jealousy.

Nor did the passage of time lead to much improvement. High school phys ed brought further humiliation, as it was taught by the head basketball coach, and my prowess on the court was even less impressive than my dexterity on the diamond. It could not have surprised him to observe my utter incompetence with layups, the mechanics of which were a true mystery to me. I saw others dribble toward the hoop and toss the ball in with ease, but my own attempts were executed with all the grace of Frankenstein's monster. Obvious as my lack of talent was, it nevertheless perplexed our teacher when I was unable to complete an obstacle course due to its final element: a successful shot from the free throw line. He watched in disbelief as I missed again and again, unable to sink one until I was allowed to move embarrassingly close to the net.

As senior year loomed, everyone of my acquaintance knew better than to rely on me to help lead a sports team to victory. This was something of a relief, as it meant that I was generally left alone to fulfill my non-athletic destiny without suffering humiliating interludes of awkwardness. You wouldn't waste your time trying to train the family dog to take pinochle tricks, right? Some efforts are simply unnatural and, consequently, fruitless.

However, I occasionally found myself once again a bumbler among the graceful. During a co-ed summer leadership camp,

I watched nervously as girls were assigned to the outfield for a friendly afternoon of softball. The sexist assumption of the team captains was that boys would make the best infielders. Having ascertained that I was a male, they put me at third base. No one but I knew what a dreadful mistake they were making.

I can still see the mischievous smile of my new friend, Mark, as he strode to the plate and cockily pointed the bat at me, telegraphing his intentions. Sure enough, he sent the first pitch hopping just inside the third base line. I remembered from my CYO days that fielders are supposed to get down in front of ground balls to stop them, even if it meant taking a bad hop to the face. I tried to do just that, but the ball zipped underneath me and continued deep into the outfield. The girl playing left field intercepted the ball and sidearmed it back toward me with an athleticism ten times greater than my own. Really, her arm was strong and bulls-eye accurate. The ball landed a mere foot in front of me, and though I ordered myself to get down there like I was taught to do, it once again hopped beneath me and followed the foul line to home plate. Mark jogged onto third base and laughed at his good fortune. Two between-the-legs errors on one play by the same player is, I feel safe to say, statistically rare.

Not long after that notorious incident, I distinguished myself on the tennis court during a game of mixed doubles when I served into the back of my partner's head. Such an action is pathetic under any circumstances, but being a guy and clobbering a girl in the noggin with an overhead smash is just mortifying. She took it in good humor after recovering from the shock, having neither seen nor expected the offending projectile. Still, I played the net after that.

These and other personal bloopers ran through my mind as I considered Brian's request to join him for some prison softball. Ultimately, I agreed, succumbing to sibling pressure while harboring a kernel of hope that I might somehow find redemption for my past errors. When we arrived at the correction facility, the dismal results of Brian's recruiting efforts became coldly apparent to me, as we didn't even have enough guys to field a team.

Playing against prisoners didn't sound too bad to me, because if I made some dumb mistakes, it would only benefit them. But this meant that we would be playing with some inmates as well. I wondered how they would take having a misfit like me on their team, and the thought turned my stomach.

We passed through security and were escorted to a rectangular courtyard surrounded by high brick walls. There didn't seem to be anything particularly intimidating about the guys who had been permitted to play, and I was pleasantly surprised to find my inmate teammates treating me with good-natured camaraderie. For the first time in my life, I was asked to play left field, and the gray clouds of my third-base fiasco began to threaten my optimism. But when the opposing team stepped up to the plate, I realized that every single batter was pulling for right field. This was because the dimensions of the courtyard made the right field wall much closer than the left field fence. It was conceivable that a ball might possibly clear the courtyard wall for a home run, but at the very least, the right fielder was going to face a difficult rebound off the bricks.

I managed to avoid total embarrassment at home plate, flying out and grounding out rather than striking out. And once, incredibly, I got a double. Out in quiet left field, I watched with gratitude as ball after ball bounced off the right field wall. Then someone who either swung too soon or decided to take advantage of my milquetoast game sent a high fly ball into my territory. Like the terrifying interval between skidding tires and crashing cars, time slowed down to the accompaniment of my thundering heartbeat. I followed the arc of the ball and tried to visualize the end of its trajectory. I held my oversize glove open and kept my right hand ready to trap the ball. There was a sudden thwack in my mitt, and I willed myself to react with nonchalance. It was by no means a tough play to make, and I couldn't expect to be taken seriously if I sank to my knees in ecstasy.

"You know," I said giddily to Brian during the drive home, "I actually did have fun. And I can't believe how nice our teammates were. I really thought they'd give me a hard time, but they couldn't have been nicer."

"Mmm," Brian nodded, and we traveled on happily. Redemption at last.

Years later, when I recalled the extraordinary cordiality of our hometown's minimum-security prison inmates, Brian cleared his throat and added an asterisk to our experience.

"Yeah, well...they were nice. I didn't think it was necessary to tell you at the time, but..."

"But what?"

"Well, I told them that you had never played baseball before."

"You *what?*"

I looked at Brian in open-mouthed astonishment, and just as suddenly it dawned on me how great a brother's love can be. He had been looking out for me, and I hadn't even suspected it. We started to laugh, and we didn't stop for quite a while.

A Nearly Perfect Circle

I imagine that Dick Ireland, were he alive today, would be surprised to learn that a former student fondly and frequently recalls his old geometry and physics teacher nearly forty years later. Once our mortarboards arced through an overcast spring sky and clattered onto the asphalt parking lot, I never returned. Nor did I bother to contact any of the instructors who were an integral part of my life all those years ago. Somehow the thought of keeping in touch with my alma mater and its faculty seemed like moving backward instead of forward. Yet in a minor irony that I never foresaw as a teenager, I eventually became a teacher myself.

Like most former educators, I wonder about the lasting impact of my instruction and guidance. It's been years since I signed off on my last report card, and I hope that I made a net positive difference in the lives of my students. But I'll never really know. Students move on, just as I did. It took me years to truly appreciate what the best of my teachers had given me, just as I had to reach a certain level of maturity to understand how and why the worst of my teachers had shortchanged me. Good or bad, my lasting impressions of them have little to do with the content they labored to teach me.

Mr. Ireland was too eccentric to fade from any student's memory, but I remembered him more often after I took on the responsibilities of a teacher. In fact, there were three distinct triggers that summoned his visage. Whenever I drew a circle on the board, I would see Mr. Ireland with chalk in hand. If a student happened to gasp in a moment of sudden, dawning comprehension, I would hear his gruff baritone. And on those occasions when I took notice of the clacking keys of my laptop as I rapidly transformed thoughts into processed words, I remembered some of the best advice that I was given in high school.

"Hunt!" he barked in his customary fashion of addressing students by their surnames. He was talking to my brother Brian, eight years my senior, some time well before I ever set foot in his classroom. "Is there a limit to how thin a bubble can be?" Brian thought it over a moment and answered affirmatively, whereupon Mr. Ireland expanded upon his correct response with a lengthy lecture about molecules and the building blocks of matter. My brother's attention soon wandered to his lab table's empty post hole, which was a receptacle for mounting Bunsen burners. With a small wad of paper at the ready, it also made an excellent mini-golf green.

Perhaps twenty minutes elapsed before Mr. Ireland finally reached the end of his educational monologue. With a lawyer's flair for drama, he sought to wrap up his argument with a theatrical reiteration of his original premise. "So," he asked almost rhetorically, "is there a limit to how thin a bubble can be...Hunt!"

Only my brother had not been listening. He was somewhere on the back nine, lining up another putt. The room fell silent at the mention of his name, and he looked up to find Mr. Ireland staring at him expectantly. Brian's intuition told him that he was expected to answer a question, and weighing his chance for success at even odds, he took the plunge and replied, "No."

"WHAT?!" roared a wide-eyed Mr. Ireland. Like the thinness of bubbles, his patience had a limit.

I had heard many Mr. Ireland stories before the day I became one of his pupils, tales of melodramatic moralizing, salty language, and legendary classes in which his passion for delivering life lessons eclipsed any curricular content. I was not disappointed. He was as unconventional and entertaining as promised. In addition, he knew his stuff, and he radiated a humble self-confidence in his academic knowledge. Even as addled as I was with the self-absorbed mindset of the typical teenager, I perceived Mr. Ireland as someone to whom it was worth listening.

Circles were a prominent focus of our geometry lessons, and Mr. Ireland was forever inscribing them on the chalkboard. Although he had a large, wooden compass that was probably a product of the same ancient purchase order that procured his oversize protractor, he preferred the rapidity of drawing circles freehand. It was marvelous to watch. Over the years, his right arm had become its own compass, and the ovals he produced were stunningly regular, their beginnings and ends overlapping to form invisible seams. Sometimes after stepping back to admire his work, he would note that a circle is, by definition, the set of points equidistant from one point on a single plane. Then, with a smirk of satisfaction, he would boast that his freehand circles were as close as you could get to the real thing without using a compass.

Mr. Ireland spoke reverently about what he called the Aha Experience, that moment when you suddenly realize that you understand something that was only moments ago a mystery. He promoted it as a transformative experience, the very essence of education. To that end, he was always chiding us to stay on the alert. "Get your brain in gear!" he would thunder whenever he sensed that we were losing focus. It was a helpful admonition in geometry, which I grasped easily, but it wasn't as applicable for physics. No matter how hard I tried to kick-start my grey matter, it never produced the level of success I was able to attain by allying myself with a smarter lab partner.

Perhaps because his duties were divided between the disciplines of geometry and physics, Mr. Ireland seemed unable to resist going off on a tangent. Our eyes snapped to eager attention at those times, because the longer we could encourage him to talk about something other than math or science, the less energy we would have to expend on learning. His war experiences were a reliable source of distraction, and they could be deeply entertaining, disturbing, funny, and sometimes all three at once. No one who heard his graphic depiction of the ravages of wartime syphilis (on his comrades, let me clarify) is likely to forget it. Though we welcomed his tales because we preferred them to the rigors of a challenging course, it was during one of those yarns that I absorbed advice for which I have been forever grateful.

At that time (the mid-1980's), the more visionary members of our high school faculty observed the advent of the personal computer and foresaw the likelihood that our professional lives would be intertwined with the digital domain. Mr. Barnhart, our algebra and calculus instructor, even pioneered an extracurricular class teaching BASIC programming on old TRS-80 computers. In a nod to our changing world, the administration changed the name of the typing class to keyboarding. But aside from using some early typing education software, we were still buying correction tape and clacking away at IBM Selectrics. Keyboarding was a recommended yet elective class, and I wondered why I should trouble myself with it.

Mr. Ireland had an answer, though far from being visionary, it was rooted in his military service. Apparently there came a decisive moment when a secretary was needed for some strategic purpose. Among the rank and file, Mr. Ireland was the only one who happened to know how to type. He was immediately chosen for the position, a fortuitous circumstance that he claimed kept him out of combat. He urged all of us to sign up for the keyboarding class, because we could never know when that coveted skill might give us the leg up on our competition.

And here I am, my hands resting comfortably on the home keys as they obediently take my mental dictation. Thanks to Mr. Ireland, I can effortlessly record my thoughts almost as quickly as I think them. It's a practical skill that has served me well over the years. It hasn't yet kept me out of combat, but it has saved me plenty of time. And on more than one occasion, it earned the admiration of my elementary school students.

"Wow!" one of them would exclaim as they saw me dash off a sentence lickity-split. "How do you do that?" I couldn't help but smile and think of Mr. Ireland, just as I did whenever I saw one of the kids having an Aha Experience, or whenever I constructed a Venn diagram by drawing a pair of overlapping circles on the board. And I tried to pass along a tiny bit of his legacy.

"I learned how to type. You can, too. You'll never regret it. In fact, you may not believe this, but I once knew someone whose life may have been saved because he knew how to type..."

Turkey Bowl

It was a sacred tradition for a number of years, a ritual no less important to its participants than the national holiday on which it occurred. Every Thanksgiving morning at 9:00, a ragtag group of brothers and friends assembled on a frozen field at Robb Park for a spirited game of touch football. Victory with all of its bragging rights was awarded to the first team to score five touchdowns. By that time, great patches of dormant grass would be stripped away, leaving a muddy pit as testimony to the annual battle. Soaked through, sore, and grimier than any other time of the year, the players trudged home to clean up in time for heartily appreciated turkey dinners.

The Turkey Bowl began as a smaller affair, nothing much more than my three older brothers and a few of their friends running some plays on Thanksgiving morning. Things changed when my brother Richard taught 7th and 8th grade math and science at his alma mater, the same Catholic school that I attended.

"I told students I was a tight end at Cal Poly Pomona," acknowledged Richard. "They didn't know any better."

Thus the game was transformed into a contest between two mismatched teams: the students against the Hunt brothers and their friends. Although all of my peers played on the student team, I tagged along as a member of the Hunt team by birthright. Given my athletic skills, my peers must have been delighted.

"Oh, the memories," recalled student team veteran Dave Ruen, who lived just down the block from the Hunt household. "Years and years of training, defeat after defeat. That was enough to motivate us youngsters against the elders. It was classic David and Goliath stuff."

Teammate Dave Moskwinski concurred that the middle schoolers were fighting an uphill battle in those early days. "I remember Mr. Hunt being like a lightning bolt when he got the ball! We were fast at our age, but he was a step faster!"

As years went by and the game got bigger and bigger, so did the student team players. The age advantage enjoyed by the Hunt team was leveling out, well on its way to becoming a liability. One year during that transitional era, my brothers and I were rummaging through an overstock discount store looking for the warmest hats and gloves that we wouldn't mind having caked with mud. To our delight, we discovered a cache of cheap football cleats. Not only did it enhance our traditional, two-block walk from our house to the park with the staccato cadence of a military march, it helped us on the field.

"The only thing I remember," student team member Dan Hickey told me, "is not having any cleats and the field being six inches of watery mud. During one play, your brother David pushed me completely off the field, which at the time was embarrassing since David was only about half my size."

Ah yes, the mud. No one forgets the mud. "The weather always played a big part of any Turkey Bowl I was a part of," said Joe Landwehr, who played for the Hunt team. "The weather was never good; snow, cold, rain or mud. Sometimes two or three of them."

"How could I forget the endless number of prayers I would start saying the week of Thanksgiving just for snow or rain?" asked Ruen. "The crappier the weather, the better the walk of fame... or shame. The endless times my mom would ask about getting all muddy and then having to wash the clothes two or three times."

My brother David spoke of the messy aftermath back at the homestead. "We'd be covered in mud and go straight down to the basement to get out of our muddy clothes."

Though the mud was a constant, a victorious Hunt team was not.

Neighbor and Hunt team perennial Jeff Felkey remembered the tide turning for the elders. "I recall beating the students Richard taught until they got bigger, stronger, and older; then they kicked our butts."

Richard Hunt agreed: "Once they went to LCC (Lima Central Catholic High School) and learned how to play defense, we were cooked."

Indeed, a proper defense proved to be a daunting obstacle for the Hunt team, which had often profited from distracting the opposition with strange and unpredictable formations. The Turkey Bowl was notable as much for its unconventional plays as it was for its utter lack of officiating.

"Penalties? What penalties?" Ruen summarized succinctly. He recalled a game rule that required the offensive line to count off five seconds before rushing, observing that it was never followed. When it came to the Turkey Bowl, there were few prohibitions and even less enforcement.

"The adrenaline and excitement to try plays and positions that may not have been allowed on an organized team!" rhapsodized student team player John Gillotti at the thought of some of the ploys that were well outside of regulation football.

One gem involved Hunt team offensive lineman Dave Shine, who purposely fell to the ground at the start of the play, waited until his defensive counterpart dropped his guard, then sprinted forward to catch a pass as planned. Then there was the classic Roman Candle, a single-file vertical formation that dispersed all but the quarterback into wild receiver patterns. When things got really desperate, juvenile humor was occasionally effective.

"My favorite play was the 'Balls, Balls, Balls' play," admitted Felkey, "where upon the hike we all stayed still and chanted 'balls, balls, balls' while covering our privates with our hands, before going out on our routes." It may not have worked in the

NFL, but it was novel and naughty enough to incapacitate a few adolescents.

The Turkey Bowl continued to grow in popularity, especially as the student team began to trounce the Hunts. One year, more students showed up than there were members of the Hunt team. To even things out, one of the extra guys was handed over to play for the Hunts.

"I don't know if you're aware of this," confided newcomer Mike Saylor, "but I'm the LCC quarterback."

"That's okay," deadpanned Richard Hunt, "we'll take you anyway." ·

Tongue-in-cheek trash talk was all part of the game. Student team player Garry Tabler (TAY-BLER) was routinely put down by my brothers, who made a habit of mispronouncing his last name and referring to him as "the Tabbler girl." Garry always took it in the spirit with which it was intended. Whether it was verbal sparring or the game itself, a lighthearted atmosphere prevailed. "Nobody took it seriously," said Richard. "Everyone was just out to have fun."

I can attest to that. I had no business being on a football field, but no one ever gave me a hard time about being there. The better players ragged on each other and left the worst players alone. "It was inclusive and fun," remembered Gillotti.

"As I recall, I was always the MVP," proclaimed my brother Brian, demonstrating the swaggering confidence that was part and parcel of the experience. He described a play in which he rushed the quarterback, tipped the ball into his own possession, and continued downfield for a touchdown. "It sounds more impressive than it was," he added, explaining that one of the least experienced students had been permitted to step in as quarterback on the play.

Even so, the Turkey Bowl was a game that sometimes granted genuine elation to its players, as well as genuine suffering. David Hunt experienced, if not the ABC *World Wide of Sports'* thrill of victory and agony of defeat, at least the joy of a perfect play and the searing pain of injury. As for the joy, David remembered a touchdown pass that Brian threw to him. "What made it special was that as we lined up, I told the defense what my route was going to be, and that Brian was passing to me. At the snap, I ran straight ahead, and when I passed the goal line, I went right five or six steps, turned, and the ball was right there. I dropped to my knees and caught it. Touchdown!! Brian threw a perfect pass. The best thing about it is that after all these years, we still talk about it whenever we talk about the Turkey Bowl."

But all was not roses for the star receiver. One year, "I broke a bone in my left hand. An innocent enough play, but I stumbled forward and fell into an opposing player, my left hand split on his thigh – instant pain. And for the rest of the game, throbbing pain, especially if my hand was below my heart. I sucked it up and played the rest of the game, but later that day I went to the ER and found that I'd broken a bone in my hand."

Eventually, like all good things must, the Turkey Bowl came to an end. I was one of the first to bow out, leaving sometime in the late eighties, my lack of athleticism having rendered me increasingly ineffective even though I was the youngest member of the Hunt team. Others retired not long after, though some carried on for the long haul.

"I bet we played for twenty years," estimated Felkey. "I think my last one was circa 1997 or 1998. Forget what I did, but it was at least a bruised rib. I think it was then that my body was saying enough is enough."

Though the cherished tradition is long gone, it has not been forgotten. "I remember it was magic!" said Gillotti. "Especially as a young kid, being able to take on the mysterious and magical elder Hunts."

"The Turkey Bowl was the most fun we all had as young men!" enthused Moskwinski. "It would be fun to have a Turkey Bowl Reunion – Old against Older!"

"It was always fun playing in the mud," recalls Richard Hunt.

Perhaps Ruen put it best. "Man, did I love the Turkey Bowl."

COLLEGE DAYS

I Say Potato, You Say What?

Don Ward and I were utterly out of sync, from the day we met until the hour we last parted. We were baffled by each other, somehow forever falling short of achieving pleasant and productive conversation. Under any other circumstances, we never would have interacted at all. Fate had intervened, however, and he was as stuck with me as I was with him. For four inscrutable years, Don Ward was my appointed college adviser.

That was not the original plan, at least according to an initial schedule. Having declared my major in Photography and Cinema midway through my freshman year at Ohio State, I was assigned to receive academic counseling from an associate professor who had been with the department for over a decade. I had heard good things about him, and he had the bearing of a wise and approachable mentor. But when I tried to make my first appointment, I learned that I had been inexplicably reassigned to one of the newer faculty members.

Perhaps therein was the initial dissonance that created disharmony between Don Ward and me. For all I know, he might have been as surprised to see me as I was to have been directed to him. The Photography and Cinema Department was housed in a ramshackle building that had been erected in the twenties. Its ominously creaking elevator seemed to be of that era as well. Don Ward's office was a tiny room in one of its shabbier corners, adjacent to a work area where students cropped and mounted prints fresh from the black-and-white photo lab. I walked in to introduce myself.

I found an owl-eyed man with a disheveled mop of sandy hair sitting at his cluttered desk and staring up at me through large, circular lenses. "Professor Ward?" I asked, and a corner of his mustachioed lip curled as though no one had ever addressed him with such formality. It made me slightly uncomfortable when, upon learning my name, he thereafter called me "Mr. Hunt." Something about the way he said it suggested to me that he was dryly amused, but I was not in on the joke. Little did I know at that time that he would address me exclusively in this fashion for the next four years. Even in class, where he called on others casually by their first names, he persisted in referring to me as Mr. Hunt. Was it a subtle insult? A deliberate taunt? An indicator of familiar fondness? His idea of a joke? I was never to know. It became emblematic of our mysterious relationship, two people operating at opposing wavelengths, their thoughts occasionally intersecting but generally at odds.

Professor Ward had an unnerving habit of staring silently from behind those thick lenses, taking just a tad longer than the social norm to respond, as though he were perpetually preoccupied. He took himself seriously as a video artist and filmmaker, and on a couple occasions he shared some of his work, which I found as ambiguous as its creator. Was it serious? Was it satire? Was it good or bad? I couldn't tell. I also took myself seriously as an aspiring director of film and video, and that was half of the problem between Professor Ward and me. He was inevitably flippant when I was sincere, yet he received my rare attempts at humor with grave annoyance.

He turned on me in class once when he solicited our opinions about what we would like to see in the way of improvements to our video editing facilities, modest equipment that was insufficient to meet the student demand. I interpreted his request as a purely hypothetical exercise in defining a fully adequate studio. He was actually trying to determine how to spend severely limited funds. I did not know this, though, and as was his habit, he called on me to respond.

"Mr. Hunt, what would you like to see in an editing facility?"

"Well," I pondered, my eyes and imagination rising to the ceiling, "I suppose we would all like to have our own editing decks and as much time as we liked to use them."

There was an uncomfortable pause.

"Mr. Hunt," Professor Ward said curtly, "get real." And then he stared at me for just a little too long, his lips pressed together in stern disapproval. I was dumbfounded.

Some time later the same quarter, Professor Ward was in a jolly and almost offensively solicitous mood. He was dropping the name of an alternative band in what seemed to me to be a desperate attempt of a man in his thirties to curry favor with a small group of very young adults. In fact, he was getting downright silly, and much to my disgust, the rest of the class was going along with it. It was a pendulum swing from his customary air of disdain. I was not about to brown-nose, and so I sat expressionless amidst the false hilarity. This bothered him, and he attempted to get me involved.

"Wouldn't that be great, Mr. Hunt?" he asked animatedly. I was in no mood for frivolousness. The others could laugh like bleating sheep if they liked, but if he insisted on dragging me into his farce, I was going to call him out on it.

"No," I said emphatically, without a trace of amusement. The very air evaporated from the room. Professor Ward trained his owl eyes on me and scowled as if to say, "What in the world is wrong with you?!" Which was precisely what I was thinking about him.

Which is not to say that he was totally unsupportive. He actually expressed his admiration for much of the work that I produced for his class, going so far as to slow down the playback and discuss the merits and creativity of individual shots. But not always. Once I made the mistake of debuting my final, which I had finished early, for our TA during a class that Professor Ward could not attend. It was a satirical piece that earned some good laughs from my classmates. When Professor Ward was present for the next session, he played all of our final pieces.

Mine ran to complete silence, as the class had already seen it. He had nothing good to say about my work that day.

As my adviser, Professor Ward had to approve my Photography and Cinema course choices, which meant that I was regularly going into his office to have him sign off on my proposed schedules. These were usually awkward encounters with little meaningful interaction. Toward the end of my time at Ohio State, he was trying to encourage me to attend grad school at his alma mater in Iowa.

"You can't do anything with a bachelor's degree in cinema, not unless you're going to be happy stuck behind a TV news camera for the rest of your life."

But I had seen enough of the obsessive world of film and video to know that I was unwilling to devote every minute of my young life to the craft, which seemed to be what was required to make a success of it. I let him know that I had no plans for grad school at that point, and we regarded each other with mutual puzzlement.

Perhaps what he wanted for me was simply what he desired for himself. He eventually became an internationally known video artist whose work has been exhibited in some prestigious venues, and he continued in education at a university out west. Well over a decade after I last saw him, he became a target of disgruntled students on one of those awful websites that allow anonymous educator reviews.

> *"His work is worse than many students. He really shouldn't be a teacher."*
>
> *"Avoid his classes at all costs."*
>
> *"Quite possibly the worst teacher ever."*

I smiled as I read those words, simply because they reminded me of a certain young man who was also perplexed by this unknowable professor. As such, I took their opinions with the mandatory grain of salt. I really have nothing against Professor Ward. I just never could get a handle on who he was. I suspect he might have said the same about me.

On my last visit to his office, I was determined to get in and out as quickly as possible. He must have noticed the earnestness in my face. Midway through our brief appointment, the beeping alarm of my digital watch unexpectedly interrupted us.

"Time for a hamburger!" he smiled.

And at last, he made me laugh.

A nervous laugh, perhaps, but still...

Hip Hop

As a summer job, it wasn't bad. Working for my hometown's small parks and recreation department gave me a steady 40 hours a week with weekends off. Although it was for minimum wage ($3.35 an hour at the time), the full-time seasonal position allowed me to earn enough money for the textbooks and miscellaneous expenses of a further three quarters of undergraduate study. Furthermore, one's employment there made the prospect of being re-hired the following season likely, and so it was that my college experience was interspersed with a trio of summers spent keeping the parks beautiful.

The colorful characters I met there could have populated a lowbrow sitcom. Each day began and ended in a dingy office area within the maintenance garage, where assignments were given out in the morning and the same four regulars concluded each afternoon with a few rounds of euchre. Many of them had been working for the parks department for years, and the atmosphere was very casual and wisecracking. On my first day there, another "temp" and I were assigned to the most casual and wisecracking of them all, a small and rotund man who went by the nickname of Hop.

Hop's regular duty was to run the department's trash truck, which was dispatched to empty the plentiful green barrels that dotted each of our city's parks and playgrounds. In the summer, he was given a pair of seasonal workers to accomplish this, which meant that he spent most of his working day bouncing along the springy bench seat of the truck cab. I was a little nervous that first morning, sandwiched as I was between Hop and a beefy returning seasonal named Doug. Not much was said as we rattled and creaked toward our first destination, and I hoped I would be able to do my job well. When at last we pulled into the parking lot of a hamburger joint on the other side of town, I was confused. What were we doing here?

"Breakfast time!" announced Hop gleefully, and the three of us trundled out of the cab for coffee and donuts. And here I was worried about keeping my job. Welcome to Parks and Recreation.

Working with Hop would turn out to be one of my favorite assignments, although the actual labor wasn't too desirable. Doug and I would jump onto the back of the truck whenever we reached a park entrance, holding onto a handle and perched on little running boards as we traveled from can to can. Our hands protected with heavy work gloves, we would roll each rusted metal can toward the back of the truck and hoist it along the lip of the hopper to empty its contents. I soon got used to the sickeningly sweet smell of picnic trash that had stewed in the summer heat for days. Many times, we had live maggots wriggling in the toxic soup that would slosh around the bottom of the bin until we periodically operated the compactor. On the rare occasions that we emptied trash at an active playground, the kids thought Doug and I had the coolest jobs on earth.

I enjoyed working on the trash truck only because it put me in the eccentric company of Hop and his infamously crude sense of humor. He was an unapologetic man who had obviously long ago stopped caring what anyone thought of him. The rumor that I would eventually hear was that Hop had once been one of the most industrious employees in all of Parks and Recreation, but when he was overlooked for a promotion that he felt he deserved, his demeanor changed. Apparently, he had been sticking it to the man ever since, doing precisely what was asked of him and nothing more. It must have been cathartic for him, because far from being a bitter soul, Hop was as jovial and carefree as a lazy boy whiling away idle summer days.

"Ohhhh....we ripped and we snorted and we shat on the floor, wiped our asses on the knob of the door!" sang Hop lustily to the tune of "Turkey in the Straw." Attempting to shift into third gear, he struggled for a moment as the cab vibrated with a terrific crunching noise from the transmission. Hop was undeterred. "Ground me a pound!" he grinned, and the hulking trash truck lurched forward. Decelerating at a four-way stop, he looked both ways before asking rhetorically, "Anybody comin'?" Doug and I learned to wait a beat for the punchline. "Anybody breathin' hard?"

In the overwhelmingly male parks department, vulgarity was as commonplace as it is wherever juvenile men are allowed to speak freely. But whereas less creative minds were known to pepper their speech with mere profanities, Hop eschewed such reflexive utterances in favor of more artistic fare. For example, if an attractive woman (or nearly any woman, for that matter) used the crosswalk as we waited at a stop, Hop might appreciatively refer to her undulating brassiere as an "over-the-shoulder boulder holder." And like any great actor, the performance was much more than words. Hop delivered his crude remarks with such gusto and relish that he was nothing less than endearing. It either made him happy or was a byproduct of his existing happiness; either way, you couldn't help but be happy with him.

Hop's imperturbability extended to all aspects of his work. Nothing seemed to faze him. At one routine stop I opened the padlock that secured a trash can to a tree and was startled to discover a pair of wide eyes staring at me from the depths of the container. I called out to Hop for assistance, and he dismounted from the cab to see what was wrong. "Nothin' but a possum," he observed, but when he tilted the trash can onto its side, the animal refused to leave its shelter. I watched in astonishment as Hop got on his knees and reached into the can, emerging with a large and frightened opossum that had its tail coiled firmly around Hop's forearm. The terrified marsupial was momentarily motionless, then it abruptly untethered itself and ran into the woods. Hop treated the strange encounter with such aplomb that he made pulling a wild animal out of a trash can seem like nothing more than an everyday annoyance, like retying one's shoes. He brushed some debris from his pants, smiled, and got back into the cab.

Hop was also an engaging storyteller, though his tales tended to be as bawdy as his humor. He told me about a childhood incident in which he and a friend were out exploring in the woods when nature called. His friend found it necessary to produce a bowel movement, and consequently the absence of available toilet paper became an issue. This was remedied by the application of some nearby leaves, which were later identified as poison ivy. Snorts and chuckles interrupted Hop's speech as he recalled his friend spending the rest of that summer on his stomach, humiliated by the attention of his mother to his most basic needs.

Not long after my last summer with the parks department (and perhaps a decade before Hop's death), I ran into Hop in the concourse of a shopping mall. Contrary to all appearances while on the job, there were things about which Hop did care, and among them was wildlife conservation. He was manning a booth devoted to the cause, and when I approached him, he admitted sheepishly that he could not recall my name. He had worked with many seasonal temps over the years. I introduced my fiancée, whom Hop received with such genteel politeness that she could scarcely believe my tales of his vulgar comments. We said goodbye to Hop and sauntered onward.

"Really," I explained, "it's the same Hop."

"He seemed normal to me."

"Well, sure." We strolled along as I mulled over this truth. "I guess if you really want to know him, you have to be one of the guys."

I Once was a Man
who Lived in a Shoe

Ohio Stadium is not quite what it used to be. Though its tradition of hosting Buckeye football games continues unabated and the structure itself remains an unmistakable landmark for sports fans and aircraft pilots alike, a piece of it that thrived for six decades is missing. You might be forgiven for walking within it and failing to notice this omission. Even when it existed, few people seemed to be aware of the Stadium Dorm.

Make that The Ohio Stadium Scholarship Dormitory, as it was officially known. Its genesis was a spartan facility constructed inside the southwest tower in 1933, a mere eleven years after the stadium itself was built. From that humble beginning as a no-frills campus residence for 78 men of limited financial means, the dorm gradually expanded along the west concourse into a much larger, coed residence hall. The additions were elevated structures, their three floors of rooms suspended from the underside of the stadium seating. In its final form, the Stadium Dorm was comprised of five major sections accessed by tiny entrance foyers featuring a flight of stairs leading up to the "first" floor. Up to thirty students lived in each of the fifteen gender-segregated floor units, sharing communal bathrooms, taping posters to the paper-thin walls, and taking meals in the dorm cafeteria. Meanwhile, throngs of Buckeye supporters sauntered beneath these quarters on many a football Saturday without noticing that a vibrant and lively dormitory was hanging above them.

By the time I lived there in the late eighties, its longevity had done little to raise its profile, nor to rectify popular misconceptions.

"What's it like to live with the football players?" a classmate would ask without a hint of irony or sarcasm.

"Nobody on the football team lives in our dorm," I would politely explain. "One of the cheerleaders lives there, but that's about it as far as I know."

"Oh," the inquisitor would respond with disappointment. "Still, it must really get loud during a game, huh?"

Actually, no, at least not on the lower floor where I lived. In fact, you could easily go about your business without ever knowing that nearly 100,000 people were making a day of it in your backyard. The one and only time I could ever sense their presence was after a particularly exciting moment during a Michigan game. I was reclining on my bed, watching the game on TV while it was being played only yards away from my room. As I watched images of the crowd going berserk, I detected the slightest tremor in my bedsprings, much as someone paying very close attention might notice a slight natural aberration hundreds of miles away from the epicenter of a mild earthquake.

In earlier days, I might have enjoyed the privilege of accessing games by the ramp doors that adjoined each section as emergency exits. For years, dorm residents (including my three older brothers) were able to simply step from their own living quarters into the frenzied excitement of a major college football game, like idle children discovering a magical land beyond the back panel of their wardrobe. The powers that be eventually got wise to that and saw fit to equip the doors with emergency alarms. During the era in which I lived there, residents were threatened with expulsion from the dorm for exiting to the ramp at any time other than a genuine emergency.

We still had plenty of opportunities to get into the Horseshoe, however. Occasionally we were granted special access, as in the case of Primal Scream Night, on which our dorm was invited to gather at the 50-yard line for a midnight catharsis to

122

relieve the stress of studying for finals. In the spring, we hosted an annual formal in the press box. While other dorms rented hotel ballrooms, we had the pleasure of being able to step away from the loud music with our dates onto a tranquilly deserted C-deck, whereupon we could sit quietly and admire the silent football field. All of this was before the university installed the high-tech turf that is still used today, and it was not unusual for the stadium gates to be open to everyone on any given weekday. Frequently the track was enjoyed by recreational runners, and the field was home to countless Nerf ball touchdowns. When I needed to find interesting images for a photography class, it was a fruitful and convenient location.

And on one very special occasion, living in the Stadium Dorm happened to be *incredibly* convenient. In the spring of 1988, the campus was giddy with excitement over the announcement that Pink Floyd had been booked to play the first-ever concert in Ohio Stadium. Students queued up in amazingly long lines to snap up inexpensive tickets, and *The Lantern* reported breathlessly for weeks on every development from the rapid sell-out to construction of the enormous stage. A few enterprising guys in our dorm went so far as to devise an elaborate scheme by which they were able to bootleg the show in stereo from their own room. When the highly anticipated night finally arrived, it was all the more pleasurable to simply enjoy the quiet comforts of our dormitory home right up until showtime. Go downstairs, exit, walk ten feet to the gate, and show your ticket. Afterwards, retrace your steps and enjoy the afterparty in your own private room inside the venue. Fat cat CEOs in their luxury boxes never had it better.

Of course, it wasn't all fun and games. The Stadium Dorm was cooperative housing, meaning that its residents enjoyed a lower rate for their rooms in exchange for participating in a modest work-study program. Everyone contributed several hours a week to keep the place running smoothly, though it usually fell to the freshmen to perform all custodial and culinary duties. After a year in the cafeteria, I became a sophomore security guard, checking IDs at the main door after hours and making the rounds down the aptly named Long Hall (so long, in fact, that the curvature of the stadium prevented a person at one end from seeing a friend at the other) to ensure that all exterior doors were shut and locked.

The latter half of my Stadium employment was spent in the cushiest of positions as a staff writer for the dorm newspaper. Cleverly titled *The West Side Story* in homage to both Bernstein and the side of the stadium that we occupied, this featherweight rag was derisively referred to by most residents as *The Wuss*, a snide corruption of its acronym. There was no small amount of resentment among the student dishwashers and toilet scrubbers that a fellow stadiumite could get away with paying off his work-study debt by dashing off a few bad articles a week. Those of us lucky enough to secure this non-work were given very wide latitude to write almost anything we wished, and I enjoyed composing a series of articles that dryly presented outrageous lies as fact. Among the whoppers I reported was a confirmation of rumors that professors accessed academic buildings via an underground labyrinth of tunnels, the revelation that the white squirrel seen frequently on The Oval had been imported from Italy, and a stunning announcement that administrators were planning to build a dome over the stadium. I don't know if anyone believed it. For that matter, I can't say whether anyone even read it. But it kept me out of pots and pans, that's for sure.

Like any college dormitory, ours was not immune from the pathetic excesses of young men and women enjoying unprecedented freedom and minimal supervision. Floors became sticky with the resin of spilled beverages, and occasional bouts of hallway roughhousing resulted in various crevasses and holes along the flimsy drywall. Most of it was harmless enough, although I happened to be in my room one evening when an extraordinary outburst of violence erupted just outside my closed door. A young woman with an axe to grind, or more precisely, a baseball bat to wield, was expressing her displeasure with one of the guys who lived across the hall. There was much shrieking, thunderous pounding, and the shattering of glass. Miraculously, no one was injured. When it was all over, there was a frightening dent in the ex-boyfriend's mini-fridge, and the hallway was a rank debris field of broken bottles, puddles of perfume, and scattered prophylactics. The unhinged ex-girlfriend was later banned from entering the dorm, but the damage had been done. Not physical damage, but rather the long-term psychological consequences. During the course of her rampage, she made a vociferous and insulting anatomical reference to her embattled boyfriend using the rather impressive word *minuscule*. It burned in my mind as a brand seared on a hide, and even today the word *minuscule* is inescapably suggestive to me. God help me if a psychiatrist ever uses it to prompt me in a word-association exercise.

Yes, we experienced it all in the Stadium: laughter, tears, violence, love...and even death. I recall the late winter evening when my roommate, Ken, walked in the door with surprising news.

"Hey, did you hear? Woody's dead!"

I looked up from my book and silently turned his words over in my mind. I furrowed my brow in disbelief and cried out to him, "Woody Allen is dead?!" Ken regarded me with the exasperated compassion of a straight man tolerating his hopeless sidekick.

"No, Bob. Woody. Woody Hayes is dead."

It was the solemnest occasion on which the stadium gates were left open to the public. We went down to the field to take in the surreal sight of mourners trickling in and placing mementos upon a makeshift memorial as the image of Coach Hayes shone from the scoreboard. That night, the very same setting for so many raucous football crowds was transformed into a contemplative and reverent sanctuary, as much as any church has ever been.

Ah, football. As young adults immersed in our college years, it was difficult to see ourselves as anything other than the very center of the world in our humble Stadium Dorm. Did we ever realize how insignificant we were in the vastness of the temple we inhabited? Had we ever considered that this majestic edifice was built solely to embrace the gridiron, and the fact that we lived there was merely a footnote to its legacy? Probably not. But it was football for which Ohio Stadium was built, and ultimately it was football for which the Stadium Dorm was destroyed. As the century drew to a close, my old dormitory was demolished to make way for major renovations that significantly increased seating capacity on football Saturdays.

And so the fabled campus dorm that was a secret to many is now all the more legendary. When I last visited Ohio Stadium, it was strange to think that the former residence of so many alumni was simply gone. But I cannot forget the quirky campus digs that I once called home. Especially when I hear the word *minuscule*.

Stranger Danger

Twice in my life I have been momentarily convinced that a total stranger was about to kill me. Given my sheltered upbringing and habitual avoidance of risky behavior and potentially unsafe scenarios, it seems an unlikely statistic. Both incidents occurred when I was a college student engaged in the most humdrum of pursuits. One moment I was just another Joe Average going about his ordinary business, and then suddenly I was staring death in the face. Or so I thought.

My first brush with mortality happened on an otherwise dull September evening. I had moved into my dorm room a few days earlier than most students due to required training for my work-study job. As a member of the dormitory security staff, I would be expected to know what I was doing by the time the rest of the residents arrived. I didn't mind getting a head start on campus life, especially since it was easier for me to move in while almost everyone else was still out.

An unusually quiet atmosphere transformed the boisterous dorm with which I was familiar into a strange and contemplative place, a tranquil chamber with echoing halls that fostered deeper thinking and even some serious reflection. It was the dawn of a new academic year, I mused, the beginning of three more quarters' worth of new ideas and opportunities. Like the final hours of New Year's Eve, the circumstance called for resolutions and a renewed commitment to self-improvement. An investment in sound nutrition seemed like a good place to start. Yes, I resolved, it was time to cut out the chips and fries and fill up instead with fruits and vegetables.

Determined to embark on this course of action before my enthusiasm could wane, I immediately pulled on a jacket and bounded down the stairs. A gentle autumn chill wafted through the early evening darkness as I strode purposefully across campus. There were no grocery stores nearby, but a United Dairy Farmers was conveniently located just a short walk away. I was fairly certain that I had once spied a tiny amount of produce in one of their refrigerated cases, and with any luck I would find their kitchen gadget shelf stocked with vegetable peelers. I envisioned myself back in my dorm room, setting forth on my journey to better health to the resounding crunch of raw carrots.

The shortest route to the convenience store included a trip through a covered passageway that connected adjacent buildings with the same roof. Though its path was entirely above ground, we were in the habit of referring to the narrow space as a tunnel, as its dim interior produced much the same effect. By day it was merely unsightly, but nighttime lent it a vaguely sinister air. Even so, plenty of students used it at all hours. It was much quicker than walking all the way around the block.

On this particular evening, I happened to be the only soul using the popular shortcut. Its emptiness made me just the slightest bit uneasy, but I moved forward briskly with the confidence that I would soon reach the other side. Nearing the end of the passageway, I made out the silhouette of a lone figure standing there motionless, as if waiting for someone. The person was of small stature, and I checked my flight reflex with the counterargument that my sudden fear was only silly paranoia. After all, there was nothing particularly threatening about this stranger, save for his loitering spot. I picked up my pace to pass him quickly, and that's when he darted forward to intercept me.

He was a young man like myself, clad in jeans and a light jacket. He stared at me with disturbingly intense eyes, and his voice was a grim monotone that befitted his grave countenance. "Do you believe in life after death?" he demanded in an aggressive manner far more intimidating than his size would suggest. It never occurred to me not to answer.

"Um...I don't know," I stammered, true to my agnosticism of the time. Then came the kicker.

"Would you like to find out?" He reached into his jacket, and I felt the sort of adrenaline rush that accompanies close calls in rush hour traffic. I didn't exactly see my life flash before my eyes, but I was dumbstruck with terror and simultaneously overcome by the irony of it all. *Oh my God!* I cried out silently, somewhat unfaithful to my agnosticism. *He's going to kill me! I'm going to be shot and killed because I decided to walk to United Dairy Farmers for a bag of carrots! It's not like I was going to indulge in unhealthy snacks, either – I was going to buy carrots! This is what I get for trying to be healthy?!*

And then he pulled out his gun. Only it wasn't a gun. It was a small pamphlet entitled *Are You Going To Hell?* The words were printed in a bold red font above black line art of a man's face contorted in agony. The evangelistic thug had to know that he had just scared me nearly unconscious. But he said nothing more, so I stuffed the fiery tract into my pocket and continued on my vegetable quest. Somehow the relative nutritional merit of one food versus another seemed rather insignificant in light of my brief flirtation with nonexistence. But I bought the carrots anyway, and my trembling hands found a peeler as well. As for the pamphlet, I found its message less than persuasive.

My second not-so-near-death experience happened not long afterward, this time not on campus but rather among the grassy hills of a city park in my hometown. I had a summer job with the parks department, and I was entrusted with the mowing of one of our larger properties. It took about a week to mow the entire park, by which time the section that had been mowed first needed to be mowed again. As dull as the routine was, I enjoyed the independence I was given. Someone from the parks department would drop me off at the maintenance shed every morning and come back to pick me up in the afternoon, and it was up to me to stay busy in between.

One sweltering day after lunch, I had taken the riding mower up into the northwest quadrant for a few more hours of grass cutting. By this time my tasks had become so repetitive that I found it necessary to keep myself in a state of preoccupation in order to make it through the day. A portion of my brain guided the mower along its course as the rest of my mind was far away, usually lost in an endless mental loop of whatever music I had been listening to recently. We were required to wear jeans on even the hottest days, and so my senses were further dulled by the oppressive heat.

The park to which I had been assigned had a reputation for attracting odd characters. Its acreage included many tall trees and undulating hills, affording visitors seeking seclusion a number of unpopulated options. This gave it tremendous potential as a venue for hide-and-seek, but it also created the dependable lack of bystanders that is craved by nefarious types. I was told that it was unwise to trespass its grounds after dark, but I always felt safe enough fulfilling my parks department job there. I was mindlessly turning the mower around for another pass when I caught sight of a shirtless man walking toward me.

I stopped the mower, wiped the sweat from my brow, and tried to discern whether or not what I thought I was seeing was real. I had heard of strange people roaming the park, and this man certainly fit the bill. He wore only ragged cutoffs and sandals. With his long, matted hair and unkempt beard, he looked like a Woodstock refugee who was unaware that it was no longer the Summer of Love. The incredible part, though – the thing that chilled the sweat on my back – was his posture. He was walking toward me with his arms stretched before him and his hands clasped together. In fact, he was obviously pointing something at me. *Oh my God!* I panicked irreverently once again, *he's pointing a gun at me!* There was nowhere to run, the riding mower was far too slow to effect an escape, and so I simply stared in helpless horror as the crazed hippie drew closer. To have survived the menacing evangelist only to perish like this!

Whereupon it suddenly became clear to me that he was, in fact, holding a squirrel. Yes, a squirrel, and apparently an injured one at that. This latter-day St. Francis had found the poor animal and was seeking aid, although precisely what was wrong with the critter was unclear to me. When he saw me astride a riding mower in my official parks department green t-shirt, he assumed that I represented the nearest thing to a naturalist authority that he had yet encountered. But I was just a college kid sweating through a summer job. I didn't know anything about squirrels.

"What should I do with it?" he asked.

"Um...I don't know," I stammered, true to my veterinary ignorance. He looked at me for a moment with disappointment in his eyes, and then he wandered off with his squirrel. *How should I know?* I thought to myself indignantly. *Good God, I'm lucky just to be alive!*

Loving in Fall

I don't remember taking a walk along a lake with my mother on a chilly fall day, but the gentle moment is documented in a faded color photograph. I was no more than a toddler at the time. Looking at it now, I can imagine how fresh and exhilarating the sensation must have been for me, a novice to the cyclical changes of turning seasons. The sharpness of the cool air, the windblown rustle of decaying foliage, and cascading waves of pinwheeling leaves would have captivated me. Autumn must have been a wondrous and beautiful contrast to the vibrant skies and sweltering sun of summer.

Whatever wonder I associated with the season would dissipate within several years, however. My annual return to school became the most memorable event in autumn, and I soon developed a distaste for what I gradually perceived to be a depressing time of year. Summer was a joyous freedom from responsibility, a chance to impulsively indulge every whim, an endless vacation with so many hours of daylight that you could wake up late and still have more time than you ever wanted to ride your bike for blocks with no agenda whatsoever. Fall came to represent the absence of these cherished things, and so it held little charm for me. Deciduous trees aflame with color and crisp strolls through the apple orchard? Who cares? Summer's over.

Of course, I would eventually adjust to the departure of summer and enjoy the unique pleasures of autumn like any other kid. I was right out there with the rest of the neighborhood children, raking up leaves for the sole purpose of jumping into massive piles of them. Trick-or-treating on Halloween was certainly a highlight, and Thanksgiving was always a treasured holiday. But those were little islands of happiness within a greater sea of anxiety. I didn't like seeing the cold and empty darkness envelop our street a little earlier each night. Just hearing the droning of *Monday Night Football* announcers from the living room as I lay sleepless in my room aggravated my apprehension of the perils I might face the next day at school. *What if I get in the wrong lunch line again? What if I get called up in front of everybody and have to find a place I've never heard of on the big map? What if we do another one of those horrible times table relays?* Yeah, I was a neurotic kid.

Though my neuroses ebbed as I matured, my disdain for autumn did not. I was no longer wasting my thoughts worrying about the next day's potential unpleasantness, but I still regarded fall as a time to endure rather than enjoy. At least winter brought the gradual lengthening of daylight hours and the possibility of a good snow day or two. Aside from the welcome distraction of its holidays, autumn offered a bleak forecast: things are going to get worse before they get better.

These days I see it all quite differently. Rather than belittle the falling temperatures and longer nights of October and November, I now revere fall as my favorite season. No longer does the revelation of skeletal trees lead me to despair. The deepening chill that forces us to close our windows and turn on the heat cannot cool my enthusiasm. I love autumn, and even when its arrival still signaled a certain loss of freedom for me during my years as an elementary school teacher, that fact would not dampen my affection.

What prompted this drastic change? Surely just growing older has been a significant part of it. In a way, it reminds me of how my childhood preference for bright music in major keys was ultimately subverted by a growing appreciation for the bittersweet ache of contrasting minor chords. Whereas I once found sad melodies disturbing, I am now likely to find the very same pieces uplifting and even life-affirming. There is some of that in autumn as well. Leaves are dying, the wind is blowing, and the sun isn't sticking around like it used to. There is a certain sadness to the season. And yet, here we are, living through it, taking the crisp air deep into our lungs, somehow confident that a satisfying coda awaits.

But I know that there is more to it than that. A lifetime of negative autumnal associations evaporated during my college years. It was there that I experienced a different and more rewarding freedom while enjoying the company of new and interesting friends. Most importantly, it was the means by which I came to know the wonderful young woman whom I would later marry. We met early in our freshman year, started spending a lot of time together in the spring, and tearfully said goodbye when we returned to our respective homes for Summer Quarter.

That summer seemed to last forever. We were just a little ahead of our technological time, stuck as we were in that lonely darkness just before the dawn of email and the glorious day of unlimited cell phone calling plans. Our communication was limited to handwritten letters and a 1-hour, landline call every Saturday night at eleven, when the rates were lowest. We were fortunate to enjoy a few cross-state visits, but otherwise our time was spent far away from each other, and we longed for the day when we would be together. For the rest of our undergraduate experience, summer became the season of absence, and every autumn brought a joyous reunion.

Like so many other couples whose meeting was fated by their choice of university, we married after graduation and never left town, finding a home only twenty minutes from campus. Years went by, yet despite our proximity to our alma mater, we rarely walked among its familiar buildings and landmarks. Not literally, anyway. But we would reminisce about our college days now and then, especially each autumn. It's almost impossible not to when college football is a major focus of the local media, and images of those buildings and landmarks seem to be everywhere come September. Each fall takes me back to a place and time when I became reacquainted with a sense of enchantment that I had not known since I was very young.

Why do I love autumn? Perhaps because I cannot experience it without recalling a dark and rainy late September evening over thirty years ago. I am nineteen again. My parents have helped me move my belongings back into my windowless dorm room. They have treated me to one last good meal out before my return to cafeteria food. Now we wind through the lamp-lit avenues of campus toward another dormitory, our windshield wipers furiously swishing away the swelling rain. As we reach our destination, I hug my parents and promise to call them from time to time.

A slanting rain pelts my face when I emerge from the car. I lean into the wind, my jacket billowing, and trudge toward the door. In my arms I am cradling a dozen red roses, keeping them safely sheltered from the strong gust that is scattering leaves across the pavement. The weather, some might say, is awful. And I have never been happier.

Focus Study

The photograph was a surreal, black and white portrait, just the sort of clumsy stab at art that one might expect from a college student in an introductory photography course. Its subject was a young woman whose eyes were obscured by the pair of oranges she held before her face. Perhaps it was its humor that earned it a spot on the wall of Haskett Hall, where I stopped to regard my handiwork each day after class. Passersby might have mistaken my look of concentration for the solemn focus of critique, but my motivation was shallow. The truth was that I had something of a crush for the model, and standing for a moment in front of her portrait allowed me to stare at her captivating image and daydream of impossibly good things.

Making films and videos interested me far more than capturing stills, but having declared my major as Photography and Cinema, I was obligated to learn the rudiments of picture taking and photochemistry. The lecture section of my introductory class was taught by Tony Mendoza, who was known at the time for a whimsical series of black-and-white photographs featuring his cat, Ernie. His artistry was inspiring, but as I was to discover, creativity was only a fraction of what was required to produce good photographs. The technical side of it – everything from light meter readings to focal lengths to maintaining the proper temperature for photochemical solutions – was daunting. I was long on ideas but short on technique.

My shortcomings were made painfully clear (all too literally, I'm afraid) when I received my first roll of negatives back from the department lab. A few hours of traipsing about campus and shooting whatever caught my interest had produced nothing more than unexposed film, apparently the result of loading the camera improperly. Mind you, this was well before the advent of digital photography, back when pointing and shooting would get you a good image only if you knew what you were doing. My borrowed SLR was a bit of a mystery to me at first, but gradually I came to appreciate the subtleties of aperture settings and shutter speeds. Oh, and making sure the sprocket holes of a fresh roll of film are fully engaged before setting off to take pictures.

My TA was a short, curt woman whose brusque manner seemed affected in order to weed out anyone who was taking the class as an easy elective. She was brutally honest rather than unconditionally encouraging. One weekend we were assigned the task of creating, printing, and mounting an image that suggested motion. The obvious route would have been to take a prolonged exposure of a car passing by at night, its taillights extending like phantom lightning bolts, but I was not about to succumb to cliché. I wanted to impress my TA with my creativity, and so I embarked on a photographic expedition in which I shot a game of bowling, snack bags falling out of vending machines, and various objects being tossed back and forth. Not satisfied with the result of any single image, I hit upon the idea of creating a four-panel collage of my roommate attempting to catch a soccer ball, which I cleverly titled The Catch. I smugly submitted my work and pitied the efforts of my conventional classmates.

My TA hated it. She absolutely lambasted my work, tarring my effort with a grade I was not accustomed to earning. I pleaded for a second chance, and she graciously allowed me to redo the assignment for full credit. That evening, I strolled out of my dorm, stood at the edge of Cannon Drive, dialed up a slow shutter speed, and snapped a few frames of passing cars. Later I printed the photographic world's most pedestrian image of streaking taillights. My TA loved it. Or maybe she just felt sorry for me. Either way, she gave me an A.

By that time, I was beginning to have a few misgivings about my major, not only due to its technical challenges but also because of the somewhat odd crowd that the courses attracted. I felt little affinity with many of my photography classmates, perhaps because I failed to understand their work. There was one outgoing young woman who had engaged me in friendly conversation every so often after class, and one day she seemed excited to share with me her latest series of photographs. Standing outside our department building, she handed me a stack of black-and-white prints, and I tried to maintain a blank expression of earnest critique as I flipped through them.

"That's my boyfriend," she explained. Indeed it was, or parts of him anyway. Her creative license involved laying on the floor and aiming the camera upward to capture her model *au naturel.* "What do you think?"

"Wow..." I murmured, glancing nervously around us with the paranoid suspicion that my reaction was being documented for some sort of feminist *Candid Camera.* I quickly ascertained that in the art world, there was only one politically correct answer. "It's, uh...wow, these are great."

Things picked up a little as I gained confidence and started taking a few artistic risks again. My TA liked my self-portrait, a high-contrast close-up in which I had shielded half of my face with the black fabric of an umbrella. That inspired me to go a little further while taking portraits of my roommate's girlfriend's roommates. Probably I made the suggestion to hold up a pair of oranges as faux eyes for the basest of reasons: to make a pretty girl laugh. I can't remember. In any case, I chose to print that image, and my TA liked it so much that she allowed it a place of honor as part of a hallway display.

My final project that quarter was a portfolio of stereo images taken around campus. Caught up once again in the naive enthusiasm of doing something novel that I thought would distinguish me from my peers, I unwittingly committed myself to twice the amount of work. Every image had to be photographed once with the left eye and again with the right, resulting in double sessions of enlarging, printing, cropping and mounting. In addition, every pair of prints had to have the same overall texture and contrast, and I found that neatly affixing twin images to gallery display boards required a lot more time than mounting just one photo. Were it not for my brother's generosity in setting up a free darkroom in his apartment, I never would have finished. As it was, my efforts were largely wasted, for although my portfolio earned a good grade, my TA was unable to manipulate her eyes in the manner necessary to view the images in three dimensions. Having reached the end of the quarter, she favored encouragement over criticism and assumed that the work was impressive, if only she could see it properly.

Aside from a history of photography class, I never bothered with still images for the rest of my major. I did, however, coax the girl with the oranges to act in and provide technical assistance for some of my film and video projects. In fact, much to my surprise, I learned that sometimes impossibly good daydreams come true. We've been married for over thirty years. And still, I find that mysterious and oddly humorous portrait as captivating as I ever did.

ADULTHOOD
(apparently)

The Dark Sides of the Room

I used to work in total darkness. Not all of the time, mind you, but I experienced the complete absence of light for an average of an hour every working day for a few years. And no, I wasn't sleeping. As the manager of a micrographics department within a small records management firm, it was my responsibility to handle raw film stock and process every exposed reel. As a result, I spent a fair amount of time squirreled away inside a darkroom.

Our digital age has rapidly transformed the very notion of a darkroom into an antiquated concept. Forthcoming generations will grasp the idea only through its representation in old movies and television shows, with their romanticized, red-tinted photo labs inhabited by outcasts who discover startling evidence upon retrieving an enlargement from a chemical tray. Such a cliche never once happened in real life, I guarantee you. Dramatic moments of unexpected revelation might occur when a photographer is projecting a negative with an enlarger prior to exposing a sheet of photo paper, but unanticipated compositional elements never emerge from a fixer bath. I guess the truth is too complicated or dull for visual narratives. In any case, that isn't the kind of darkroom in which I worked.

My darkroom had no red-filtered safety lamps. There was no need for them, as I never worked with photo paper. We bought our unperforated 16mm microfilm on 100-foot reels, which had to be wound by hand into the lightproof cartridges that were inserted into our cameras. After a reel was exposed and rewound, the film had to be extracted from the cartridge and placed on a much larger reel for processing. Both of these processes had to occur in total darkness, or else we would compromise the carefully calibrated exposure of up to 3,500 document images on each roll.

When I was first trained to do this, these routine tasks were daunting. To load a roll of film into a cartridge, for example, required performing a sequence of precise movements without looking at what you were doing. First, attach an empty cartridge to the special receptacle on the left rewind of a loading board. Find the trailer and extract it from the cartridge. Then grab a box of film stock, tear off its label, and remove its reel. Peel the safety paper off the film, then attach the reel to the right rewind, making sure that the film spools to the left from underneath the reel. Next, take the leading edge of the film and hold it so that it abuts the end of the trailer. With a free hand, pull off a tab of splice tape and secure the underside of the connection, then pull off another tab and secure the top. Ensure that the film is positioned underneath the guide roller, or else it may get scratched on the lip of the cartridge. Now you're ready to reel! Turn the crank on the left rewind counterclockwise until all of the film has spooled into the cartridge. Now find the end of the roll and pull it out of the cartridge. Take the end of a black leader and hold it so that it abuts the end of the film. With a free hand, pull off a tab of splice tape and secure the underside of the connection, then pull off another tab and secure the top. Wind the leader into the cartridge, and *voila!* You're done. Easy, right?

Actually, it *was* easy, but only after you established a routine and got used to it. Consistency was the key. Provided that all of the necessary materials were gathered and placed in designated locations prior to turning out the lights, everything went smoothly. I was surprised how quickly I could adapt to the utter lack of visual information, and soon my darkroom tasks became as automatic as tying my shoes. The danger was the tedium. As dull as it could be to sit in darkness doing the same task over and over, I couldn't afford a lapse in concentration. A bad splice on a cartridge trailer could result in a couple hours of wasted microfilmer labor due to the exposed film remaining stuck in the camera (its retrieval requiring its exposure to light).

A worse fate was possible if I mishandled preparing exposed film for processing. It was cartridge loading in reverse, with up to 14 rolls of film spliced together onto a single reel that was then concealed within a light-tight magazine. For splicing, the rolls had to be overlapped in a particular manner and secured with five staples. Failure to do this within a certain measure of accuracy would cause a splice to become jammed between the magazine and the processor, a harrowing occurrence of costly potential. Despite my best efforts and those of the employees I trained, a jam would occur now and then, and I became as attuned to the call of my processor alarm as a new mother is alerted by the wailing of her infant. Disaster was avoided many times, but it was far easier on the nerves to take the time to make precise staple splices that were sure to travel smoothly through the mechanism.

Maintaining a diligent focus on quality control was challenging in a silent darkroom, which is why a radio tuned to the local NPR affiliate became as essential as a fresh roll of splice tabs. The thinking part of the brain needed to stay active in order to keep the automaton awake. In this manner I wound and rewound hundreds of thousands of feet of microfilm whilst blind and pondering the state of current affairs. It actually became a rather enjoyable part of the day. Everyone knew that when I was locked behind the double doors of the darkroom, I couldn't interrupt my work for anything short of an emergency. Alone in the dark, I could toil away to the accompaniment of *Morning Edition* and the soft gurgling of our deep tank film processor. Sort of a single-sensory deprivation therapy.

Not that I miss it. It was mindless robot work. I'm happy to never again have to sightlessly manipulate microfilm. But I do credit my years in the darkroom with what is perhaps an above average level of comfort in low-to-zero-level lighting environments. It does not bother me to traverse my home in the middle of the night without turning on a light. The mind adapts easily to operating blind within familiar spaces. Descending the steps, maneuvering around the couch, and grabbing a water glass from the kitchen cabinet? It's as easy as making the next microfilm splice.

Deebies!

When our eldest daughter was quite young, my wife supplemented our income by providing child care in our home. Amber seemed to enjoy the company of her daily playmates, one of whom was a boy her age named Dylan. The two of them got along well, whether they were building with cardboard bricks or guiding a toy school bus through the living room. One day, however, the mood suddenly turned sour, and that's when my wife first heard it.

"Deebies!"

Was it a nonsense word, or was it simply an approximation of something one of them had heard? While its origin would remain a mystery, its meaning would not. Over the next few days, the word *deebies* resurfaced, sometimes arising in a moment of anger and other times sputtered in mock frustration followed by giggles. We looked at the little ones in amazement. Apparently, they had invented their very own swear word.

Once we realized this, we implemented one of the strangest rules ever to be declared in our home. All utterances of the nonsense word *deebies* were strictly verboten. Lest one assume that we overreacted, I must explain that Amber and Dylan were using their invented invective with all the percussive emphasis of a passionately delivered profanity. The word itself sounded harmless out of context, but it lost its innocuousness the moment one of them spat it out between clenched teeth. They might as well have been saying – well, you name it.

The whole episode sounds silly, and it was. Yet it wasn't, at least not completely. For the natural behavior of these two toddlers suggests to me a key to understanding the etymology and offensive power of swear words. Why does society condemn certain words as obscene? Context and connotation. It's not only where, when, why, to whom, and how you say a word, it's also the emotional baggage attached to that word.

One of the best examples of this idea that I have seen appeared in, of all places, a Saturday morning cartoon. In a 1999 episode of the ABC series *Recess*, the character of T.J. Detweiler inadvertently sparks a firestorm of controversy after he expresses displeasure by using the invented expletive *whomps* (as in, "Man, that whomps!"). The expression catches on with the rest of the student body, causing the faculty to go into a tizzy. Eventually, the utterance of *whomps* is banned at school.

It's all very silly and entertaining, what with mature adults getting worked into a froth over something so trivial and apparently inconsequential. Yet, as a former elementary school teacher, I can envision such a scenario playing out in real life. At issue is the intention of the speaker. If a child uses an invented word in the place of a profanity in order to express the same level of disrespect, contempt or subversion that would have been conveyed by an actual expletive, then the effect is much the same. Thus, the nonsensical word becomes, in that context, as offensive as a swear word. And since it is the offensive connotation of expletives that makes them objectionable in the first place, *faux*-profanity may justifiably be banned in circumstances that prohibit the real thing.

I have seen children attempt to worm their way out of trouble by ignoring this fact and clinging to the most literal interpretation of student conduct rules. They will, for example, try to use the foulest profanity against a peer by subtly modifying the expletive into an invented, sound-alike swear word. They will put their phonics knowledge to use by employing the beginning sound of a forbidden word and then suddenly finishing with an unexpected, inoffensive alternative. And when filthy words fail them, they will attempt to circumvent the ban against rude gestures by confronting a classmate with an extended ring or index finger.

"I didn't flip him off," desperate students will cry out when caught, "I was doing *this*!" They will argue and emote with the vehemence of a trial lawyer. That is when educators may capitalize on the so-called teachable moment and deliver a memorable lesson on the vital difference between the letter and the spirit of the law. In essence, it's what you mean, and not necessarily what you say, that matters.

It's an important point that we may easily overlook, and when we do, it makes the whole concept of obscene words seem ridiculous. George Carlin, the late comedian whose forte was observing and deconstructing language, knew this and exploited it to his advantage. His brilliant "Seven Words You Can Never Say On Television" routine (and all of its subsequent incarnations) worked because it masterfully emphasized the absurdity of profanity while deftly downplaying the sociological mechanisms that render any given speech as inappropriate within a particular setting. Indeed, why should any word get labeled arbitrarily as "bad" and thereafter become unsuitable for everyday use? Taken out of context, Carlin's infamous seven words sound hilariously inoffensive.

The fundamental truth is buried in the collective psyche of humankind. The average person, whomever and wherever he or she may be, will consider certain ideas and expressions to be offensive to the degree that such things are better left unsaid. Just what is considered objectionable varies widely according to individual tastes, hence the perpetual battles over obscenity. However, I will speculate that we are offended when that which we esteem is not regarded with due respect. Whatever we define as profanity is merely an extension of this.

Personally, I am not offended when a friend uses R-rated vocabulary in the course of a private conversation. Nor do I mind the employment of blue words in entertainment, providing there is some artistic or aesthetic point to it. However, if I'm walking down the aisle of the local supermarket and another shopper is mindlessly dropping f-bombs while loudly talking on a cell phone, I'm offended. Same words, different context. I'm offended because the coarse stranger is showing me no consideration, and I believe that I am due a modicum of respect in a civilized society. Likewise, I feel a moral obligation to at least consider the sensitivities of others and respond appropriately.

That is why *deebies* simply had to go. Not because there is anything inherently wrong with it. Not because it sounds objectionable. But if you had heard Amber and Dylan using it, you would agree. Those toddlers were cursing like sailors. And in the context of our home, at least, the use of that sort of language from such tiny mouths is considered offensive.

And if you don't like it, I guess that just whomps.

Alice in Limaland

I was the one to blame for one of the most improbable and unusual adventures experienced by my parents. By the time it was all over, our quirky story had been covered twice by the local newspaper. Mom and Dad became small-town celebrities for a brief time, recounting the incident for everyone from fellow church parishioners to Dad's doctor. They came across favorably as loving parents who gamely went along with a bit of outrageousness solely to indulge their youngest son. I was 32 at the time; they were 67.

The story began more than twenty years earlier, though none of us could have known that at the time. Who would have thought that a few nonchalantly expressed words from my father would have such a long-range impact? Who could have foreseen how the longevity and vicissitudes of an aging rock star's career would one day illuminate those forgotten words with the intensity of an enticing marquee? But that is what happened, and Dad saw to it that he was a man of his word, even if it meant fulfilling a casual promise decades later.

Around the time that I was seven years old, I became aware of shock rocker Alice Cooper. Everything about him resonated with my formative artistic sensibility: engaging music, over-the-top theatrics, and a macabre, dry sense of humor. I found Alice to be thoroughly entertaining, and so I had no qualms about parting with five bucks for the first new record album I ever bought, *Alice Cooper Goes To Hell*. My parents were not so enthusiastic about my increasingly engrossing interest, but they were nevertheless quite tolerant, allowing me to amass my favorite artist's back catalog by picking up bargains at used record stores. Nor did they mind that I would buy any magazine that had even minimal content pertaining to my hero. It was all harmless enough, they believed, and they grew to accept my fascination with all things Alice as just another eccentric dimension of my personality.

However, they drew the line at attending concerts. This was rarely an issue, because my hometown of Lima, Ohio did not often host headlining rock acts, and the pre-Internet age made it a challenge for any small-town kid to know when a favorite artist's tour itinerary might swing within a hundred miles. But in the summer of 1980, I was ecstatic to learn that Alice would be playing Detroit on the very same night that my brothers were planning on attending a Tigers game. I begged my parents with the tenacity of an obsessed 12-year-old, but they wouldn't budge. Neither would I cease my campaign.

Finally, worn out by my persistent pleas, my father found a way to keep me quiet. "You cannot go to Detroit to see Alice Cooper," he said firmly, "but I promise that if Alice ever comes to Lima, I will take you to the concert."

It was a brilliantly diplomatic bit of parenting. Like an insurer calculating the risk of a new policy, Dad knew that the odds were highly in his favor. The promise assuaged my angst without really promising anything. After all, how likely was it that Alice Cooper would ever perform in Lima?

Ah, but showbiz is a volatile world, and when it comes to promises, a boy will maintain an elephant's memory well into adulthood. Twenty years passed. Alice had seen his career dip and rise like a rock and roll rollercoaster. Coming into the new millennium, he had a new album to plug and wasn't above promoting it at smaller venues. I had just abandoned my job of ten years and was well into the graduate studies that would allow me to make a career out of teaching. I had also bought that new Alice album. And then I saw the itinerary for the Alice Cooper *Brutal Planet* tour. One of the dates stunned me into a state of open-mouthed shock.

"Do you remember a certain promise you made to a little boy a long time ago that you would take him to see Alice Cooper if he ever came to Lima?" I wrote Dad in an email. "Guess who's coming to the Allen County Fair?"

I was being a little cheeky, poking fun at Dad for making a promise that he was certain he would never have to keep, yet I truly did want to see the show. In fact, with or without Dad, it was my intention to go. I don't know how he reacted when he read my message, whether he tittered with amusement or recoiled in horror, but by the time we spoke with each other, he made it clear that he fully intended to deliver what he had promised.

"You don't have to go, Dad," I clarified. "I mean, I am 32 years old, I can go on my own."

"No, no," he insisted, "I promised you I would take you to see Alice Cooper, and I'm going to keep my promise."

Our family was abuzz. Dad, whose musical preference was primarily classical (and certainly not encompassing classic rock), was actually going to subject himself to an Alice Cooper concert. Mom was worried. Afraid that he might be overwhelmed by the experience, she decided that she would accompany us. Now I was a bit worried, and my concern would turn out to be prescient.

Meanwhile, news of the latently fulfilled childhood promise spread into the wider community. Kim Kincaid, features writer for *The Lima News*, got wind of it and gave Mom a call. "I heard a story this week that reminds parents to be careful what we promise our children," her column began. "You never know when one of those promises could come back to haunt you."

Her article summarized how it came to pass that one of the city's senior citizen couples felt compelled to put themselves in such a fish-out-of-water circumstance. Quotations from the interview revealed Mom's accurate discrimination of Alice's polite offstage manner from his evil onstage persona, her positive anticipation of the show, and her admission that she really wasn't sure what to expect. Kincaid concluded her column by noting, "Although their son is now married and living in Columbus, the Hunts are still looking forward to making their little boy's dream come true."

The fairgrounds was not an ideal venue for a general admission concert. There was an unusual upward slope to the ground in the first few yards nearest the stage, which was set up opposite the grandstand. It seemed to influence the crowd to bunch even tighter together than they might have otherwise. We were right in the thick of it, having inserted our earplugs before edging our way up front during the tepidly received opening act. As I looked around us in the lull between acts, I was struck by the nature of the crowd. Never before (nor since, in fact) had I sensed such a grim hostility from an audience. Perhaps the security had something to do with it. Rather than employing the typical beefy college guys in bright yellow "STAFF" t-shirts, the promoters had hired grizzled, leather-clad, tattooed, bandanna-wearing bikers who looked like they wouldn't be bothered by a little violence.

The concert boasted a spectacular opening in which an elevated box was wheeled to the front of the stage. It was opened to reveal a gruesome sight that would have rivaled any sideshow attraction: the upper body of a man, his exposed spinal cord and pelvis trailing beneath him. The half-creature addressed the audience, gesturing with his arms and hands as he spoke. The freakish effect fit right in with the post-apocalyptic theme of *Brutal Planet*, and the crowd roared as the poor soul advised everyone, "Go! Go now while you have a chance! Before it starts...before it's too late!"

I grinned at Mom and Dad, who appeared to be taking it all in the proper spirit of amusement. The band tore into the title track of the new album, and there appeared Alice, looking like the demented overlord of a fallen civilization. The show was terrific, a visually stunning showcase for the *Brutal Planet* concept, and I was enjoying it immensely. So, apparently, was much of the rest of the crowd that was mashed together near the stage. A strong marijuana odor permeated the air, and some of the revelers were getting a little rambunctious in their partying. I positioned myself so as to protect Mom from getting pushed.

The show ambled along, me having a good time, Mom and Dad tolerating everything good-naturedly. Still, the audience near the stage was a bit unsettling. A few of them seemed to have imbibed or ingested enough illicit substances to make them utterly unconscious of their surroundings and totally insensitive to the people crushed around them. One young man in particular was whipping himself to and fro and upon everyone in his immediate vicinity, which unfortunately included me. I stood still as a rock as he bumped into me repeatedly, determined as I was to shield Mom from being jostled.

Eight songs into the set came "Wicked Young Man," a new number that revealed the twisted psyche of the sort of person who would plot a Columbine tragedy. It was dark and thought-provoking, like much of the new album, but the neanderthal next to me wasn't getting it. In fact, he seemed to be the embodiment of a wicked young man, and when he crashed into me with enough force that I couldn't stop careening into Mom, I had had enough. The next time he pushed, I pushed back, and that is when the sociopath lost his temper.

From the crazed look in his eyes I knew instantly that this was a battle not worth fighting. He screamed at me as I backed off with my palms held up in a show of submission. I looked about and saw that the security toughs were not interested in my plight. God knows what somebody would have had to do to get ejected from the show. It was a time to cut my losses, and so I considered it a moral victory that I escaped being eaten. Mom and Dad decided to retreat to the grandstand for the remainder of the show, and I went with them, having no desire to hang out with the thugs who were taking over the front of the stage.

That nasty business cast something of a pall over the rest of the evening, as Alice's act seemed insignificant in the face of blatant aggression. Oddly enough, the incident only underscored the pessimistic social commentary of *Brutal Planet*. I'm sure my psychotic friend did not catch the irony.

A few days after the show, *Lima News* Managing Editor Jim Krumel complimented Mom and Dad in the "Roses and Thorns" section of his editorial column, awarding them a rose for being valiantly true to their word. "I think this is probably our first and last rock concert," Mom was quoted as observing. "We wore earplugs and could still hear the music perfectly well. In fact, we live on the north end of town, and I wouldn't doubt if we could have heard it there, too." She underplayed our violent encounter: "We were in a mob of young people. I wanted to see what he looked like up close. We kept getting jostled from all the kids dancing with wild abandon."

Yes, Mom and Dad were true to their word. As it happened, the Alice Cooper show at the Allen County Fairgrounds was, indeed, their first and last rock concert. And as for me, I'm all out of promises left unfulfilled.

Smile

It neither bothers me nor excites me to be photographed. You won't see me rushing to insert myself in a hastily posed group picture, nor will you hear me begging to be excused from becoming the subject of an unexpected snapshot. Like most people, I appreciate a portrait that makes me look good and wince at those that do the opposite. But whether my likeness is captured thousands more times or never again, it's pretty much all the same to me.

However, there is one photographic ritual that I have always disliked, and that is the annual taking of school photographs. I don't recall enjoying the experience much when I was a student, and I had no enthusiasm for it as a teacher. Somewhere along my sixteen years as an educator, I learned to simply grin and bear it. And that is exactly what I appear to be doing in most of my teacher portraits: grinning and bearing it.

I blame the conventions of assembly-line portrait photography for some of this. You're led before the camera and made to sit on what appears to be the upended crate in which the photographer totes his gear. As you remind yourself to stay loose and comfortable for the most natural pose, he is contorting you into a position you would never assume even by accident. For some reason, your knees are pointed away from the camera so that you must rotate your torso to face the lens, a practice that has never made any sense to me when taking head shots. If you wear glasses like I do, and if your nose is particularly long as mine is, you will be made to push your spectacles up the bridge of your nose until they can advance no further, an ocular setting that you would ordinarily avoid so as not to smudge the insides of your lenses with your eyelashes.

The worst indignity, however, is a final adjustment in which you are required to tilt your head slightly to one side, presumably to make your pose appear less staged and to deemphasize your asymmetrical features. What it actually does is evoke the dopey countenance of a dog that thinks it may have just heard one of the few magical words it recognizes, like *walk, ride,* or *treat.* So there are a lot of strikes against you even before the shutter clicks. Despite this, I always tried to relax within the constraints of my unnatural pose, imagine myself in a situation that might prompt a smile, and flash an authentic expression of carefree joy for the camera.

So far, I have described what everyone must endure in their brief encounter with the school photographer. It is a challenge for anyone to look natural under the circumstances, but it is especially difficult for a teacher. This is because teacher portraits are usually taken at the same time that their students are photographed. As any teacher will tell you, it is advisable to keep your eyes on your students at all times. Of course, it is impossible to do this during the minute or two that it takes for the photographer to do his or her job. This truth does not escape the attention of students, any one of whom may choose to take mischievous advantage of it.

At my elementary school, photos were taken on the stage in the gym, which doubled as our cafeteria. The backdrop was placed at the lip of the platform facing a rear corner of the stage, preventing students from observing the posing of their classmates. When my fifth-graders were called down to the gym for pictures, it happened to be the lunch period for half a dozen other classes. We lined up along the perimeter of the gym and waited patiently as our queue slowly ascended the stage steps, each student exiting the makeshift studio by walking among our lunching classes and lining up at the door.

It was not an ideal situation, for though the photographer worked quickly, my attention was soon divided between two groups of students on opposite sides of the gym. Whether they were waiting to be photographed or lined up to leave, the patience of my students diminished at about the same rate. By the time half of us were done, it was clear that no one wanted to stay in line any longer. Nevertheless, I tossed out directions on both flanks, calling out the names of kids whose minor infractions threatened to multiply into classwide mutiny.

The bolder ones would wait until I turned my attention to the other side and simply continue their petty insubordinations until they found themselves again under my surveillance.

When my last student had been photographed, I was summoned by the photographer, and as I did every year, I was rapidly compliant to his every suggestion in order to get the whole thing over with quickly. Greater than the physical discomfort of my unnatural pose was the mental strain of knowing that I could no longer observe my class. I had my back to them, and there was a backdrop and a sea of kids eating lunch separating us. Despite the presence of adults supervising lunch, the fact remained that I was responsible for a class of students that I could not see, some of whom were surely weighing their chances of getting away with some form of misbehavior that they otherwise might not try. This knowledge made my brief time before the camera seem much longer.

I pointed my knees to the left, rotated my torso to the right, pushed my glasses up the bridge of my nose until they bumped into my eyebrows, and tilted my head to one side. "Smile!" commanded the photographer, and as I heard the noise level in the gym rise in the manner that it might when a distant line of fifth graders notices the absence of their teacher, I tried to force myself into a state of blissful relaxation. *Click.* The photographer eyed the results and invited me to look at his monitor.

"Happy with that?" he asked as a formality. I think he knew as well as I did that there was no way that I would pose for another picture.

"Looks great!" I enthused immediately, having regarded my digital image for a nanosecond. I had already rotated my torso toward the stage steps when I heard him chuckle.

"I understand."

I turned and regarded his sympathetic grin. If only he had taken my picture at that very moment, we would have captured the elusive and highly coveted unguarded smile. Alas, yet again, my official faculty photo depicted me with all the confused excitement of Fido about to take a ride.

Next year, I swore, *I will not tilt my head.*

The Mighty Pegasus

Both my wife and I grew up as the youngest of six children, raised by loving parents who nevertheless had grown weary of the trouble and expense of caring for family pets. There was a dog named Sam whom I barely remember, and Julie once had a hamster, but much of our childhood was spent without animal companionship. That might explain why we went through a small menagerie of creatures in our first few years together. It started with a white lab mouse (Buster) that I impulsively brought back to my dorm room after learning that any unclaimed rodents would be destroyed. Five more mice (Philco, Chiquita, Abilee, Melba and Krema), a rat (Frebis), and a pair of guinea pigs (Po and Gois) followed. We stuck to the easily manageable small animals that tend to not be prohibited by apartment leases.

Then we bought a house.

It was a new build, and thus its every molding, railing, and square inch of carpeting was in mint condition when we signed our mortgage. As a childless couple, we might have kept it that way for years. But just several weeks after we moved in, a co-worker started bending my ear about the dog for which her family was seeking a home. "He's free," she kept repeating, and my head began to fill with idyllic visions of leisurely strolls through our pristine suburban neighborhood with a faithful canine at my side. It seemed like the next logical step for us. With the careless optimism and naivete of youth, we decided to accept the offer.

His name was Sparky, a moniker we instantly disliked. He was a skinny Doberman mix with floppy ears and an orange, studded collar. Still a puppy, Sparky was undeniably cute, but we were wary of his behavior. He jumped up at my co-worker's children and tore at their shirts. It didn't seem like he had been trained to obey any commands. However, he had been disciplined.

"If he gits outta line," drawled the husband, "jest take yer fist like this, stick out yer knuckle, and punch 'im on the snout. He'll understand." Julie and I glanced at each other and considered the situation. This was no way to raise a dog. We could give the poor beast the care he needed, feed him properly, have him checked out by a veterinarian, and maybe take him to obedience school. We could change his name. We could get rid of that ridiculous, studded collar. Without fully understanding the consequences of our commitment, we coaxed the dog into our car and took him home.

The trite name was the first thing we changed. There was a somewhat dopey, silly quality about our new dog, an endearing trait that was the opposite of dignity. Naturally, I searched for a name that would highlight this characteristic. I thought of the mythical Pegasus, a majestic winged horse, and it made me laugh to look at this scrawny specimen in such a context. Pegasus it was, then, which we quirkily abbreviated to Gus. And then we gave Gus a collar that made him look less like a junkyard dog.

We had been told that Gus was housebroken, but we spread newspaper over the unfinished basement floor and kept him down there while we were at work as a precaution. In the first few weeks, he missed the newspaper numerous times, tore insulation from the roughed-in wall under the stairs, and chewed through the cord to a phone extension. We consoled ourselves with the fact that his shenanigans were limited to the basement, but he soon expanded his repertoire.

One of his exploits became legendary. In later years, we would refer to it as "the milkshake incident." That is because it began when we descended the stairs to discover what appeared to be a thick milkshake deposited prominently on our living room carpet. We would have been grateful if the brown blob had indeed been a milkshake, but instead it was the foul aftereffect of putting Gus on a different brand of dog food. It was such a desecration of our new home that Julie actually cried. As for Gus, he would never surpass this offense, with the possible exception of a wee-hours crisis in our bedroom that become known as *The Gus-Log Archipelago*.

We devoted time, money, and energy into transforming Gus into the sort of dog we envisioned he should be. Some of our endeavors worked better than others. The portable kennel, for example, transformed Gus from a puppy who still wasn't quite sure whether it wasn't okay to sometimes go on the carpet into a dog who fully understood that pooping in the house was always wrong. Not that he didn't occasionally do it anyway. On the other hand, Gus proved to be embarrassingly incompetent at his humane society obedience classes. The only trained skill he ever mastered was a "sit – still – down" combination which he would faithfully execute whenever a Milk-Bone was at stake. Techniques designed to stop his chronic barking were a total failure. When it came to the art of the heel, Gus was simply incapable of it. Taking him for a walk was an upper-body workout. He actually stretched the circular link at the end of his choke chain into an oval.

Gus could not be trusted outdoors without some form of restraint. Until we built a privacy fence, we had to let him out into the back yard on a lead. For several seasons, we had a ring of dead grass caused by his frantic running whenever he detected another living creature within a hundred yards. A few times he actually tore up the sod and ate it. And whenever he got the chance, Gus would bolt out the front door and tear down the sidewalk, roaming free until we could find him and lure him into our car.

Incorrigible as he was, Gus was our dog, and we regarded him affectionately. In fact, we practically doted on him the first couple years, as evidenced by the number of photographs we took of him during that time. Things changed, though, with the birth of our first daughter. Gus was immediately demoted to a position of lesser importance. In retrospect, he took it well. Probably he had no idea. Or maybe he appreciated the delicacy that is dirty diapers, which he lustily consumed on more than one occasion. When our second daughter was born, Gus was pushed even further from the center of our attention.

Over the years, he matured into a somewhat mellower dog, relative to his tumultuous puppyhood. However, sheer excitement was never far away for Gus. One needed only to mention the name of one of the handful of other dogs he had come to know, and he would start to race about the house in a frenzy, searching for his friend. The word *David* had the same effect, due to my brother's generous habit of bringing quantities of dog treats with him whenever he visited. Also magical was the phrase *post office*. In those days, when we actually had the need to regularly mail things via the U.S. Postal Service, we would take Gus along for the ride, which he enjoyed more than anyone might think was possible.

Julie and I maintained a running debate over just how intelligent our dog was, and we most often concluded that the answer was "not very." Sometimes, though, he surprised us with the complexity of his thought processes. One winter afternoon, Julie was enjoying a good book and a cup of tea in the living room. She happened to observe the most curious yet subtle change in our dog's expression as he meandered past the coffee table. He eyed the tea momentarily, almost as though he was taking note of it while trying to appear inconspicuous, then he coolly walked across the room and lay down. We left the house shortly afterward on some errand, and when we returned, Julie discovered that her mug no longer contained the ounce or two of tea that she had left in it. The cup itself was otherwise undisturbed.

Years passed by, the girls grew older, and so did Gus. He started to slow down as he approached his twelfth year, taking longer to gingerly rise from a resting position. Eventually, his back end became a burden to him, and he sometimes yelped from the pain in his arthritic joints. Even the two steps from our kitchen into our back yard became difficult for him to navigate. When we had to carry him out and back, we knew that our pet adventure was nearing its inevitably sad ending.

I got a flat tire on the way to work on the cold February Friday on which we had scheduled Gus to be euthanized. It was strange, anyway, all of us going off on our normal routine knowing what was coming at the end of the day. It was stranger still to grapple with changing a tire totally devoid of irritation, my mind occupied with a weighty concern that made a flat seem insignificant. He was alive, and soon he would be dead. It would be our fault that he would be dead, yet it would be for the best. I sighed as I thought of how much more difficult it would be for our daughters.

My brother David, always loved by Gus, went to the vet with us. Gus was always thrilled to go to the vet, and so he was the least stressed of all of us. The whole procedure was over quickly, and we drove out to David's rural home to bury Gus. While Julie and the girls stayed up at the house, David and I set up flashlights in a spot near the stream and got to work. It was cold and dismal, the rushing of the water interrupted by our labored breathing, which sent condensing fogs swirling up into the darkness. The soil was mercifully soft, and when at last we were done, we sat at opposite ends of the grave, our legs dangling over the sides, and took a measure of satisfaction in our grim work.

Julie and the girls joined us for the solemn ceremony. We comforted each other with the thought of how beautiful a resting place it was for Gus, just the sort of natural setting that he loved to explore. We shared our memories and regrets, and then we trudged back up to the house. No dog ever had a more dignified funeral. Nor had any goofy dog a more majestic name than the mighty Pegasus.

The Old Man and the Sea

There's nothing like an unqualified pummeling to inspire a practical respect for the power of nature. I thought about that as I lay curled in a fetal position on the hotel bed, enduring waves of nausea and wanting nothing more than to drift off into unconsciousness.

"Are you alright?" asked my wife, and I assured her that I was just fine, only I could use a few more minutes of resting limp as a rag doll, if she didn't mind looking after the girls during that time. To my surprise, I felt remarkably better within an hour, and we were able to resume our vacation with no further delay. For a brief period, however, I felt like I had been set upon by a gang of thugs and left for dead in an alley. All because I didn't have the good sense to recognize the difference between harmless fun and obvious danger.

We were on our first real family vacation. With our daughters having reached the ages of 7 and 4, Julie and I decided that we were ready for a driving trip to the east coast. We packed our compact sedan with plentiful snacks and diversions, doling out dollar store trinkets every so often along the hundreds of miles we traveled from Ohio to North Carolina. Our destination was the Outer Banks, where we had reservations at a seaside Comfort Inn in Kill Devil Hills, a mere primitive flight away from the Wright Brothers Memorial. The ocean would be good for a day's fun, we reasoned, and there was much else to see in the area.

Naturally, the girls were enchanted by their first encounter with the Atlantic. We walked down to the shore as soon as we arrived, and their initial tentativeness quickly dissolved into a giddy series of splashes and waist-high immersions. Should have put their swim suits on first, I suppose. But Julie and I found ourselves caught up in our children's enthusiasm for the ocean, so much so that we spent far more time in the water than we had anticipated. Our Outer Banks adventure became a swimming vacation with a little sightseeing thrown in.

It was I who was the most surprised by this turn of events, for I had originally pooh-poohed the beach as worthy of no more than an afternoon of our precious time. I'm sure my peculiar perspective must have been based on my experience as a child, when I accompanied my family on a trip to Florida in 1976. Wary of the ocean themselves, my parents instilled in me what they surely intended to be a reasonable respect for marine danger. There was talk of an undertow, a mysterious force that could grab you without warning and cast you out to sea. Jellyfish could sting you, and a Portuguese Man o' War could kill you. Not to mention sharks, which went without saying, as *Jaws* was being relentlessly promoted everywhere.

Put it all together with weather that was never particularly hot, and the result was that we never really went into the ocean. Sure, we put on our suits and pranced along the surf, but up-to-the-waist was about the extent of my oceanic fun. I had not yet learned to swim (that would have to wait until college!), so to venture any further out into the water seemed like a blatant request for disaster. It was only natural, then, that I would grow up to have an ambivalent opinion about the merits of ocean swimming.

My attitude changed completely during our Outer Banks vacation. The weather was warm, the sun shone down from a vibrant blue sky, and getting out there up to my neck in the Atlantic was a joy. Were it not for our girls and their unrestrained happiness among the waves, I might never have known what I had been missing all those years. Suddenly the other tourist spots on our itinerary seemed more like an inconvenience, inasmuch as we would have to get out of the water in order to see them.

Our enjoyment of the water was enhanced by a gift presented to us during our first full day at the beach. Another family who had arrived in a compact sedan discovered that the pair of foam boogie boards they had purchased at the beach would not even come close to fitting in their trunk for the drive home. We gratefully accepted their generosity. The highly buoyant devices were a novelty to us, and I don't think we ever would have thought to buy them for ourselves. We attached the tethers to our arms with the Velcro wrist straps and plunged into the water to try out our new acquisitions.

The four of us were delighted. Relaxing atop a boogie board and lazily riding the swell of incoming waves was great fun. We all took turns, and sometimes either Julie or I would swim a little further out to ride some bigger waves. It was an altogether agreeable sensation, and had the weather not changed to brisker fare, who knows how many days we might have stayed on the water? As it was, the cooler air enticed us to pursue some of our original plans, and we spent some time exploring the Wright Brothers' old flying grounds and visiting a nearby aquarium.

As our remaining time at the Outer Banks was dwindling and the weather became even cooler and windier, I lamented the fact that I would not enjoy the bliss of ocean boogie boarding again until I might visit the ocean anew some time in the future. Julie and the girls were preparing to take a dip in the hotel's outdoor pool, and though that was the sensible way to swim under the current weather conditions, it seemed like a sacrilege to forsake the adjacent, majestic ocean for a pedestrian pool. And then I thought, why should high winds and cool temperatures stop me? Julie looked at me like I was either crazy or stupid (perhaps both), but having been married for over a decade by that time, I was used to it. Besides, I knew what I was doing.

The fact that no one was on the beach, save for a middle-aged couple bundled up in jackets, might have given most aspiring boogie boarders pause. But I looked out into the ocean and marveled at the waves that were considerably bigger than what we had experienced just days before. I thought about how fun it had been to ride those modest waves, and I concluded that it would be even more fun to get tossed up and down by these larger waves. It was simple, really. I trudged toward the surf for one last dose of extra-intense ocean fun.

The first few meters into the water was a depository of pebbles and small shells, the sort of surface that makes you wince and arch your feet until you reach the soft sand beyond it. The water was cold, and I grimaced at the stinging droplets carried along the stiff wind. At last I ventured out far enough to stand comfortably, where the water reached my waist and waves smacked my shoulders. This was going to be great. I turned around, hopped on the board, and anticipated the next wave, which soon crashed over me and threw me down with a force unlike anything I had ever experienced.

I had been pushed forward and smacked down onto the pebbly bottom, and it was all I could do to get up on my knees before the next wave arrived and threw me down again. This caused me great alarm and no small amount of pain. At once I realized how tragically stupid I had been, and it occurred to me that if I didn't somehow scramble up onto the beach, I might drown in a few feet of water. I managed to rise up to breathe again and felt the smack of another wave against my back, but this time I kept my head up and let the momentum carry me forward. As the middle-aged couple looked on from a distance, I staggered up the sand as nonchalantly as I could, vainly attempting to project an attitude of *I meant to do that*.

My head was reeling and I started to feel sick to my stomach. Julie and the girls were still in the pool, but I passed by and went directly to our room. Removing my trunks in the shower, I heard at least a pound of pebbles clatter against the tile. Minutes later I was curled up under the covers, calmly awaiting my imminent death. How unfortunate that my wife and children should discover my lifeless form, but I was resigned to my fate. In fact, as the nausea increased, it was starting to sound pretty good.

Of course, I pulled through quickly, having actually suffered nothing more than getting the wind knocked out of me. To her immense credit, my wife simply let this unfortunate life lesson speak for itself. Nature had already humbled me in a violent way I would never forget. There was no need for her to crow about her astute recognition of my stupidity.

It was painfully obvious.

Hostel is a Homophone

"Nothing just happens! Nothing just happens!" thundered the evangelizing voice of T.D. Jakes as I gnawed on fried chicken from the comfort of my hotel bed. The congregation shouted its approval of their leader's assertion that there is no such thing as a coincidence. I pondered the idea for a moment, took another swig of cola, and clicked the remote. Now *The Andy Griffith Show* flickered from the screen. It was an episode I recognized, the classic "Man In A Hurry," in which a stranded big-city motorist finds his patience tested by the leisurely pace of Mayberry as he waits for his car to be repaired.

"Ah, what luck," I enthused before it occurred to me that T. D. Jakes would presumably disagree.

I was determined to squeeze whatever enjoyment I could out of my accommodations, as my room was costing me four times what I had budgeted. Perched high atop Harpers Ferry at the edge of the Catholic cemetery, my lodgings were in every way a far cut above my original reservations. In order to justify the indulgence of attending a five-day educational conference at my own expense (along with opportunities to do further research for my historical novel set in the area), I had intended to stay a little further down the Potomac, just across the river. There at the base of Maryland Heights is the small community of Sandy Hook, where a humble hostel offers shelter to Appalachian Trail hikers, assorted vagabonds, and fiscally prudent educators.

The idea of staying in a hostel held no appeal to me beyond its minimal cost. Multi-bunk barracks and community bath facilities are not what I would consider to be positive amenities. In addition, this establishment was only open in the evening, overnight and morning hours, outside of which the doors were locked. Still, I anticipated a busy week, and what more would I need from my accommodations but a safe bed and a shower? As I was traveling alone, I did not need to consider the comfort of my family. I could handle roughing it for a few days. It might even make the whole endeavor more fun, allowing me to assume the role of the itinerant writer, a rugged intellectual who cares not where he sleeps so long as he may practice his craft.

I arrived at Sandy Hook early on Sunday afternoon, pulling into the deserted gravel lot of the white, two-story house that would be my hostel home for the week. It wouldn't open for hours yet, but the quiet surroundings looked like a nice place for a relaxing walk after my long drive. If I changed my mind, I could always drive into Harpers Ferry and find something of interest. I shut off the engine and emerged from the stale cabin of my Saturn into a pleasant August breeze.

Almost immediately the gentle rustling of the trees was accompanied by a stirring in the grassy area beyond the lot, and I turned to see a lone figure emerge from a midday nap. A short, middle-aged man in rumpled hiking attire loped toward me and extended a pudgy hand in greeting. The graying hairs of his frizzy beard offset a balding pate, and his sad eyes stared at me from bulbous, wrinkled sockets. I noted with amusement that he resembled the latter-day Billy Joel.

"Hey," he offered, "you staying here tonight?"

"Yeah. You too?"

"Uh-huh. But they're not gonna open 'til six. I'm just hangin' out 'til then." He peered more closely at me. "You hiking the trail?"

"Oh, no," I laughed. "I'm here for an education conference at Harpers Ferry. Plus I'm doing some research while I'm here."

"Mmm..." he nodded, "I need to head into town myself. Maybe you can give me a ride on your way in tomorrow?"

"Sure, sure," I heard myself say as my head bobbed up and down affably. It disturbed me a little that I had just promised a ride to a total stranger, but I just as quickly chastised myself for being so uptight and judgmental. This was all part of the hostel life, a casual community of good-natured travelers who believe in random acts of kindness and paying it forward. Just because circumstances had afforded me the luxury of a car while Billy Joel had none, did that give me the right to keep it all to my selfish self?

I smiled my widest smile. "My name's Bob. It's nice to meet you."

"The pleasure's all mine, Bob. You can call me Matt."

Perhaps this was the genesis of a rich and rewarding friendship. There was an almost collegiate air about Matt that made me conclude that he probably had a few interesting stories to tell. I decided to give him an opening. "So, Matt, what brings you to Harpers Ferry?"

'Well, Bob, I'm on my way back to D.C., which is where I spend most of my time. I've been doing a lot of research in the libraries there, and I've got files full of evidence to show every congressman and senator who'll listen to me just what the government's been doing to me for the last ten years."

"Really?" I politely responded. "What is that?"

He looked at me conspiratorially. "Bob, have you ever heard of directed energy?"

"Um...directed energy..."

"I'm ex-military, Bob. The government's been experimenting with directed energy for years. Picture a microwave without the microwave oven. Imagine being able to torture somebody halfway across the world just by bombarding their body with hyperfocused energy beamed by satellite. They've been doing this stuff to me for years, Bob. I didn't always look like this." He spread his arms to indicate his haggard frame. "I used to be a specimen of perfect health. That's what directed energy will do to you."

"Um..." I muttered, trying to think of a good response while fighting my flight reflex, "why would the government want to do that to you?"

"Because they don't want you to know the truth," he said matter-of-factly. "I found out they put a damn chip in my head when I was in the army. I didn't even know it until years later, after they started hitting me with directed energy. I didn't know what it was at first, but as soon as I found it, you can bet I started raising a stink about it. I've got enough evidence in my files to put half of 'em in jail! Once they knew I wasn't going to stay quiet, that's when they started using the chip. Oh, yeah. They use voice-to-skull technology just to harass me."

"Really."

"They'll wake me up in the middle of the night, sometimes just one guy, sometimes three or four of 'em talking at once. Doesn't matter where I go, voice-to-skull works anywhere. I've had nights when I haven't had a wink of REM sleep because they won't let me. Just to harass me. They'll tell you things like your wife is having an affair, or go jump off a building, anything to drive you crazy. But that's just mind games. It's the directed energy that's caused me so much pain I've had days when I can't even walk."

"Wow," I managed, trying to look and sound sympathetic to the plight of this madman. A short pause ensued, Matt staring at me intensely while my relatively normal brain searched frantically for a swift and sure escape. After a few quick calculations, it returned the following insights:

1. *Do not give Matt a ride to Harpers Ferry tomorrow, or to anywhere at anytime, for that matter.*

2. *Do not stay at the hostel unless you're okay with being the victim of axe-to-skull technology.*

3. *Get away now, and do not return.*

"And now the VA wants to cut my benefits," he started in again. His rambling speech became an aural blur as I smiled and nodded compassionately, waiting for the right opportunity to announce my departure. It was essential that I not imply in any way that he was welcome to come with me. I contemplated my options while paying scant attention to Matt's concerns, though I was careful to display every social cue that would indicate my complete engagement.

'That's incredible," I deadpanned at one or another of Matt's implausible revelations, and he continued unabated as a lonely man might if he were delivering a monologue to his wide-eyed cat. My legs were starting to ache. When at last I thought I could endure no more, Matt gave me the great gift of proclaiming his intention to take a walk and invited me to accompany him.

"I'd love to, but I have a few errands to run before the hostel opens." I beamed at him, willing myself to look like someone who just couldn't wait to get back and listen to more tales of covert government torture.

"Oh," he reacted pleasantly, "I'll see you later, then."

Within the hour I was calling my wife from my locked hotel room, explaining that the sting of our forthcoming credit card bill might be trumped by the comfort of having me alive to pay it. And as it happened, staying at that location was quite advantageous, expenses notwithstanding. The Catholic cemetery was home to headstones relevant to my research, and I was only a few minutes away from the conference site. The hot sausage gravy and biscuits each morning didn't hurt, either. By the end of the week, I was almost grateful to my psychotic friend for scaring me away from the hostel.

I left Harpers Ferry as soon as the conference ended around noon on Friday. I was looking forward to returning home, especially because an uncommon alignment of the planets (i.e., both of our daughters spending the night somewhere else) was about to provide my wife and I with a rare evening to ourselves. But halfway across West Virginia, my Saturn lost all power, and I glided to a stop on the berm along Route 68. A call to AAA and one long tow-truck ride later, my vehicle and I were deposited in the crowded lot of a Morgantown mechanic. I begged the owner to look under the hood and replace my battery before he closed up shop for the day.

"It ain't your battery," he informed me after a quick diagnostic inspection. "It's your alternator. I could try to charge your battery up a bit, but you won't get too far on that. Where'd you say you're from?"

"Ohio."

"Right. Nah, you'll never make it out of West Virginia, I'd say. And our supplier is..." he looked at his watch, "just about to close. We can get to it first thing tomorrow morning, though."

I sighed heavily as the promise of dinner and a movie with my wife vanished like a swirling eddy of vaporizing exhaust fumes. Add an expensive car repair to my list of Harpers Ferry trip debits. And another night in another hotel. *But wait,* as they say in the notorious TV merchandise offers, *there's more...*

"Ah am sew sorry fer yoo," drawled the mechanic's receptionist as she returned the phone to its cradle. She had offered to help me arrange a room for the night, but after a few calls around town, her fear was confirmed: there wasn't a room to be rented in Morgantown that night. Not when parents were bringing their college kids back for another year at West Virginia University. Not when the Mountaineers were playing at home tomorrow afternoon. And so, the bitter truth became all too clear. I would be spending the night...in my car.

With the prospect of an uncomfortable night's fitful sleep ahead of me, I decided that a good, head-clearing, leg-stretching walk was in order. As I ascended the hills toward downtown, a grumpy pessimism got the better of me, and I began to resent the very land upon which I trudged. Of all the places to break down, why was I stuck in a little college town where a lousy football game can fill every hotel room? What kind of a hick garage can't lay their hands on an alternator on a Friday afternoon? How long will it be before I can get out of this place?

I soon tired of looking down at my shuffling feet and raised my gaze to the horizon. That's when I saw the billboard for a car dealership, unremarkable in every detail but its location: Don

Knotts Boulevard. My ire rose again. *Don Knotts Boulevard?!*
What kind of a town would have a Don Knotts–

Suddenly a tattered fragment of trivia broke loose from a
cranial recess and tumbled into my awareness. I was stranded
in Morgantown, West Virginia — the hometown of Don Knotts. I
was the man in a hurry.

You are free to make of this what you will, of course. But I know
what T.D. Jakes would say.

Kill the Wabbit

Expectations are founded on previous experience, so when we welcomed Tony into our home, we had no reason to believe that he would behave much differently from the recently deceased Sam. Sam had been something of a Halloween miracle, an emaciated stray who appeared during Trick-or-Treat and boldly leapt onto my lap as I sat outside distributing candy. We put out some food for him, and he soon became a fixture below our front window. Plummeting temperatures eventually persuaded us to let him in one night, and with the exception of visits to the vet, Sam never left the comfort of the great indoors. For two years, he was the gentlest and most contented house cat. Then one Sunday morning, we found him inexplicably dead on the kitchen floor.

Julie and I did our best to console our young daughters, who had become accustomed to Sam's comforting presence. Not long afterward, we heard of another stray that looked similar to Sam and had been hanging around our friends' house, agitating their house cat. It sounded like taking him in would be a win-win-win situation. Little did we know that there was no such thing as "taking in" this cat, nor was his personality anything like that of his predecessor. Perhaps the fact that he hissed at us during our initial encounter should have alerted us to that fact.

The first few days were a period of adjustment for family and feline alike. Tony exhibited some feral tendencies, boldly attempting to climb into the open refrigerator and then letting loose with an indignant meow upon being denied. He seemed nervous in his new surroundings. Often, he stood before the front door and brayed, and when we failed to let him outside, he would lash out at us. As Tony's hostility toward us increased, it became clear that this was not an exclusively indoor cat. Reluctantly, we let him out one afternoon. We went to bed that night with no sign of our newly adopted stray. Nor did he return the following evening. But on the third day, when we had just about lost faith, he showed up again.

Eventually we began to acclimate to our altered family dynamic. It was easier to get along with Tony when we accepted that he was not anything like Sam. And perhaps Tony began to come to grips with the imperfection of the humans who now filled his food and water bowls and provided a warm, predator-free place to sleep. Whatever went through his little cat brain, he settled down somewhat. As long as we faithfully responded to his demands to go outside and be let back in, he was usually docile. Not that you could depend on it, though. Bonding with Tony required a special patience and quick reflexes. What seemed to be an affectionate rub could instantly devolve into the bearing of fangs.

One evening not long after Tony had established residence with us, I opened the door to find that he had killed a small mouse. I suppose I should have been appreciative, but having had mice as pets, I instead felt empathy for the tiny creature that lay motionless on our porch. What a way to go. Then Tony began to play with his limp prey, grabbing the mouse in his mouth and tossing it into the air so that he could bat it down again. He seemed to really enjoy this activity, and seeing as the mouse was already dead, I decided to let Tony have his fun before I disposed of the unlucky rodent. I closed the door and went back to my evening routine. When I returned a half hour later, I was horrified to discover that Tony was eating the mouse, head first. *Crunch, crunch, crunch.* It was a stark reminder that no matter how much I preferred to see the similarities among us fellow mammals, there were unavoidable differences that put us at opposite ends of the continuum from civilized to savage.

The mouse was but the first of many small animal conquests. Tony dispatched whatever birds he could get his paws on, usually little finches and wrens. Evidently he didn't find them palatable, however, as their corpses were generally unmolested. Invariably their necks were broken, and it seemed like the fun was all in the catching. Like a disinterested child abandoning a broken toy, Tony walked away from lifeless birds.

Rabbits, though, were a different matter. For Tony, they were apparently a delicacy to be pursued at every opportunity. As cuddly as your average bunny is on the outside, I can assure you that they are generously stuffed with viscera on the inside. I know because I sealed many a half-rabbit into a Ziploc bag before tossing the remains into the trash. Just as many people start on their chocolate Easter bunnies at the ears and work their way down, so did Tony prefer to consume the head before digging into the rest. Often we found the back end of a rabbit in the vicinity of our front or back doors. Sometimes we discovered nothing more than a quartet of tiny legs.

And once, near the service door to our garage, we came upon what appeared to be, incongruously, a pair of blueberries. Upon closer inspection, we realized that they were rabbit eyes. It is difficult for me to convey the full measure of our disgust at this gruesome sight, nor can I adequately explain our cat's behavior. What *did* go on in that peanut brain of his? After all, he had just eaten nearly an entire rabbit, from its whiskers to its cotton tail and everything in between. Was he so full that, like the Pythonic Mr. Creosote turning down a "wafer thin mint," he simply couldn't manage another bite? Or having consumed his fill of brains, intestines, and crunchy bones, did he find the idea of consuming eyeballs revolting? *Oh, sure, I'll eat the innards, but eyeballs – THAT'S where I draw the line!*

Helpless as we were to keep Tony from roaming about the neighborhood, we were powerless to curb his savage bloodlust. We would have much preferred that he simply leave the small creatures of the neighborhood alone. When we would find yet another victim in his scarlet string of serially killed mice, birds, and rabbits, we sometimes shook our heads. "Ugh," we recoiled at the spilled remains, "Sam would never have done that."

And then we would remember that, although the cat we acquired as a successor to Sam may have looked like his gentle predecessor, he was a different breed altogether.

Sweet Home, Perstai

Y ou should get a home in Perstai, Dad," urged Melinda. I had reservations. I was not looking for new ways to occupy my time, and I had seen how willingly Melinda would sacrifice a free hour here and there to amble about her virtual world. I couldn't quite get it. It seemed like her avatar never did anything of much significance, yet unwinding within this mythical land apparently provided her much pleasure. I had to admit that *Animal Crossing*, the Nintendo Wii title that made Melinda's imaginary journeys possible, was a clever game. Its designers had crafted a tightly controlled environment that gave a satisfying sense of individual freedom within a dynamic fictional society fueled by limited artificial intelligence. Melinda was well aware that she was playing a game by herself and that her illusory interactions with pixelated neighbors were nothing more than simple, scripted encounters. But she didn't care, because it was fun.

"Maybe," I said, by which I meant, "No."

She had already persuaded Mom to establish residence in the small village of Perstai, and I had noticed Julie starting to take almost as much pleasure in this digital alternative existence as Melinda did. Sometimes one of them would watch the other strolling about town for a while, then the one playing would log off and the one watching would log on. It didn't seem to make much difference who was actually playing, as both gamer and observer appeared to be equally absorbed by Perstai culture.

"Look," one of them would say, "Bones just clapped when I caught that fish!"

"Ha, ha!" the other would guffaw, and I would glance at them with withering condescension. Time wasters. It would be a cold day in Perstai before I indulged myself in that sort of pointless activity.

And so it was. Snow covered the ground not only in Perstai but in Ohio as well, and as I was enjoying that most magnificent of perks that come to elementary educators – namely, the annual two-week break at the end of the calendar year – it seemed harmless to idle away a few of those hours in a virtual way. Melinda would be pleased by my interest, and maybe it would even be a little fun.

"You'll start by working for Tom Nook," Melinda informed me.

"Who?"

"Tom Nook. He's the raccoon who runs the store. He'll give you different jobs around town, and when you're done, you can pay off your mortgage."

"My what?"

"It's like rent. He'll let you expand your house, and when you pay it off, he'll let you expand it again. When that's all paid, you can get a second floor."

"Why would I want that?"

"More room for your stuff!"

I wasn't quite sure if I liked the rather materialistic bent of the game, as it seemed to eerily parallel the reckless home-buying practices that ignited our nation's housing crisis. "Don't worry about the money, just pay me back as you can," is the message parroted by Tom Nook, who seems eager to lend without any evidence of consumer responsibility. In fact, he never even mentions interest, which conveniently does not exist in this virtual paradise. Pay off your house renovations, however, and he's all over you to expand again, hinting that you must be somewhat dissatisfied by your current lack of space.

178

I diligently began running errands for Nook, and soon I had enough money to enlarge my squalid starter shack into something more comfortable. There didn't seem to be much point in the whole endeavor, although I did register a twinge of pleasure at replacing my standard-issue cardboard box and candle with a decent end table and lamp. Soon afterward my indentured servitude to Nook was rapidly fulfilled, leaving me free to seek my own fortune.

Seeking one's fortune in *Animal Crossing* involves participating in a cycle of redundant activities to generate income. Sometimes just shaking trees and banging on rocks with your shovel releases currency, but most money is earned by acquiring goods and selling them to Nook. Picking fruit, catching fish, and digging up fossils are the beginner's route to financial freedom. Oranges go for 100 bells apiece in Perstai, and some of the rarest fish can fetch up to 15,000 bells. The bell, by the way, is the official monetary unit used in every *Animal Crossing* town. If ya wanna make it big, ya gotta have bells.

I had noticed Melinda and Julie scurrying about Perstai trying to generate bells by engaging in these mundane tasks. As a mere observer, I perceived only irony in their efforts. Why would anyone fritter away their free time on work? Virtual or not, that's what it was. Run here, run there, fill your pockets with oranges, go sell them to Nook, run here, run there, fill your pockets with fish, go sell them to Nook. You wouldn't do that for less than minimum wage in the real world, but *Animal Crossing* players gladly do these things for no real recompense.

Having a go at *Animal Crossing* myself gave me some insight into the human condition. We are definitely a goal-oriented species. It does not matter if the objective is particularly meaningful, nor must it be real. Provided that all basic needs are met, give your average *homo sapien* a sufficiently stimulating challenge and he or she will not rest until that aim is accomplished. As I became immersed in Perstai life, I chided myself for having once dismissed this virtual existence as pointless. I had been terribly closed-minded. Because now that I had increased the footprint of my home to its maximum area, I was only 248,000 bells away from adding a second floor. So it wasn't like I was wasting time, because I was actually accomplishing something. I was saving bells.

But it wasn't all about making money. Well, mostly it was. Yet in addition, I had become charmed by the pre-programmed residents of Perstai. The amiable dogs Bones and Marcel. The endearingly boastful bear Teddy and the similarly macho eagle Pierce. The girly-girl bear Tutu and the lady rhinoceros Rhonda. Even the somewhat bitchy duck Mallory. They would tell me amusing little anecdotes and sometimes send me on errands for which I'd always be rewarded in goods or bells. Once in awhile, one of them would suggest a game of hide and seek, and my inevitable victory yielded even more loot.

And they are wonderfully gullible. The residents of *Animal Crossing* towns love to use catchphrases and customized greetings, and they will frequently ask for suggestions along these lines to keep conversation fresh. If, say, Marcel approaches you for some help in coming up with a clever new phrase, and if you propose something that is less than tasteful, and so long as the game designers did not foresee the sort of drivel your deviant mind is capable of concocting, then Marcel will henceforth trot happily about town repeating your crude remark. This simple pleasure does not get old as quickly as you might think.

Plus, if you take the time to write them letters with an enclosed gift, they will ecstatically return the favor. Your mailbox will soon be flooded with a bounty of free furniture, clothing, and exotic fruit. The best part is that they are thrilled with whatever you give them, even if the items are totally worthless. Thus, I write a flowery love note to Tutu and enclose an old tire. She gushes with appreciation and sends me a lovely violin. I give Marcel a smelly boot that I fished out of the river, and he presents me with a computer. This delightful practice also does not get old with any rapidity.

As life in Perstai evolved from Melinda's solitary preoccupation into a family pastime, more and more evenings included the warm, animated glow of *Animal Crossing* emanating from our television. Only eldest daughter Amber remained a staunch holdout, declaring the whole enterprise a total waste of time. We regarded her sympathetically, as zealots look upon the unsaved.

It was somewhere around this time that Julie and I became more frequent visitors to Perstai than Melinda. One of us – I can't really remember who – wondered naively if there might be some useful information about *Animal Crossing* on the Internet. It so happens that there is far more to our virtual existence than we had ever anticipated, and once we discovered this, there was no turning back. No longer contented innocents, we were compelled to fulfill our destinies. There were so many more species of fish for us to catch, a plethora of insects still uncaught, and untold varieties of fossils yet unearthed. If you had enough bells, you could even add a basement. And there was something that Melinda had not yet tested: the stalk market.

Every Sunday morning, a warthog named Joan shows up with turnips for sale. She always has one red turnip seed that can be turned around for a 14,000 bell profit on a 1,000 bell investment, providing that you remember to water it daily for a week. Even more enticing are the white turnips, a highly volatile commodity. One week, Julie bought a few at 108 bells and waited to sell until Nook offered her a buying price of 459. That was all it took for us to start dropping in at Perstai on a fairly regular basis.

On my most recent trip, I had been logged on for no more than five minutes when I had the good fortune to land a rare stringfish, a great catch at 15,000 bells. Melinda was watching.

"Go sell that stringfish to Nook and let me play."

"But I just got on," I protested. She looked askance at me, and I surrendered the controller.

"At least I'm not addicted to it," she added reproachfully. "Unlike some people I know."

Ice Folly

Last weekend I laced up a pair of rental skates and ventured tentatively onto the slick surface of an ice rink for only the third time in my life. It was an impulsive decision, brought about by our attendance at eldest daughter Amber's synchronized skating team banquet. There was a lull in the proceedings after dinner and awards, with an hour of open ice before the broom ball activity anticipated by youngest daughter Melinda. What to do until then? No one was interested in skating, until I jokingly suggested that I might give it a try. Then the whole family was interested.

"Oh! Dad! You should do it! You should! If you go skating, I will seriously get on the ice with you," vowed Melinda. I had painted myself into a corner with my careless talk, and now I saw only one honorable way out. The burden of rescuing my family from an hour of boredom was on my shoulders. If I refused to hit the ice, I would be a hopelessly dull, stick-in-the-mud dad who would have to endure our children's complaints of ennui and potential sibling bickering. But if only I gave it a try, we would all be entertained for a while, and I'd be hailed as a heroically Fun Dad. If I didn't break anything, that is.

Ice skating is about as natural to me as extracting oxygen from water with gills. Had I the opportunity to develop the necessary skills as a child, perhaps things would have turned out differently, but as it happened, I never put on a pair of blades until I was eighteen. Just as learning a foreign language is more taxing to the mature mind, so is gliding gracefully across the ice a greater challenge for the adult body. All of the vital neural connections between body and mind are already set in their ways, and reprogramming oneself to acquire the requisite motions has all the success potential of a Microsoft operating system upgrade. Better to wipe the slate clean and start from scratch. That first painfully slow lap around a rink saw me hunched over like a showbiz chimp, and only the firm grip of an understanding college friend kept me from smacking my knees on the ice.

I wouldn't attempt ice skating again for more than ten years. My wife and I took our two very young daughters to a December display of holiday lights at the zoo. The festive mood was heightened by the presence of hot chocolate vendors, kiosks selling roasted chestnuts, and a miniature ice rink constructed within an open-air pavilion. Accompanying my family on the ice seemed like the responsible and sporting thing to do, but I was dismayed to find that skating was just as challenging for me as it had been the first time. In fact, it was just a bit worse, as I was already noticing the subtle decline in agility that a decade of adulthood will bring. I valiantly clung to the boards and made a mental note for future reference: remember that you can't ice skate.

If there is irony to be found in my incompetence, it rests in the fact that I am the father of a proficient figure skater. Amber makes spins and jumps look as effortless as walking. Simply moving along the ice is automatic for her, and I have little doubt that she could simultaneously eat dinner, read a novel, send text messages and do laps around the rink if she so desired. As for me, staying upright on skates requires my full concentration.

So as I wobbled along on my tightly-laced rentals toward a third encounter with ice skating in as many decades, it was not without well-founded trepidation. I disliked the amount of play at my ankles, as I would have preferred to completely immobilize the joint, leaving one less variable open to failure. Others trotted confidently before me and zipped onto the ice in one fluid motion, while I cautiously gripped a railing so as to firmly establish verticality before daring linear progress. One thing at a time, you know. Having assured myself that I was not in imminent danger of falling, I set about trying to move forward.

Now older and wiser, and with the spacious luxury of an uncrowded rink, I was able to be a little more analytical about the challenge. I extended my arms outward for balance and pushed off, trying to build and preserve momentum while maintaining a straight course. Soon I realized that I was experiencing much the same annoyance and frustration that must hinder babies as they learn to walk. Just how is all of this supposed to work, anyway?! Accomplished movers take a good deal for granted, but there is a whole lot going on that means all the difference between successfully getting from here to there and the humiliation of falling flat.

For example, there is a sweet spot of skate alignment, wherein the blades are held vertical and kept at a parallel distance. This ensures straight coasting and maximum conservation of momentum. I found it a difficult position to consistently maintain, especially since I had to keep disturbing my alignment by making alternating propulsions forward. That required me to stay balanced on one foot while the other pushed off at an angle, and then I had to do it the other way around, and back and forth it went. Which brings up timing, another crucial element that came to my attention. And it also helps to relax, as one's feet will soon ache when kept in a tense grip against the boot sole.

By paying close attention to these details and through a series of diminishing errors and overcorrections, it wasn't too long before I won the admiration of my wife and daughters, who had wondered whether I would be able to do more than stand. *Hey, look at Dad! He's actually skating!* And so I was, though precariously. I would relax enough to set a steady pace and build up some speed, but then a small wobble would be enough to set my arms flailing. That combined with no practical knowledge of how to stop made me a bit dangerous. But sure enough, I was skating better than ever.

As I attempted small refinements in propulsion, timing and alignment, I had an important revelation that gave me some insight into my failure as an ice skater. Each time I've stepped out onto the ice, I have brought with me a lifetime of overpronation.

That is, my feet roll too far inward when I walk. It's not too much of a problem under ordinary walking conditions, though it's bad enough that I prefer wearing motion-control shoes. On the ice, it's problematic. I think I'm standing up straight, but my feet are inclined toward each other. When I force them into a position such that my blades are plumb to the ice, it feels like my feet are splayed outward. You can imagine how difficult this makes it to skate. What I really need is a pair of motion-control ice skates, with the blades moved in about a quarter of an inch.

On the other hand, there is something to be said for the puzzling allure of clumsiness. We would like to be good at everything, yet we are sometimes endearing in our awkward failures. I've learned to never discount the charming potential of my ineptitude, as I've profited from it in one major way. That understanding college student who held my hand as I braved the ice for the first time? We've celebrated many wedding anniversaries since then. At the time, we were both too shy to get that close under any other circumstances. But there's nothing like a chimp on skates to break the ice.

If It's Tuesday, This Must Be Africa

There is something truly disconcerting about a one-ton beast staring down your vehicle from a mere yard away. He stands there, feet planted firmly upon the dirt road and head cocked to one side, his massive horns tilted like a pair of sharpened goalposts set askew after a rowdy collegiate victory, and you are forced to confront your own shallow materialism. Because rather than reacting rationally with a measure of concern for your personal safety, you are instead preoccupied with a silent plea: *Please don't hurt my car.*

The creature lumbers forward toward your window, which you have left down because you have already become addicted to the thrill of witnessing large animal heads poke into your car in search of grain pellets and carrots. Like a trained dog, that is all this immense quadruped is really after – a treat. Yet he cannot insert his gigantic head very far into your vehicle, as those enormous horns will not allow it. You hear them clatter and scrape against the roof, and as you reach for a carrot, you repeat your prayerful mantra: *Please don't hurt my car.*

Such are the highs and lows of life on safari, at least as it exists within the decidedly non-African climate of Ohio. We found this particular wildlife park in – of all places – Port Clinton, just a shed antler's throw from the shallow shore of Lake Erie. With its garishly painted billboards promoting the display of a white alligator and brochures touting pig races and animal rides, the facility reeked of roadside tourist trap more than it evoked the sincerity of a nature preserve.

We waited in a slow-moving double line of cars approaching the safari enclosure while listening to the amplified, big buildup

186

for the adjacent pig race. Spectators were divided into sections of stands and accordingly encouraged to root for particular pigs, including Pig Daddy, Dale Swinehardt, and A. J. Oink. Meanwhile, we studied the signage surrounding the safari gate. There were instructions on how to safely feed the animals, among which was a warning to surrender your feed cup to any animal that seemed determined to snatch it. Also posted was a notice releasing the wildlife park from all liability in the event of property damage or personal injury. We had plenty of time to ponder the implications of that policy, and I could not help but be reminded of an incident that occurred during a two-family vacation over forty years ago.

We were traveling with the Monforts, in whose station wagon we entered the grounds of a South Dakota attraction called Bear Country, USA. Visitors were told to keep their windows rolled up as they drove among unrestrained grizzlies. According to the proprietors, it was early in the tourist season, and our hopes of seeing a bear up close were likely to be met, as the creatures were still curious about passing cars. As it happened, they were more curious than we would have liked.

One of the standout vacation memories of my childhood is the image of a frantic Ruth Ann Monfort flailing at her window with an umbrella in a vain attempt to shoo away a bear that was showing its menacing teeth just on the other side of the pane. We all heard alarming sounds of claws upon metal that did not bode well for the station wagon's exterior. Nestled among our luggage on the journey home was a mangled strip of chrome that had been pried loose from a side panel.

The very real potential for vehicular damage was foremost in my mind, then, as we finally reached the safari gate and purchased several large cups of grain pellets and a bag of carrots. No sooner did we drive through than we observed the cars in front of us set upon by a half-dozen or more antlered animals that were not at all shy about begging for food. Moments later, we were surrounded as well. The ravenous beasts stuffed their muzzles into our cups and vacuumed up whole carrots. One of them clamped its crooked teeth on the lip of a feeding cup and wrenched it away, and we quickly realized that our supposedly ample supplies would be rapidly depleted unless we put up our windows and moved along.

Progressing through the park, we encountered bison, which are impressively large from a distance and even more so when viewed within twelve inches. One bull galumphed alongside the car and stared at us with its left eye. Its head was far too big to pass through the window. We gave it a carrot, which disappeared instantly, and a moment of silence ensued. Then, from somewhere deep within its cavernous oral cavity, there resounded an ominous crunching. We moved on.

Farther along the path was a huge and unfamiliar animal that we would only later learn was a Scottish Highlander. It was shaggy and clumsy, as though someone had figured out how to transform one of Jim Henson's monster Muppets into organic reality. So gigantic was it that we only caught glimpses of its features when it closed in on us. It exhaled snot into our car, gulped down a carrot, and peered into the back window, looking for more. Every so often, a writhing tongue of about the diameter of my biceps emerged from its mouth and licked about its face, producing an almost comically loud slurping sound. This was not the kind of animal one would ever want to provoke, I decided. I am, in general, wary of creatures whose heads are four times bigger than my own.

The park saved its marquee animals for the end of the trail, which ran alongside wire fences behind which roamed zebras and giraffes. These animals, too, had become carrot lovers, and they easily managed to crane their necks over obstructions in order to accept visitor offerings. I had heard that zebras were, in fact, rather hostile and unpleasant animals, but these specimens appeared as docile as dogs. We patted their snouts, and they munched away contentedly. As for giraffes, I know of no better way of appreciating their outrageous height than to try to gaze at one's face as it stands beside your car. It is, of course, impossible, and only by poking my upper body out the window upside down could I locate a giraffe head and snap its picture.

When it was over, we pulled into the parking lot and gave our vehicle the once-over. No scratches or dents were readily apparent, but both sides of the car were slathered with dirt, slobber, and whatever viscous matter covered the snouts of the animals that eagerly accosted us. We were alive and unscathed, yet we had been changed. We would never look at a carrot the same way again.

Con Market – Manet Cork – Knot Cream

The human brain, that incessant maker of meaning and perceiver of patterns, is wont to seek engagement rather than endure monotony. Even when there is little at hand to provide mental stimulation, the mind will resourcefully make do with whatever it finds. I am reminded of a particular instance of this phenomenon that occurred, of all places, high in the balcony seating of a sold-out pop concert.

We had been enjoying an entertaining set by Elton John, who was touring to promote his 2004 release, *Peachtree Road*. It was a great and engrossing performance until we heard the opening lyric, "She packed my bags last night, pre-flight." The audience responded predictably, greeting "Rocket Man" with a resounding ovation, but we were less than thrilled. Having seen Sir Elton a few times before, we knew that he had just embarked on a journey that would, indeed, last "a long, long time."

Not that there's anything wrong with "Rocket Man," a nicely crafted hit when it clocks in at its originally recorded length of 4:45. I will also acknowledge that it can be great fun to hear a band stretch out and improvise a few variations on a familiar theme, even if that results in a song lasting several times longer than it otherwise would. However, in the case of Elton John's titanic concert renditions of "Rocket Man," this is a bit of shtick he's rested on for so many years that it must be inconceivably pleasurable for him to execute, as any less enjoyment would surely drive a man mad after so many years.

Not to belabor the point, but the Economy-Size "Rocket Man" includes several peaks and valleys, a few frustratingly false codas, and in its moment of grossest excess, a four-bar, letter-by-letter spelling of its title. It's great the first time you hear it, interesting the second time, tedious the third time, and generally intolerable after that. You sit there and start thinking about two or three other Elton John songs that you might have heard but won't thanks to this interminable exhibition. You wonder if there's time to make your way to the restroom and return before the next song, then you kick yourself when the end finally arrives, and you realize you would have had enough time to leave the arena for a quick repast, all without missing anything of interest.

The routine is inevitably a hit, which is apparently why Sir Elton keeps doing it. This places me solidly in the minority, but I know that I am not alone. Sitting next to me was my brother Brian, who sighed and looked at me with a weary gaze as though we were colleagues asked to break out the Post-It notes and chart paper for a team building exercise. I tried to make some enjoyment out of the varying stage light display, and when that failed to occupy my attention, I passed a few minutes following the tangled paths of catwalks along the arena ceiling. When I glanced at Brian, I saw that he was not looking at the stage. Instead, his expressionless gaze appeared to be fixed at some point above us, where there was nothing except the reverse side of several sponsor logo signs. He appeared as vacant as *Seinfeld*'s David Puddy on an intercontinental flight.

"Do you realize," he said to me at length, "that you can rearrange the letters in *Giant Eagle* to make *eating a leg*?" And there it was. My brother's brain, its functioning threatened by the mind molasses that is fifteen minutes of unrelenting "Rocket Man," clung to survival by anagramming the first words it found. It was a moment of salvation for me, too, for although I was ultimately unsuccessful, I spent the rest of the song trying to come up with an even better anagram. *Agile gnat* left me with a stranded e, and *elegant IGA* wasn't as funny. Still, it was a lot better than that cursed R-O-C-K-E-T-M-A-N.

Brian is a formidable Scrabble player, at least within our amateur circle, so generating anagrams comes naturally to him. I find it somewhat difficult to do without having tangible letters to move around, which frees my mind from having to keep track of what letters I have and have not used. When I think I've come up with a brilliant anagram solely through mental effort, I usually find that I've left out a letter or added a duplicate.

Nevertheless, is there any better testament to the playful eagerness of our brains to simply think than the mind's capacity and thirst for anagrams? Other than achieving one's own amusement, it's a pointless exercise. As amusing, pointless exercises go, however, it's a great time filler.

During a lull one weekend afternoon, I picked out my name in Scrabble tiles and started moving them around, looking for credible aliases. My favorite anagram for *Robert Gerard Hunt* is *Arthur T. Rodenberg*, which sounds like the namesake of a liberal arts grant benefiting NPR. ("Funding for *Morning Edition* is provided by the Arthur T. Rodenberg Foundation, a tax shelter with an attractive veneer of philanthropy.") I also found the mysterious *Garrett Durrebohn* (a German spy, perhaps?), *Darren R. Butterhog* (whom I envision as the wealthy founder of a pork rind franchise), and *Brother Andergurt* (a menacing monk). Plus, my name can also be rearranged to form the phrase *darn hotter burger,* though I'm hard-pressed to explain why anyone might utter such words.

Of course, one man's anagram is another man's complete waste of time. I received Brian's brilliant *eating a leg* with admiration, whereas many would respond with a flat "Big deal" (which, by the way, can be rearranged to make *I Be Glad* or *GI Blade*). Those of us who enjoy the odd anagram now and then have come to recognize stony silence (*Tony's license* or *Let's ice Sonny*) as the universal signal of anagrammatic discouragement. So in the interest of risking no further alienation from valued readers, I shall anagram no further.

Except to note that the letters in Elton John can be rearranged to make a cautionary message regarding the handling of poultry (*Jolt no hen.*)

Okay, I'm done. (*Nook may die.*)

Sorry.

Wait, Wait

Y ou've been through this before. There is a valuable object that you must physically attain, but it's going to take a little bit of bureaucratic interaction to make it happen. An indeterminate amount of waiting may be involved. In this case, the treasured item is a West Campus parking pass for The Ohio State University, a necessity that your daughter ordered online. Armed with a day off, you are charged with the task of picking up the pass in the morning so that she may use it to attend her first college class that evening. You take the precaution of calling ahead to confirm that you are permitted to retrieve the pass on your daughter's behalf. You look over a map of West Campus and find the small visitor lot where you've parked before, the one that is a short stroll from the Traffic and Parking offices. You double-check to make sure that you have your daughter's university ID card and a printed receipt for the parking pass. Then, satisfied that you have taken all reasonable preparatory measures, you embark on your journey.

Your destination is a popular one on this first day of Winter Quarter, but several spaces open up after you circle the visitor lot once. There is a "Pay and Display" system in place that requires the purchase of a timed pass from an automated machine. You approach it and fish out the coins you brought along for this purpose, depositing three quarters and three dimes. It's 9:00. There are more coins in your pocket, but the machine says that you have just bought 42 minutes of parking time, which seems more than adequate for the purpose of picking up a previously purchased parking pass. You chastise yourself for the wasteful habit of padding parking meters with unnecessary time simply due to an irrational aversion to the unlikely prospect of purchased time elapsing. Next time, you think, you'll spend a little less instead of fattening the coffers of Traffic and Parking.

Though it feels as though you have all the time in the world to accomplish your mission, your paranoid mind tells you that there is no sense in taking any longer than you must, and so you eschew the right-angle path in favor of traversing its snow-covered hypotenuse, gaining perhaps a minute in the process. Shortly you find yourself opening the door to Traffic and Parking, and there is the long, customer service counter, nearly empty but for a pair of customers receiving service. Again, you reprimand yourself for buying a ridiculous 42 minutes of parking time. There is a large sign nearby, and it notes that you must walk past the counter in order to reach the end of the waiting line. Peering down the hall, you see just one person standing at that point, the intersection with a perpendicular hallway. You stride confidently past the counter, and as you approach the corner, you note that there are, in fact, several people waiting, but no matter, as you have plenty of time to spare. Then you round the corner and try not to betray your astonishment at the sight of thirty or more people waiting along the length of the hallway.

Taking your place at the end of this grim and eerily silent line, you realize that you were not paranoid about buying parking time, that you should have pumped all the change you had into the stupid machine, and that you have just set yourself up for a pins-and-needles wait that might last well beyond the 42 minutes you had allotted. You are familiar with the university's Traffic and Parking enforcement officers, who patrol lots like vultures circling the sky in anticipation of the magic moment that a dying desert traveler becomes carrion. You know that there is no irrationality in fearing that one of them may pounce on your Civic at minute forty-three. And then what? A ticket? Would an appeals officer see the irony in your plight, that you ran a few minutes over your purchased 42 minutes of parking time because you were waiting in line to pick up your daughter's previously purchased parking pass? Were you to intercept a ticketing officer just as he is about to slip the notice under your windshield wiper, would he listen courteously to your story and graciously tear up the ticket? Perhaps. But you have been here before, and in all your experience with Traffic and Parking officers, you have never known them to show any flexibility. Nor to smile.

So you sigh and try to accept your fate without worry, noting that the line has already moved a little, and thinking that there might just be some sliver of hope that you will return to your car either before your time runs out or before a Traffic and Parking officer notices that your time has run out. Others in the long line hold postures that suggest either nervous tension or slouched resignation. Someone apparently thought it amusing to apply a dashed yellow median along the length of the hallway floor. The line snakes along, incongruously, to the left of the line, as mandated by nearby signage. Other attempts have been made to brighten up the windowless hallway. Safety posters and an enlarged aerial photo of campus adorn one wall. A life-size "Pay and Display" machine has been awarded a prominent space. From the ceiling hang a pair of silent TV monitors, one of which is showing a succession of weather graphics, the other featuring a morning show chat with a bedraggled and effusively gesticulating William H. Macy.

The thick silence is broken by spontaneous conversation halfway up the line: a cheery young man with a broad face and recurring smile has struck up a conversation with a pleasant young woman whose blond hair flows from beneath a knitted winter hat with hanging tassels. You can hear every word they say – everyone can – and though their talk is amiable and altogether unremarkable, you cannot decide whether their public discourse is an annoyance or a welcome distraction. For just beyond them, at the far end of the hall, is the LED marquee that advises aspiring customers to have all forms ready, lists accepted forms of payment, and periodically flashes the time. 9:20. You count the people in front of you and decide against applying mathematical reasoning to the situation, as your numerical intuition tells you it doesn't look good. Instead, you hang on to the undeniably promising fact that one person who was in front of you has left, apparently unwilling or unable to wait any longer. If only several more of the sad sacks in this line follow his lead, it just might work.

But who are you kidding? There is no way that you will have concluded your transaction and returned to your vulnerable Civic in time. It is merely a question of whether or not the transgression will be noticed by the Gestapo. And you know it will, you just know it. And you further know that they will not give two buckeyes about some fat, old alumnus who was too cheap to plunk all of his change into a parking meter. They will be merciless, just like the time you failed to remove your father's Oldsmobile from the stadium parking lot before midnight, the deadline by which they started to tow vehicles in anticipation of the sacred marching band's dawn practice. Not that you're still bitter about it. But you hold no illusions about their charity. It's now 9:25, and those buzzards have probably already made note of your 9:42 expiration. Time to face the music. You were stupid! Stupid!

And then...a miracle. An angel appears. Admittedly, there is nothing angelic about her rather ordinary appearance, but she whisks down the line and calls out like a carillon's worth of church bells, "Did anyone already pay for their pass on the Internet?" You are nearly too stunned to speak, and the angel almost turns away, but you recover your senses in time to thrust your arm upward and croak, "I d-did!"

You reach your car at 9:33, alive with adrenaline and a deep gratitude for the unexpected windfalls of intervening fortune. Others, you know, will not be so lucky. Like the absentee owners of the cars across the lot, a row of vehicles under surveillance by an expressionless officer sitting inside an idling Traffic and Parking cruiser. He was coming for you next, you think. But not today. Not today.

Everybody Clap Your Hands

There is a celebrity educator renowned among teachers for his bestselling books and the extraordinary commitment he has made to fostering the success of disadvantaged students. His achievements and advice are laudable, as is his practice of funding his school with the honorariums he earns as a popular speaker. Anyone would be thrilled to have him looking after the learning of their child. And yet, despite my admiration for all that he has done for children and teachers alike, there is one quirky aspect of his personality that makes me cringe. He is known for spontaneously mounting desks and tables and proceeding to dance.

Now, I have nothing against people dancing. For all I care, the whole of my community can shimmy about as a choreographed flash mob the next time I'm out and about town. I will smile charitably and perhaps even enjoy the display. Just don't ask me to boogie along. Primal as the urge to dance supposedly is, I have never felt the compulsion to bust a move. Just the opposite, in fact. Never am I happier to remain seated than when a group of revelers is dancing. My reluctance to dance is little different than, say, your dismissal of foods you do not like. It's just not for me. I simply do not enjoy it.

But the dancing celebrity educator sees it differently. Not only does he literally put himself on a pedestal and shake his groove thing, he expects everyone else to follow his lead. Whether he is addressing his student body or a convention hall full of teachers, he expects every last soul to clap along.

As with dancing, I do not begrudge anyone their right to clap along, whether in response to a prompt or simply out of sheer joy. Occasionally I will even clap along myself, if that is what I truly feel like doing, though such instances are rare. But I loathe a relentless exhortation to clap along, especially when delivered with furrowed brow and the implication that anyone who chooses not to participate is a sociopathic blight on the community. Must we obey every command to bang our hands together?

Of course, mandatory audience participation does not stop at mere hand clapping, and this is where human nature amazes me. There seems to never be a shortage of people who are willing to indulge the whimsy of a suit at a lectern, no matter how ridiculous or humiliating the manipulation may be. They will parrot whatever phrases they are told to repeat. They will obediently hold onto their abdomens while forcing out belly laughs. They'll strap on the red, rubber noses concealed beneath their seats. And always, always, they will clap along like a thundering herd of sheep.

Should you ever wish to instill in me a leaden psychological weight of purest dread, you need only inform me that I am about to be subjected to a motivational speaker who is known for an ability to "get audiences moving." You can increase my despair and possibly even drive me to consider self-destruction by telling me that I will be seeing a Joyologist or a Certified Laughter Leader. Too often, programs that are sold as inspirational morale boosters are merely arrogant exercises in performance art. Regardless of content, if the speaker can successfully provoke a majority of the audience to experience cathartic waves of tears and laughter, the show is considered successful. The cheapest way to achieve these emotional plateaus is to exhort the audience to become physically active and train them to respond to behavioral prompts. Unfortunately, it's a strategy that works. A good portion of any audience apparently does not mind being treated like children, at least not enough to simply sit out the stupid stuff (or could it be that none of it seems stupid to them?).

My brother Brian once suggested that the best professional development in the world would make its point by exploiting this herd mentality to its extreme. The speaker would guide the unsuspecting audience through an increasingly stupid and demeaning series of teambuilding exercises, boldly ratcheting up the ridiculousness until finally someone is brave enough to publicly dismiss the whole affair as time-wasting nonsense. The speaker would then identify that brave dissenter as the most valuable person in the organization, chastise the lemmings, and leave.

But no. Across the land, in lecture halls, auditoriums, convention centers and school gymnasiums, grown men and women are turning to their neighbors and parroting catch phrases, locking arms and holding hands, learning to appreciate cooperation by getting tied up in human knots, stepping outside of their comfort zones to understand their peers through situational role playing, humoring every offbeat command, and always, always clapping along.

Mine is a timeless complaint, and others have voiced the same displeasure, but perhaps no one has illustrated our collective docility more eloquently than Monty Python in *Life of Brian*:

> BRIAN: *Look, you've got it all wrong. You don't need to follow me. You don't need to follow anybody. You've got to think for yourselves. You're all individuals.*
>
> CROWD: *Yes, we're all individuals.*
>
> BRIAN: *You're all different.*
>
> CROWD: *Yes, we are all different.*
>
> BRIAN: *Well, that's it. You've all got to work it out for yourselves.*
> CROWD: *Yes, yes! We've got to work it out for ourselves!*
>
> BRIAN: *Exactly.*
>
> CROWD: *Tell us more!*

Back to our dancing celebrity educator. He was the keynote speaker at a professional development conference attended by hundreds of employees of my school district. I was sitting near the exit at one of the many round tables that filled the main floor. Sure enough, the time came when our speaker's dynamism could not be confined to the stage, and a whoop of audience appreciation greeted his gyrations upon a table in the center of the room. When he told us to clap along, the great majority of the attendees went with the suggestion.

However, in the age of No Child Left Behind and its legal mandate that 100% of our nation's children will be proficient in all academic areas, it can be bothersome to a celebrity educator to get anything less than the full participation of his audience. His radar detected that there were pockets of flagging enthusiasm along the periphery of the room, which he sought to remedy by dancing and scowling among the shyer sections of the crowd. Remarkably, this gambit worked, and soon perhaps 99% of the audience was obligingly clapping along.

I, however, was among the stoic 1% that refused to compromise its dignity. *I will not clap, I will not clap,* I told myself, *no matter what he does, I will not clap.* Soon our speaker was a mere table away from me, and I could see his eyes scanning the audience for malcontents. Amid the deafening clapping that filled the hall, I heard his amplified voice take on an accusatory tone.

"Sir," he called out, "why aren't you clapping?"

The adrenaline of steely resolve was surging through my system. I longed to stand up before hundreds of my peers and confront the unstoppable juggernaut of enforced audience participation. I wanted to point out that, as much as clapping along and dancing along might be a wonderful enhancement to the learning experience for most people, there are some for whom it is demeaning. Go ahead and tell your audiences and your students to clap along, but respect the dignity of those who prefer not to. It doesn't mean that they are not engaged. They just don't want to clap along.

But he wasn't talking to me. His ire was directed at an expressionless gentleman who was leaning against the exit doors with his arms folded. The celebrity educator kept after the non-participant for a bit, but the guy refused to play along, remaining still as a mannequin. At last our speaker chose to ignore his nemesis and danced his way back toward the stage. The rest of the crowd clapped along.

FICTION

Dynadormophis Up

It doesn't matter if you're dealing with a sleeper or a dynamo, every service call on a Dynadorm unit leads to an angry or incoherent customer. That's why there's such a high turnover rate for us service techs, never mind the money. I don't care what kind of debt you have hanging over your head, the first time you get assaulted by one of these people, no amount of compensation seems worth it. It's not the physical trauma of it, it's the terror of dealing with the unhinged. There's nothing more dangerous than some sleep-deprived zombie who's counting on you to get up and running again.

I've had all sorts of weapons pulled on me, dodged my share of thrown objects, and more than once I've been forced to threaten a client. Dynadormophis tells us not to in the handbook and every training session, but they know what goes on at the front line, and you do what you have to do. They'll never admit it – that's what keeps the lawyers off our backs – but every rookie soon learns that corporate doesn't care what we do so long as the green keeps flowing. And they expect the green to keep flowing.

After all, it's the service contracts that keep us in business. You can rent a Dynadorm fairly cheaply these days, relatively speaking, and outright buying one is within reach of some, but you'd be a fool to think that's the extent of your investment if you expect the thing to keep working. I see the same scene over and over again. That first call usually comes sometime in the second or third year of operation, by which time the unit is well out of warranty and its owner has become financially, emotionally, and/or physically dependent on it. They can't believe that the call is going to cost so much, swear up and down that nobody in sales ever made the cost/benefit ratio of a service contract clear to them, then finally stop stamping their feet and cursing long enough to accept our generous offer of applying seventy-five percent of their bill toward a long-term contract. After that, they're pretty much hooked.

Dynadorms are actually amazing machines, when you stop to consider it, and given the Rube Goldberg assemblage of theoretical biophysics and fairy dust that makes it all work, nobody should take for granted that they run at all. Fixing the contraptions requires the knowledge of an engineer, the precision of a surgeon, the intuition of an artist, and the faith of an evangelist. That's what our clients fail to understand. We're not overeducated grease monkeys following flow charts here. We get paid a hefty commission because very few people have what it takes to nurse an ailing Dynadorm back to health. What's more, we need a psychologist's insight and a soldier's brawn to deal with the clientele.

"Time is money, you big, fat moron!" one of my wealthier customers once screamed in my ear as I peered into his smoking console. I could smell the coffee evaporating off the unit, noticed the concentric sweat rings of a mug on his old-growth hardwood desk, but this guy insisted that he did nothing more than switch it on when sparks shot out of it. And he called me a moron.

"Mr. Reynolds," I addressed him curtly, "your contract excludes console damage due to immersion or exposure to excessive moisture or liquids, which, I might add, is why we recommend that Dynadorm units be kept away from any area where beverages are consumed. That means-"

"You son of a bitch!" he growled.

"That means, of course, that the cost of this repair will be billed to you. Should the unit be damaged beyond repair, we cannot refund any portion of your existing service contract, though we are offering a ten percent rebate on upgrades, and you can apply the remainder of your contract toward the new unit."

Mr. Reynolds was coming down, big time, and he and I both knew it. He ran his trembling fingers through a thinning tangle of graying hair and stared at the panorama of skyscrapers below us. No doubt he had a number of deals on the line this morning, if the numerous spreadsheets and legal documents on his monitors were any indication. A less hectic day might have afforded him the luxury of real sleep if necessary, but now was no time to indulge in risky behavior. Who knew when he had last slept? The wretched man was minutes away from collapsing into dreamland and staying there for the rest of the week.

"Alright...alright....," he managed in a quavering voice, "... alright then...fix it right now or give me the upgrade...I'll even sign for an emergency boost if I have to, but..." he leaned against the window, "only...only if I absolutely have to."

Some of the guys I know would have whipped out their emergency boost release and shot him up right then and there, but somebody has to take the higher ground these days. Sure, Reynolds is screwing anybody, anytime, any chance he gets for as much as he can, but that doesn't mean I have to. At least – forgive me for saying so – but at least *I* can sleep at night.

I disconnected his old 3000 and pulled it out of the rack, because you can't so much as spill an ounce of Coke or coffee on it without blowing out the circuitry and toasting its gamma drive. He was lucky he didn't ruin his storage as well, especially since he had already banked a good month's worth of repos, but his card tested clean and I was able to slip it into his new 3500. Now he could download repos online straight to his Dynadorm, if he cared to, though a dynamo like him probably bought his credits for much less through a dealer. If you're not going to sleep at all, the habit can get quite expensive.

"Okay, Mr. Reynolds, we're booted up and ready to go."

He had plugged in before I could ask him whether he was renting or buying, though for Reynolds, such questions were mere formalities. He was a different man in a few minutes – they always are – flush with adrenaline, free from tremors, and focused in the eyes. With the ebbing of his paranoia came the onset of rising confidence, evident in the speed with which he finished the transaction and ushered me out his office. He showed no signs of remorse or even knowledge of his rudeness, which was not surprising. Once a dynamo recharged, all drowsy faux pas were left behind like a bad dream.

Sleepers are a different breed, still potentially dangerous but more out of desperation than greed. I've had to threaten a few with physical violence as a matter of self-defense, but most of my intimidation of sleepers involves not-so-subtle reminders that I'm repossessing their Dynadorm if they fall behind on payments. Some of them have actually fallen to their knees and groveled at my feet. Pathetic as that sounds, it's nothing compared to the tomblike atmosphere of their squalid homes and the grim faces of their children.

I might forget to pack a gun if I'm in a hurry to respond to a fat-cat dynamo downtown, but you can be sure I never go down to the bottoms unarmed. I wouldn't even take sleeper calls if corporate didn't force us to, but ten to one it's the sleepers whose units break down, thanks in part to the reconditioned rentals we give them. Most of the time they're desperate enough to sign a service contract, and Dynadormophis probably makes more money off of them than the dynamos. For every sleeper who gets his Dynadorm repossessed, there are five more poor souls who have scraped together enough of a deposit to give it a shot. When they can't hack it anymore, others are ready to take their place. Like an infestation of carpenter ants, there's never any shortage of sleepers.

Ask any tech and you'll get the same answer: you're taking your life in your hands just getting to your sleeper. We've lost a few guys who got caught in the crossfire or were just plain jumped before they could get to the right address. You have to double-check your calls, too, because every punk knows what's inside a Dynadorm, and they'll kill you just to strip it and get a week's worth of groceries or half a tank of gas.

That's why a sleeper will always ask you to hold your tech ID up to the peephole. You stand there for a minute or so, sometimes there are shots in the distance or uncomfortably close, and finally half a dozen deadbolts turn and you get to come into some hole where you never wanted to be in the first place. Sometimes it's not even the sleeper who answers the door, it's one of the kids.

Once I was shown in by a little brown boy who couldn't have been more than six or seven years old. He had that hardened look of a kid who was raising himself, and every dirty dish on the couch and towel on the floor indicated the same. He rushed into a pitch-black bedroom and started calling out, "Mama! Mama! He's here! The sleep machine man is here! Mama! Quit wastin' your sleep! Wake up, Mama!"

Mama fixed me with the classic sleeper stare as my eyes adjusted to the dim surroundings. She was too out of it to be angry. Talking to her was like trying to wake up a teenager before dawn, and though she looked haggard as anything, she probably wasn't long past the teenage years herself.

"Ms. Johnson, it's not banking your hours?"

"Wha?" she whispered, a strand of drool stretching from her open mouth.

"Your Dynadorm. It won't give you repo credits when you're sleeping, right?"

She shook her head and looked like she might plop back down on the bed without warning. "It don't work no more. I got nothin' to sell. I won't be able to make no payment if I got nothin' to sell."

Even as she spoke, I could see the problem, and it had nothing to do with her rental unit. These sleepers, especially the young ones, get their schedules so screwed up that they don't know up from down, and then they stop taking even basic care of themselves. I don't know what happened to the cover of her docking port, but you could see all the crud that had built up on the contacts after they got exposed to everything that came in contact with her head. Probably tried to take a shower with the cover broken off. Lucky for all concerned that it's a simple and inexpensive swap-out. She didn't like it when I made her lay still and pulled her chip out, but I had the replacement in before she knew what hit her. By this time, she was so exhausted that you could practically see her income circling down the somnambulistic drain. I got her boy to sign off, and I plugged her in. If she had her wits about her when the eight-hour bank alarm sounded, she would see a nice display of repo credits before she unplugged and slept for herself.

The boy never said a word as I packed up my gear and headed for the door, but he fixed his unblinking eyes upon me as though I were likely to steal something from him. I heard the deadbolts as soon as the door shut behind me, and I'm certain he yelled something after the last lock turned, though what it was I couldn't tell. Whatever it was, he better not have disturbed Mama. Even the little ones learn quick: never wake up a sleeper on the job. That's why we have bank alarms.

No question it's a high-stress job, dangerous and demanding. But outside of our work, a tech lives a pretty good life. Sleepers spend most of their lives in bed, barely making enough to cover their costs and stumbling through their waking hours in a haze. Dynamos make more money than anyone can imagine, but then they never stop working either. We techs are like a throwback to the twentieth century: on call for forty hours a week. I get a solid six hours of sleep every night, and that leaves me with eighty-six hours a week to spend my money however I please.

And just like Reynolds likes to bark, time is money, right?

Good Friday

T hem Catholics sure know how to make themselves miserable, let me tell you. I know, 'cause I used to work with one. Fred Murphy, that was his name, he used to work down in the supply cage, only decent guy in the whole department. Everybody on the shop floor knew to go to Freddy if you needed something, 'cause he'd actually listen to you and do whatever he could to help. Maybe he couldn't always fix your problem, but he'd go to bat for you every time. I never knew anybody who didn't like Freddy, except maybe the old fart who used to run the supply cage like it was his kingdom and we were the serfs. Anyway, ol' Fred was a good guy.

Now we were all second shifters back then, including Fred, and somehow or other we started up a Friday morning bowling league. Might have been Mel Gordon's idea, he was a pretty good bowler before his heart attack. The rest of us were just in it for a good time, you know? Couple of beers, some greasy food, who cared about the score? It was a great way to unwind before the last shift of the week, and you knew the weekend was on the other side. Fred was kind of a quiet guy, not pushy at all, and it took a while before someone thought to ask him to join our league, since it was all guys from the floor. But once he joined us, he never missed a Friday, not so long as the league lasted.

We were all glad to have Freddy with us, but it turned out he wasn't much of a bowler. He said he'd bowled before, but that might just be the only lie that Fred Murphy ever told. He was tossing more gutter balls than anything else for the first month or so. And we could tell he was reading some kind of bowling books or something, 'cause then he came up with his famous approach and started trying to spin the ball. It cracked us up, and we used to ride him about it, but ol' Fred, bless his heart, he was a real gentle guy, and he must have known we all liked him, 'cause it never seemed to bother him when we kidded him about his lousy bowling. He'd just smile and order another Dr. Pepper, never any beer for Freddy. And he'd be the first to slap a guy's hand for getting a strike. Real friendly guy, ol' Fred.

And as far as him being Catholic, you never would have known it, not like he ever talked about it, except he'd pick the pepperoni off his pizza on account of it being Friday. And he'd keep that smudge of ashes on his forehead from Ash Wednesday all day long, like it was a sin to wash it off or something. Other than that, though, he kept his personal business to himself. He never acted like he was better than anybody else. He might not even have liked being Catholic, for all I know.

Anyway, one Friday morning we're putting on our shoes, and Bill Haller says, "Where's Freddy?" 'Cause Fred was always there before the rest of us for some reason.

And I said, "I don't know, he didn't say nothing about it last night." And everybody knew Freddy never got sick, and he'd never missed our Friday league since the day he joined it. So we decide to wait a few minutes, you know, out of respect, and we toss back a round, and we're just about to start without him when we see Fred come through the door looking like he'd just lost his best friend. I mean, Freddy wasn't one of those guys who goes around looking happy all the time, but he was looking pretty grim.

So I say, "Freddy, what's wrong?" But he just shakes his head and doesn't say nothing, just puts on his shoes with this grim look on his face and drops his ball in the ball return like it's got germs on it. Well, by now, Mel Gordon's getting a little hot about having to wait so long to play, so we start the games and act like nothing's wrong. But we're all worried about Freddy, 'cause that wasn't like him at all. And then it's his turn, and he picks up his ball and goes right into his delivery, without so much as a second's look down the alley, and would you believe that ball has the perfect spin on it, and his first ball's a strike! We're giving each other high fives, none of us can believe it, and poor old Freddy just shuffles back to his seat and plops down without a word. Doesn't even want a Dr. Pepper. We can't figure it out.

Next ball he does the same thing as before, just grabs his ball and throws it down the lane in two seconds, and I'll be damned if he didn't get another strike. This has never happened before, and we're going crazy. "Freddy! Freddy! You're doing great, Freddy!" But it's like he couldn't care less, and it's starting to creep us out. I mean, what's wrong with this guy? But he won't say nothing, just stays slumped down in his seat staring at his shoes, and I figure there must be trouble at home, right? That would explain why he was late. Before I can ask him about it, though, it's his turn again, and this time he leaves a Woolworth split. Now, ordinarily, Freddy was about as good at picking up spares as he was at bowling strikes, which is to say not at all. But this time he pulls off a textbook spare without taking any more time to study the lane than he did before. And the guys are going bananas, 'cause they know Freddy has bowled entire games with a lower score than he's just picked up from his first three frames.

So I plop myself down next to Freddy to make him spill the beans. "Okay, Fred," I tell him, "out with it. You'll feel better if you tell somebody. You in the doghouse with Bev?" He doesn't want to talk, but I keep at him, and every so often he gets up and throws a strike or picks up a spare, never leaves a frame open. Unbelievable. And finally, he cracks and tells me that Bev didn't want him to go bowling that morning, that he was almost out the door when she started giving him hell for going bowling.

And I say, "Wait a second, Freddy, this makes no sense. How long you been bowling with us now? You're telling me your old lady's just now figuring it out?" But Freddy says that's not it at all, and then he lays it on the line. Suddenly it all makes sense. The lateness. The haunted look on his face. The total lack of any joy from frame after frame of the best he's ever bowled. He tells me – get this – Bev didn't want him to go bowling because it was Good Friday, and it was a sin to enjoy yourself on purpose on Good Friday.

Can you believe that? And here I didn't even know it was Good Friday until Freddy told me, not like I would have cared one way or the other, but there you go. Not allowed to have a good time on Good Friday. *What the hell's good about it, then?* I want to ask him, but I got too much respect for Freddy to ride him for that. It just makes me sad, seeing him so glum and worried he's doing something awful just because he's doing what he does every other Friday, and it's not like he's not a hard worker or nothing like that. It also makes me kind of mad, because if that's what religion is, I tell myself, I don't want no part of it. Imagine, the best game a guy ever bowls, and he can't enjoy it. Freddy ends up with a 256, which is what he usually has to bowl three or four games and add up the scores together to get, and he goes off to work just as sour-faced as he came into the bowling alley. And the next week, he's his usual cheery self, and he's back to being a lousy bowler.

Some Good Friday, huh? But like I said, them Catholics, they know how to make themselves miserable.

Weird but True!

Due to administrative oversight, murder is legal in more than two dozen U.S. municipalities.

Staring upward into the moving blades of a ceiling fan from a prone position may induce hiccups.

The screw is merely a cylinder wrapped with an inclined plane!

Among the items salvaged from the Titanic debris field on the floor of the Atlantic Ocean was a nearly complete set of elephant bones.

It is physically impossible to simultaneously experience flatulence and vertigo.

The dish that we commonly call ravioli was first known as lasagna, and vice-versa.

It cost less money to make *The Wizard of Oz* than the U.S. government spends on a single cockpit toggle switch for Air Force One.

Construction of the Panama Canal was actually merely the excavation of an ancient land bridge engineered by the Aztecs.

A typical gum ball dropped from a height of 100 meters toward the surface of Mars will reach a terminal velocity sufficient to penetrate the human skull.

Jell-O was originally invented as a means for preserving medical cadavers.

Popular astronomer Carl Sagan never received any formal education beyond the eighth grade.

Plantains are deliberately malnourished bananas.

The sleeper sofa was invented in 1871 by New Jersey carpenter Leonard Couch.

A bomb with the explosive power of half a stick of dynamite can be assembled using just a battery, a fuse and a Big Mac.

Napoleon Bonaparte was known to be fond of trail mix.

Performance artist Tiny Tim was a hoax perpetrated by Jim Nabors.

Slim Whitman has sold more records than the Beatles and Elvis combined.

The first Red Lobster folded during the McCarthy hearings.

A group of twelve or more feral cats is known as a caravan.

Trading cards were introduced by the Yankee Tobacco Company in 1864 and featured contemporary Union generals.

A theremin was discovered in the possession of the Watergate burglars.

The compound responsible for the adhesive properties of Elmer's Glue is a closely guarded secret.

Contrary to popular lore, U.S. automobile license plates have never been manufactured by the incarcerated.

A one-ounce box of raisins will intoxicate an adult mouse.

Bowling alleys in the Czech Republic have 15-pin arrays.

Former Superintendent of Chicago Public Schools and U.S. Secretary of Education Arne Duncan has never held a teaching position!

The average U.S. household uses enough square feet of toilet paper each year to tile the entirety of Vatican City.

The Pythagorean Theorem has never been proven.

During the French Revolution, more citizens were killed in bathroom accidents than executed by guillotine.

Fireflies show symptoms of postpartum depression.

Walt Disney invested half a million dollars into a failed scheme to develop a car that runs on human waste.

The U.S. Mint spends $1.01 on each penny that it manufactures.

Galileo Galilei attempted to launch a dog into space using a catapult.

From 1978 through 1982, every Oscar statuette concealed a complimentary vial of cocaine.

The designer of the pioneering video game Pong was blind.

Charles Manson was a distant cousin of Leo Buscaglia.

The recipe for French Toast was acquired by Marco Polo along the Silk Road.

The movie Kramer vs. Kramer was actually the first installment in the middle trilogy of an intended nine-film series.

The FCC prohibits discussion of bodily functions during the dinner hour.

Carnegie Hall is plagued by several acoustic "dead spots," undesirable zones in which seats are generally given away for free.

The song "Happy Birthday to You" was written to the tune of a liturgical refrain from the Satanic Mass.

Lee Harvey Oswald was turned down at an audition for the Ice Capades.

The Ebola virus can survive both electrocution and lethal injection.

Famed restaurant entrepreneur Dave Thomas battled a lifelong phobia of vegetable oil.

A 2-liter bottle of Mountain Dew applied to the battery of most domestic cars will dissolve not only the battery but the engine block as well.

Industrial-grade structural concrete is less dense than the human femur.

Pencil shavings are toxic to baboons.

Ownership of the Statue of Liberty will revert to France in 2386.

In medieval times, horses were thought to be the marine offspring of sea horses and consequently were permitted to be eaten by Catholics on Fridays.

The apparent birthmark on the head of Mikhail Gorbachev is in fact the scarred impression of a surgically removed Marilyn Monroe tattoo.

An unopened letter dated February 2, 1862 and addressed to Abraham Lincoln was discovered during renovation of the White House mail room in 1953; the missive was from a young adult admirer named William McKinley, who warned the President to be on guard against assassins.

Ludwig van Beethoven allowed mice to live inside his piano.

Beloved radio broadcaster Paul Harvey's life was devoid of irony.

The common house fly has no long-term memory.

Light bulbs sold in the Southern Hemisphere are threaded for counterclockwise insertion.

The basic principles of the Internet were discovered by Leonardo da Vinci.

If our planet were to rotate just one mile faster than it does, the resulting centrifugal force would be sufficient to overcome the centripetal force of gravity, causing everyone and everything to fling off into space.

Cheddar cheese is banned in Iran.

Diners wearing belts are statistically five times less likely to overeat than those wearing elastic waistbands.

Ed McMahon was a certified doctor of divinity.

Astronauts must massage their abdomens to avoid constipation in space.

The furniture in the Oval Office is fixed to the floor.

Cell phone technology is a byproduct of the Manhattan Project.

Whiskey, vinegar and uric acid can be combined to make a primitive embalming fluid.

Charles Dickens was illiterate until a year before he wrote his first novel.

A crocodile's reproductive organs are in its mouth.

The San Francisco Earthquake of 1906 destroyed the first functional prototype of a television.

Newspaper magnate William Randolph Hearst bought the Great Wall of China for an undisclosed sum in 1895 from a visiting delegation of Chinese diplomats. The Chinese government later refused to acknowledge the sale.

Jazz trumpeter Dizzy Gillespie had only one Eustachian tube.

The Eiffel Tower, though constructed of iron, repels magnets.

Trick or Treat

An icy wind cut through the fabric of my jeans and numbed my legs as I paused under the streetlight at the end of the block. When had it ever been so cold in October? And where was everybody? Our dark street was as deserted as it might have been on the bitterest winter night. Even the dry and brittle leaves seemed lonely as they scratched along the pavement of the empty road. My gloved fingers fumbled with the pillowcase that contained all that I had to show for the evening, a take that seemed disappointingly modest compared to the great hauls I recalled from Halloweens past.

With every exhalation, I could feel my breath condense against my perspiring face, which was concealed behind the stifling latex of a full-head Frankenstein mask. I pushed back the bulky cuff of my heavy coat to reveal my watch. 7:09. Still nearly an hour of trick-or-treating left. As I trudged onward, a rivulet of sweat trickled from the back of my mask and descended between my shoulder blades, causing me to shudder. I let out a short gasp against my unforgiving mask, adding more moisture to the rubbery enclosure that was turning my expedition into an alternating series of smothering heat and quivering chills.

Where were the Reilly kids? Where was Chuck Martin? Did everybody just give up this year and go home early? I reached Wiltshire and peered up and down the street in search of house lights and other signs of life. Not a soul haunted the sidewalks, and only a smattering of homes had their porches illuminated, spread out down the block like cold and distant constellations. I thought about turning around and going home, but I couldn't let myself give up. Mom had said that this year was it; trick-or treat was for kids, and next year I would be too old to put on a costume and walk around asking the neighborhood for candy. This wasn't the way I wanted to remember my last year.

I didn't really know anyone on Wiltshire, except for Mr. and Mrs. Runyon, whose back yard ran right up against ours, and I knew they wouldn't be home because Mom had told me they went out to eat every year so they wouldn't have to hand out candy. I was supposed to stick to only the houses of people I knew, but that was hardly anybody. What was the point of even going if you didn't have a decent chance of filling your pillowcase?

I lumbered toward the nearest house with a lit porch, keeping my head down and peering through the narrow slits of my mask. There was a really bad, uneven part of the sidewalk somewhere along here, and I didn't want to trip over it in the dark and smash up my face like Joey Metcalf, who once got seventeen stitches in his lip when he missed it. When I finally reached the house, I walked up to the porch and discovered a large, empty wicker basket. Taking a step backward, I noticed a little sign with someone's dirty shoe print on it under the bushes. *HONOR SYSTEM*, it read in big, curly letters. *Take ONE and have a HAPPY HALLOWEEN!*

The next home with a light on was eight houses up the street, and when I got there, I remembered that I did know some people on Wiltshire besides the Runyons. It was the Lewis house, and even with a sweaty Frankenstein mask on, I had a good enough head on my shoulders to know I should avoid it. The Lewis boys were juvenile delinquents, in trouble all the time. The older one had actually tried to poison their little sister, or at least that's what Chuck told me. I stayed away from that family, and I sure wasn't going to accept any candy from them. If anybody was putting razor blades in their Snickers, it was the Lewises.

By now I was in the middle of the block, and since I hadn't yet profited from my venture down Wiltshire, it seemed silly to do anything other than hit the homes between here and the corner. I would actually be closer to home that way, so long as I continued around the block. The next stop was a house where the curtains were still open, and I could see a television with some sort of game show playing on it. I heard a very loud ring when I pressed the doorbell, but it seemed to take forever before the door creaked open.

"Well!" croaked an old, white-haired lady with a kind, wrinkled face. "What have we here? Ooh, it's Frankenstein's monster, well I'll be!"

"Trick or treat," I uttered into my mask.

The old lady reached for a bowl brimming with popcorn balls. "I haven't had many visitors tonight. Maybe it's the cold. Or maybe you're scaring all the other monsters away, eh?" She laughed at her joke. "Here, you go on and take as many as you like. I can't eat them, you see, what with my dentures."

I couldn't tell her that I didn't like popcorn balls, and it seemed rude to take only one when she seemed so pleased to offer me as many as I wanted. "As many as I like?"

"Why, certainly!" she crowed, her eyes darting momentarily toward the droning television. She pulled her shawl tighter around her shoulders and smiled at me patiently.

"Gee..." I stammered, unsure how to proceed. She seemed very nice, and I didn't want to offend her. I thought about taking two popcorn balls, but I wondered if that was as insulting as taking only one. Three seemed like it might be the right number, yet the way the old lady pushed the bowl toward me and stretched her smile even wider across her wrinkled face made me think she wanted me to take even more. Another stream of sweat ran from my mask down my back and caused me to shudder.

"You'd better take some quickly," she added as she glanced yet again toward her TV. "I wouldn't want the cat to get out, what with the door open like this." Again she pushed the bowl toward me, tilting it forward so that a single popcorn ball rolled off the top and dropped into my open pillowcase. I peered upward through my mask and saw that she hadn't even noticed. She was watching the game show. I don't know what got into me at that moment, but suddenly the whole idea of beggar's night seemed ridiculous to me. Here I was, chilled to the core yet sweating feverishly, holding out my sack for something I didn't even want. And there was the old lady, starting to lose her grip on the quivering bowl and now totally absorbed in whatever was coming out of her television. Judging by how ancient she looked, I guessed that it was just as likely her last trick-or-treat, too. As another shudder rippled down my spine, I knew it was time for both of us to call it quits.

Before I could even consider the wisdom of my actions, I reached deep into the bowl and scooped the popcorn balls over the rim and into my bag. I needed only two scoops to get them all. At last the bowl stopped quivering, and the old lady turned from her television and stared down at the empty container. Then she looked at me expectantly.

"Thank you, ma'am," I offered.

"Happy Halloween," she smiled, closing her door quickly. The porch light went off, and through the window I saw her settle down on the couch. The clock above her television showed 7:25. I hefted my bulging pillowcase over my shoulder and headed for home.

Black Friday 2050

NEWSCASTER: And now, over to NewsForYou Nine's roving reporter Matilda Morris, who's standing by live at the Best Buy at the Big Shoppes at Birch Meadows. Matilda?

MATILDA: Thanks, Kent! For the past several months, this parking lot has been a thriving community, a curb-to-curb sea of tents and shanties that have served as a home-away-from-home for several hundred of our city's most dedicated consumers. They come from all walks of life, rich and poor, young and old, cyborg and android, but they are united in their passion for the latest in personal and home electronics at rock-bottom prices. I have with me Scott and Sara Sanderson, who moved into Best Buy Bargainville in September when news was leaked that a limited supply of portable, self-adhesive wall mural televisions would be made available at the insane price of one thousand ameros. Scott, is it worth it to put your life on hold for so long just to snag a great bargain?

SCOTT: No doubt it's worth it. Last year I waited until the end of October to get in line, and I came away empty-handed. I'm not going to let that happen again!

SARA: I told him he shouldn't even bother coming home unless he snagged one of those wall mural TVs. Our youngest boy just has old-school, painted walls, and the kids at school have been teasing him about it.

MATILDA: What's it like living here in Bargainville?

SCOTT: Well, it's like one big, extended family out here. You see the same people every year and get to know each other, so it's sort of our reunion.

SARA: That's right, we consider these people to be family.

SCOTT: Except in a few hours, when those doors open. There's not a soul out here who wouldn't trample his own mother if that's what it came down to.

SARA: And we wouldn't have it any other way.

SCOTT: That's right. You don't deserve it if you're not prepared to do what it takes to get it.

MATILDA: Thank you, Scott and Sara. And speaking of violence, I also have with me Sergeant Burt Brinkley, who is Tactical Commander of Big Shoppes at Birch Meadows security this year. Sgt. Brinkley, you and your force of over a hundred private soldiers have been patrolling the area since Labor Day. What is the mood of the troops now that Black Friday is just hours away?

SGT. BRINKLEY: A little tense, Matilda. No one has forgotten the Christmas Riot of '41. It's my duty to secure the safety of our shopping public and to ensure that never again will so much retail acreage go up in flames. To that end, we've spared no expense to stay on top of things. Today's technology allows us to know precisely where each shopper is at every moment, the identity of whichever shopper first touches an item of available merchandise, and whether or not they've already exceeded their credit limit or, God forbid, if they have no credit at all. In the event that merchandise is touched first by an ineligible shopper, the right to that item is forfeited to the next eligible shopper who has touched it. Once an eligible shopper is identified, that shopper's ID is shown on the item display, and there's no disputing it. Still, things can get out of hand, so you can bet we have a fully armored officer next to each display and every twenty meters in the aisles.

MATILDA: What do you say to critics who claim that the shopper identification technology is vulnerable to hacking and therefore may allow inequitable highly-discounted merchandise distribution?

SGT. BRINKLEY: I'd say, "Come on down here, and you deal with these nuts!"

MATILDA: Thank you, Sergeant. And finally, we have Best Buy Black Friday Regional Coordinator Gary Goins here to fill us in on the latest news behind the scenes. Gary, are you ready for this crowd of hundreds who have been waiting so patiently over the last few months?

GARY: Well, I certainly hope so. I know that Sgt. Brinkley and his troops have secured the perimeter and are doing everything they can to prevent large-scale rioting both without and within the store. For our part, we have reinforced the entrance windows and doors, installed additional padding at the ends of aisles and the vertices of all right-angled displays, quintupled the security cameras for 360-degree real-time-3D coverage, and strategically positioned a crack squad of sharpshooters in the rafters. And we're handing out turkey-shaped sugar cookies to the first twelve dozen shoppers.

MATILDA: Any concerns that your employees may not be up to the task?

GARY: Not at all, Matilda. Each of our associates is protected by custom-fit, crush-resistant body armor and has undergone a mandatory online training seminar in Black Friday crisis management. We will be rotating shifts so that no one will be out on the floor for more than two consecutive hours, and we also have a Shopper Negotiations Team standing by in case things get ugly. Really, it's all under control.

MATILDA: How profitable do you expect today to be?

GARY: Well, we'll move a lot of merchandise today, that's for sure, but anymore the actual Black Friday is just icing on the cake for us. It's the three months leading up to it that puts us in the black, thanks to the various guest services that we have found our short-term residential customers have come to expect.

MATILDA: And what sort of services are those?

GARY: To start with, anyone who takes Black Friday seriously will see the value in becoming a Best Buy Bargainville Preferred Camper, which entitles you to a minimum four-by-six plot located somewhere on the property or adjacent leased lots starting on Labor Day. Many of our customers know just how worthwhile it is to upgrade to a Plot License, which simply reserves your existing plot and gives you first dibs on its lease the following year. But the greatest value over the long run for our most dedicated customers is to invest in our Best Buy Bargainville VIP program. Those are the folks you see over there with priority Gold Circle Proximity Plots, featuring unlimited data streaming and complimentary recharging of all implanted personal electronics, plus the added bonus of being permitted to set up your living quarters and move in on the first of August. And a ten-percent discount at the Bargainville Taco Trailer.

MATILDA: Sounds wonderful, Gary, and good luck to you and your crew.

GARY: Thank you, Matilda.

MATILDA: And just a quick reminder to our viewers at home that it's not too late to come on out and join in the fun. Doors will be opening in just a few hours. Back to you, Kent.

NEWSCASTER: Thanks, Matilda. Great to see they're keeping the Christmas spirit alive down at Birch Meadows. In other news, a local group of classic car enthusiasts will do just about *anything* to get their hands on the precious oil and gasoline that makes their historic vehicles run. Details when we come back.

Two Minutes for Holding

Things had just quieted down in the east wing when the welcome silence was pierced by another bellowing shout from Room 11. "Loo-eeeeze!!"

"Good heavens," sighed Kaylee from behind the nursing station. She brushed a lock of hair from her eyes and replaced the phone in its cradle. "Doesn't that man ever stop?"

"I can tell you're new here," drawled Janice as she checked items off of her clipboard. "I don't even notice it anymore. It's like the racket them geese make out on the patio. Drives you crazy at first, but then you get used to it."

"I don't know if I can ever get used to that. It makes me want to jump out of my skin every time he does it. Imagine having a man shout at you like that! Then again, I suppose poor Louise probably got so used to hearing it that she just tuned him out like you do."

"Poor Louise?"

"Well, I'd say she was poor, having to put up with Mr. Francis until the day she died."

Janice gave a hoarse laugh that died out in a series of coughs. "Ah, honey, you know what they say when you assume! Far as we know, nobody was putting up with Mr. Francis but himself."

"What about Louise?"

"There's never been any Louise that we know of. Old Mr. Francis was a bachelor, didn't have no kids, lived alone and never saidboo to the neighbors about any Louise until they started hearing him shouting the name over and over like he does here now."

Kaylee furrowed her brow. "Well, that's...odd."

"And that ain't the half of it! Wait 'til you see him with his hockey players."

"His what?"

"Hockey players! Had 'em in a little plastic bag in the pocket of his robe when they brought him in. They got little silver sticks and everything! There's even a goalie with a little face mask on him. Oh yeah, old Mr. Francis and his hockey players. Don't even think about takin' 'em out his sight. He keeps 'em on his tray most of the time, except for the one little guy with the green hat. He sleeps with that one."

"Good heavens!" exclaimed Kaylee, her lips thinning into a grimace as she tried to suppress a giggle. It was totally unprofessional to speak of the residents in a disrespectful manner, and she feared that they were on the verge of crossing that line. As hard as it was to stifle her amusement, she reminded herself that there was nothing entertaining about the manifestations of mental illness. Kaylee cleared her throat and spoke softly. "Thank goodness poor Mr. Francis is here, where at least he's safe and cared for. He's probably just lonely. The next time he yells like that, I'll calmly walk in and see what he wants."

"Oh, but honey, that's the thing. He won't tell you nothing when you look after him. He won't even notice you're there. I really don't think the man's lonely, odd bird that he is."

"Maybe," offered Kaylee diplomatically, "but there's no way to know for sure, not if he isn't having conversations with us. The next time he gets upset again, I'm going to—"

"LOOO-EEEEEEEEEEEZE!"

"Well, here's your chance, Florence Nightingale," grinned Janice. She bowed slightly and gestured toward the hall, extending one arm like a theater usher. "Enjoy the show!"

Kaylee reflexively bit her lip and cast an apprehensive glance at the open door to Room 11. This wasn't how she had envisioned her first day. She had hoped to become a bit more familiar with the various protocols of Weber Estates before attending to any of their more confrontational residents. Now that she had claimed the higher philosophical ground, though, she would have to follow through with her good intentions.

She was halfway down the hall, just a few feet short of Room 11, when Mr. Francis yelled yet again, causing her to check her balance against the near wall. What in the world did the poor man mean by repeatedly roaring the name Louise? Was there any sense to it at all? Had he once known a Louise who had meant something to him? Might he mistakenly take an unfamiliar nurse to be this mysterious Louise? Kaylee gathered her courage and strode confidently through the doorway before she halted in a moment of unguarded shock.

The frail man sitting upright in his bed did not look like he possessed the lung capacity to produce more than a whisper, so wizened was his frame. He was hairless save for two shocks of wispy, white cotton that protruded above his ears. His cheeks were sunken, and tears gathered at the outside corners of his eyes before following rivulets down the wrinkled crevasses of his leathery skin. Most startling of all was his bizarre attitude: bony arms raised with clenched fists as though he were crossing a marathon finish line, and a defiantly victorious smile to match. An assortment of miniature hockey players littered the folds of his bedspread.

"Mr. Francis?"

True to Janice's prediction, he seemed to take no notice that someone had entered the room and was standing at the foot of his bed. Slowly he lowered his arms, and then he began reaching out with his hands and retreating repeatedly, like a child opening and closing dresser drawers. Not once did he regard her in any way, but his head swiveled suddenly and his eyes darted here and there in a long series of convulsions. At last Mr. Francis let out a prolonged and satisfied sigh before falling back onto his pillow.

"Don't worry 'bout it, honey," called Janice from the hallway. "He does that every time." Her shuffling footsteps faded until Room 11 was uncomfortably quiet. Mr. Francis had closed his eyes and was drawing long and raspy breaths.

Kaylee looked about the room for clues but found no traces of her patient's identity. All of the furniture was standard issue, and there were no photographs anywhere. No personal effects at all, except for the miniature hockey players. Was there anyone alive who could provide his history? If so, did they even know that Mr. Francis was here? Most likely the decrepit figure before her was once a highly-functioning, productive member of society, but now he was reduced to living out the rest of his existence trembling and repeating a meaningless name.

Suddenly Mr. Francis' left leg twitched violently, sending a pair of hockey men clattering to the floor. Kaylee reached down and retrieved the figures, which were painted in garish shades of yellow and red. She placed them carefully on the bedside tray and noticed that the remaining miniatures were all balanced precariously near the bedrail. One by one she extracted each little hockey player and placed it with the others until the one miniature with a green helmet remained, perched just below the pillow near Mr. Francis' gnarled neck.

Leaning in to examine it closely, Kaylee noticed the sharp edges of the tiny hockey stick's blade. If Mr. Francis were to roll over, there was a minute possibility that he could inadvertently puncture his carotid artery. Really, this was a danger that the other nurses should have recognized. Letting a senile, non-communicative resident who is prone to tremors and possibly seizures sleep with a potentially hazardous object was unacceptable. She slowly reached out and secured it in her palm.

Before she realized what was happening, a cold and icy grip was clamped around Kaylee's wrist. The old man was holding on to her! His strength was supernatural, and she could not free herself. Terrified, she tried to access the call button, but it was beyond her reach. She was on the verge of screaming for help when she saw that Mr. Francis was looking directly at her, and her voice deserted her. His gaze was steely and unrelenting. He had her wrist pinned firmly to the mattress.

Then, without breaking his stare, he raised his free hand before her quivering face. Desperately she struggled to break free, but her efforts had no effect. He was going to do something to her, she somehow knew, grab at her eyes or disfigure her in some way. She pulled back with all her strength until she saw that he appeared to be signaling her. He was extending his thumb and index finger at a right angle, curling the rest of his digits against his palm. It almost looked like he was attempting to sign the letter L.

She felt herself let go of the green-helmeted hockey player, and instantly Mr. Francis released her. A bright red mark encircled her throbbing wrist. She stepped away from the bed as the old man gathered his treasured toy into his hand and tucked it against his heart. The room was quiet once more. Kaylee stepped silently toward the door. As she crossed the threshold, she thought she heard a whisper from behind her.

"Louise!"

Three Days of Darkness

CHAPTER I

Three Days of Darkness!

"GOOD GRIEF!" exclaimed Moe Hardee as he perused the latest Parish Post. He ran his fingers through his blonde hair and cast a worried glance toward his brother, Hank. "It says here that Padre Pio has prophesied Three Days of Darkness!"

"Gee," remarked Hank, dark-haired and one year older than seventeen-year-old Moe, "that will sure put a crimp in our boating plans!" Hank and Moe were the sons of famous detective Denton Hardee, and they had been looking forward to a weekend expedition on Bartlett Bay with their Mayport High chums. "Read me the details."

"Well, according to Padre Pio, an enormous cross in the sky will signal the imminence of three days of darkness, during which the sun will not shine and demons will run loose throughout the streets."

"Holy moly!" reacted Hank, whose customary reserve and lack of impulsiveness had been rattled by the startling news.

"And that's not all. The faithful are required to take shelter in a windowless room stocked with adequate provisions, lest they accidentally make eye contact with one of the demonic marauders or personally witness God's wrath, which will condemn even believers to an eternity in hell."

"Gosh! We better tell Dad!" concluded Hank. The boys rushed through the house on their way to Denton Hardee's second-floor study, but their progress was halted by their superficially tart yet fundamentally affectionate Aunt Bertrude, who would always put the kibosh on anyone running through the kitchen.

"And just what do you two boys mean by tearing through the house like a pair of reckless hooligans?" demanded acid-tongued Miss Hardee, sister to Denton. Though she had no tolerance for nonsense, Hank and Moe loved her, for they knew that underneath her crusty and rather unattractive exterior beat a heart of gold.

"Why, Aunt Bertrude," explained Moe, "we're only on our way to tell Dad some vitally important news!" He turned to his brother and gave a sly wink. Hank grinned secretly behind a façade of non-grinning.

"Not just now, you're not!" thundered the old witch. "Your father left for New York this morning on another important case. So you can take your spoiled behinds right back where they came from, only this time walking." The boys drooped their heads and trudged out of the kitchen. "And no sleuthing!" added Aunt Bertrude lovingly.

Hank and Moe decided to take refuge in their well-equipped crime laboratory on the second floor of the detached garage. Here they could formulate a plan without further intrusion from Aunt Bertrude.

"We could tell Mother," offered Moe. Mrs. Hardee was a small and attractive woman who quietly went about her business keeping the Hardee house. Often she would pack delicious picnic lunches for the boys when they were about to embark on an afternoon of detective work.

"We could," allowed Hank, "but we better not. I think demonic marauders and condemnation to an eternity in hell would only upset Mother."

"Yeah, you're probably right," admitted impulsive Moe, who was grateful for his brother's habit of thinking things through before acting. "Let's ask some of the gang what they think." The young amateur detectives raced down the steps and mounted their motorcycles. With the enticing aroma of a fresh adventure in the air, they kicked their starters and zoomed off toward the outskirts of Mayport. Soon they were pulling up the dusty drive at the Horton farm, home to their friend Shep.

Shep happened to be squatting down on the

front porch studying an array of small objects spread around him. He was so absorbed in his task that even the roaring of the Hardee boys' motorcycles did not distract him. When Hank and Moe neared the porch, they both grinned at their stout friend's inattention. At length, Shep looked up and noticed his company. "Oh, hi fellows! You're just in time for the first-ever display of my newest collection: food that resembles other things!"

"Why, who would have guessed that you would take up an interest in food?" joked Moe, and all three chums laughed heartily. Shep was known throughout Mayport as an enthusiastic eater.

"Ah, but not just any food, you see. Consider this potato, which I dug out of the ground myself. See how it looks quite a bit like the head of our principal?"

"Say, he's right!" smiled Hank. "What else do you have, Shep?"

Their porcine pal rummaged among the other foodstuffs. "Well, there's this carrot that reminds me of a Saturn rocket, and you can see how this gourd is not unlike my jalopy's carburetor, and that stubby little zucchini over there is just like my-"

"Hey!" interrupted Moe. "Look at this rhubarb!"

"Oh yeah," said Shep, "it's like a little cluster of red Ticonderoga pencils, right?"

"No, Shep, I mean the leaves. Look at the vein in this leaf!"

"Holy moly!" exclaimed Hank redundantly. "It looks like a cross!" Shep's bulbous eyes darted quizzically between Hank and Moe, both of whom had suddenly become quite solemn.

"What's wrong, fellas?" queried the rotund one.

"Listen, Shep," explained Hank. "This rhubarb leaf reminds us of why we came here in the first place." Both brothers recounted the news they had just learned from the Parish Post. Shep's frightened eyes protruded even further from their sockets, and were it not for the constraint of his skull, they might have popped entirely out of his head.

"G-g-gee w-w-w-willikers!" stammered Shep. "I better grab my scapular collection!" Breathing laboriously what with his accumulated layers of fat, he disappeared into the house and returned shortly with a shoe box filled with various sacramental scapulars. "There's enough for everybody! This one gives you the Sabbatine Privilege, which will get you out of Purgatory so long as you're wearing it on the first Saturday after you die. Oh, and you have to be pious, too. This one is a fivefold, so in addition to the Sabbatine Privilege, you get more plenary indulgences than you can believe. This one —"

"What's all the fuss?" came a gentle voice

from behind the screen door. Moe looked up to behold Shep's sister Viola, who was as slender and pretty as Shep was not. Viola was Moe's favorite date, and it occurred to him that should he be confined in a windowless room for three days during an apocalyptic conflagration, he could do worse than to spend it at the Horton farmhouse. Hank was having similar thoughts, though he envisioned himself piously ensconced within the fortified home of pretty, blonde Keri Pshaw, whom he dated regularly.

Suddenly Viola cast her gaze above and beyond her brother and his chums. "Say! Look up there in the sky!"

Shep, Hank, and Moe turned around and looked up at the cloudless summer sky. There, plainly visible against the vibrant blue atmosphere, was an enormous white cross!

CHAPTER II

Confounded by Contrails!

ACKNOWLEDGEMENTS

How can I possibly include everyone when it comes to thanking the innumerable souls responsible for the existence of this book? A fool's folly, yet I shall attempt the Herculean task.

A heartfelt thank you to Garrett Durrebohn and everyone at Durrebohn Literary Agency for their tireless representation and unflagging belief in this project.

I am forever indebted to Roberta Rundgreth for her editorial wisdom and her repeated admonition that *less is more*. I'll leave it at that.

My deepest gratitude to the fine folks at TableChair, especially Antelle Haithcock, John Mullen, Robert Funni, Louise Weber and Shirley Toich. I could not imagine a finer publisher.

And when it comes to publicists, who is better than Bertrand Trougher? I ask you, who? That's what I thought.

Finally, thanks to each and every reader who campaigned for the inclusion of their favorite pieces in this compilation. While it was not possible to accommodate everyone, we hope that the end product is a satisfying compromise.

Oh, and a postscript thank you to my therapist, who assures me that it's not the worst thing in life to be delusional.

About the Author

Robert Gerard Hunt acquired his neuroses while growing up
Catholic in Lima, Ohio. He has since managed to live what
appears to be a normal life in Columbus, even going so
far as to get married and have children. His endeavors
as a writer, musician, and all-around creative genius
have been continually thwarted by long-term
employment as a manager, a teacher,
a letter carrier, and as a courier
for a pet crematorium.

—
—
—
—
—
—
—
—
—
—
—
—
—
—

Also by Robert Gerard Hunt:

Nor the Arrow That Flies by Day

Made in the USA
Columbia, SC
14 May 2024

35261155R00135